TO TOUCH
IS TO LIVE

THE NEED FOR GENUINE AFFECTION
IN AN IMPERSONAL WORLD

MARIANA CAPLAN, PH.D.

HOHM PRESS

Layout and Design: Visual Perspectives, Phoenix, AZ
Cover Art: Kim Johansen

Library of Congress Cataloging-in-Publication Data

Caplan, Mariana, 1969-
To touch is to live: the need for genuine affection in an
impersonal world / Mariana Caplan.
p. cm.
Rev. ed. of: Untouched. c1998.
Includes bibliographical references and index.
ISBN 1-890772-24-0 (pbk.: alk. paper)
1. Touch--Psychological aspects. 2. Touch--Social aspects.
I. Caplan, Mariana, 1969- . Untouched. II. Title.
BF275.C37 2002
158.2--dc21   2002012571

HOHM PRESS
P.O. Box 2501 • Prescott, AZ 86302
(800) 381-2700 • Fax (928) 717-1779
E-mail: staff@hohmpress.com
Web Site: www.hohmpress.com

This book was printed in the U.S.A. on acid-free paper using soy ink
06   05   04   03   02   5   4   3   2   1

I am not a mechanism, an assembly of various sections.
And it is not because the mechanism is working wrongly,
    that I am ill.
I am ill because of wounds to the soul, to the deep emotional
    self
and the wounds to the soul take a long, long time, only time
    can help
and patience, and a certain difficult repentance
long, difficult repentance, realization of life's mistake, and
    the freeing oneself
from the endless repetition of the mistake
which mankind at large has chosen to sanctify.

– D.H. Lawrence, *Healing*

ACKNOWLEDGMENTS

Dr. Joseph Chilton Pearce has become a mentor and friend. His passion to create a better world for children is unmatched among those I have known, and his support and encouragement has provided a well of inspiration. I would like to express my sincere gratitude to him, as well as to Dr. James Prescott and Dr. Ashley Montagu, each of whom is uncompromising in his message.

DEDICATION

This book is dedicated to all the children who didn't get what they needed, and to the possibility for this to change in future generations.

CONTENTS

F O R E W O R D
by Ashley Montagu

        Mariana Caplan has written a beautiful book, wonderful, courageous, and distinguished by its eloquence, soundness and originality, a book that all the world should read, for it carries a healing message, easy to apply, full of highly realizable promises, and happily rewarding, especially for those of us who have been failed during the earlier years of our lives, and who bear the scars of that trying misadventure called "bringing up" or "raising" the child. I have for long held that adults are nothing more nor less than deteriorated babies, "adulterated" by caregivers unaware of their own victimization who, more often than not, with the best of intentions were zealously devoted to doing their best for their charges. Not only that, the professional authorities, obstetricians, pediatricians, psychiatrists, psychologists, psychoanalysts, psychotherapists, educators, and other non-swimmers acting as lifeguards, have for the most part perpetuated the errors of their predecessors. With their superficial psychologies they have overlooked the essential fundamental biosocial requirements for the healthy growth and development of the person. Let me say at once that by healthy growth and development I mean the ability to love, to work, to play, and to use one's mind soundly. But these are words, and they all require definition and proof. (I have done this in my book, *Growing Young*, 2nd ed. Westbrook, CT: Bergin & Garvey, 1989.)

    Words shape our understanding, and definitions can only be soundly meaningful at the end of an inquiry rather than at the beginning of one. It is the *tested* evidence that establishes its validity. It is by such means, by experiment, that a scientist comes to believe in proof without certainty, whereas others believe in certainty without proof. Most of us tend to think in stereotypes, in clichés, in fixed conventional expressions, and so we communicate with phrases and words as if the presuppositions upon which they were based never existed. Take any word at random and ask anyone to define what they understand by it, and see what you get. You will find that in most instances people are unable to give an accurate account of the words they commonly use. Ask your friends to define a definition. Don't be surprised that they can't do it. And so it goes. Ask your students at high school or university level to define the meaning of any of the words they customarily use. Ask them to define the word "race." The answer they will give you will almost certainly be wrong, for in spite of the findings of anthropologists, biologists, and geneticists that the term "race" corresponds to nothing on earth, especially as it relates to human beings, but constitutes a social construct created by scientists during the 19th century in the endeavor to account for the perceptible differences between different peoples. The result was an elaborate "authoritative" typology and classification that led to the torture and extermination of millions of human beings. Most people, however, continue to believe that "race" is a very real thing. Plato many years ago believed that the word created the thing. He was, of course, right. As Aldous Huxley pointed out, the overvaluation of words leads all to frequently to the fabrication and idolatrous worship of dogmas. Hence the importance of education.

Unfortunately, what we understand by "education," isn't education at all: what it is, is *instruction,* a very different thing, a training by *rote* in *what* to think, not in *how* to think. Hence, it is not surprising that most of us find it easier to believe than to think, to have faith rather than to examine the presuppositions upon which our beliefs are based.

xii

It was Plato who long ago said that the unexamined life was not worth living. How right he was, and how right Mariana Caplan is, in this splendid, most readable, and important book, in which she so congenially helps us all to re-examine the basic beliefs which normally form our daily round of living. Beyond all else, as she so illuminatingly shows, there is the crying need for affection that, in a world of untouchability, is so seldom understood. This is the setting and the challenge that is dealt with by Mariana as it has never been so satisfactorily and effectively dealt with before, the behavior, the sensibility, with which we are touched into completeness. IT is that need for love and to love others, which takes physical expression through touch, in a hug, an embrace, a touch of the hand, a kiss, and more, that constitutes our principal demonstration of connectedness, involvement, and caring. Indeed touch becomes the touchstone, the true measure of our humanity, our seasoning of health, the enrichment of our being. Hence, Mariana discusses, as they have never been so creatively discussed, virtually every significant human need and behavior as it has never been so revealingly examined, analyzed, and creatively restored to understanding and usefulness, in language that abjures all technical terms, and speaks plainly and simply, both to the heart and the mind's consent. This is a considerable achievement. Enthusiasm is good, but it should not look to long at the sun, and keep others from sharing the light, the glow, of warmth that this extraordinary book communicates.

Upon the completion of the first edition of this book (published under the title, *Untouched*), it was time to write letters to colleagues in the field who might read the manuscript and write some words of approval (or disapproval if need be). My editor asked me, "Who would be the ideal person to write a Foreword?"

"Ashley Montagu, of course," I told her, "He wrote the first book on touch that sold six million copies and put out the message to the world. But surely he cannot still be alive. He was an old professor already when my mother was in college. And if he is alive, I can't imagine he would be willing to take the time for my manuscript among his other thirty or forty books."

She encouraged me to look into the matter, and when I found out that he was indeed alive, in his nineties, I decided to write him a letter, at least to express my gratitude.

Three weeks later I was called to the phone. "Who is it?" I yelled, as I was quite busy at the moment.

"He said his name is Ashley Montagu. Do you know him?"

Joy overcame me.

Thus began my correspondence and friendship/mentorship

with Dr. Montagu. Contrary to my fear that he might feel that I was stepping on his toes by writing a modern-day version of his best-selling, *Touching: the Human Significance of the Skin,* Montagu was passionately supportive and delighted that someone of a younger generation would carry forth his message. Dr. Montagu read, critiqued, and eventually promoted the book himself. His mentorship was a true blessing.

Since the first publication of the book, Dr. Montagu has passed on. The body of his work was revolutionary for its time—decades ahead of his contemporaries, including *The Natural Superiority of Women; The Elephant Man; Touching;* and dozens of others. He is a true forefather.

I wish I could say that his last words to me were a benediction and congratulations for the book. That came earlier. But Dr. Montagu was also upset with me—he was upset that I had not chosen to publish the book with a large publisher that could circulate it to the world. I had chosen Hohm Press for their impeccable integrity, and stood, and still stand, behind that decision. Thus, Dr. Montagu's final note to me read, "Get an agent! Publish in New York!"

My wish, both then and now, is that this book will reach those who need it. That even a few children will be raised more consciously because their parents read the book; that some readers will find themselves more inclined to smile at a stranger, reach out to touch a friend, abolish self-hatred and cultivate love and gratitude for their own bodies and lives, honor their sexuality, and have more compassion for the pain of those who hurt them, understanding that we were all raised in a culture of touch-starvation. May we allow ourselves to be touched by the generosity and vitality of the divine Life Force, and to extend that forth to all who pass through our lives.

You could say I had a "normal" childhood—normal in a time when earthquakes and global warming don't even make the front page; normal in a time when homicides and suicides are a daily occurrence and the threat of biological warfare is run-of-the-mill; normal in a time when it is dangerous for children to play in the streets in once-safe neighborhoods, and for women to go alone almost anywhere, anytime; normal in a time in which people do not know how to extend genuine love and respect to one another, when it is common to go for days or weeks with no physical contact with another person; normal in a time when we have all but lost our humanness.

I had a "normal" happy childhood (just as all of my therapy clients, and most ordinary people, claim to have had "normal" happy childhoods). Raised in a normal dysfunctional family (with some rare exceptions, "dysfunctional = family" in contemporary Western culture), there were expectations and rules regarding touch that were to be observed. For example, when your parent says, "Come sit on your Daddy's lap," you sit on your Daddy's lap, irrespective of your wishes as a child. When your uncle squeezes you too tightly, or slobbers all over your face when he kisses you, you endure it politely. When somebody wants to pinch your cute little cheeks, or pat your head, you force a smile. You are a child, and therefore at the whim of the unmet needs for affection that others randomly place upon you.

We were a normal family in the pre-computer era. Yes, atomic bombs were dropped at Hiroshima and Nagasaki. Sure, there was a nuclear reactor meltdown at Chernobyl, releasing a radioactive cloud that contaminated 2,000 square miles of the earth. Like all my friends, I lived through a couple of nuclear war threats, and watched the news when escaped convicts were running around my neighborhood. Yes, my innocent body was fed TV dinners and microwaved food, and I watched *General Hospital* and longed to be anorexic so I could be skinny enough—but still, I maintain, this is *normal.* I was no different from any other kid on the block. We were a happy American family just like the rest of them—dead, you could say, but at least we were normal.

Such a scenario is all too common. As evidenced by the current skyrocketing statistics on child abuse (averaging between thirty and seventy percent depending upon your source), it is shockingly common for children to be severely damaged by the weapon of touch. Whereas some perpetrators of touch crimes (often the parents themselves) are blind to the lifelong consequences that their actions will have on the child, others are simply unwilling to place the child's needs over their own aggressive impulses.

Yet to place the entirety of the blame on any single parent's shoulders is to bypass the core of the problem. For parents are simply children who have grown up in what I will refer to as a "touch-starved nation." They, too, have been raised in a culture that has lost its roots, and during a time when people are so excited by science and technology that they are all too willing to be seduced away from their essential integrity, sanity and traditional family values in exchange for the allure of television, fancy cars, an important job, a computer *with* Internet and a CD Rom, and the mindset that accompanies this. They, too, are simply the products of a growing trend that, by design, will increasingly alienate us from ourselves and therefore from others.

All children instinctually understand sanity before it is drained out of them. Tens of thousands of young children look out at the world through the safety of their innocence, at their parents drinking or fighting, sitting zoned out in front of the television or the computer, stuffing their hungry hearts with one addiction or another. From a very young age they witness abuse and violence—in the papers, on the television, in their own homes. Given today's world, it is nearly impossible to raise a secure, happy, healthy child who is untainted by the ills of contemporary culture. Even if well-intentioned parents manage to create a loving home; even if their children's bodies do not become overly toxified by the chemicals in the food and water that they ingest, or the radiation emissions from their television sets, these children are still going to be faced with the toxic and often cruel world that is just outside their doorstep.

My point is that touch-starvation is not an affliction of the few, but is spiraling outward into the culture of the masses. The awkwardness and inappropriateness of where, how and whom we touch is an issue that affects *everybody*. Whether you are somebody who is unaware that you even *need* touch, or a single man or woman who has been horny for the last five or fifteen years because you are not in an intimate relationship and the only way you know how to get touch is through sex, or even if you are surrounded by family and children who want to love you and touch you but you don't know how to take it—you *are* affected by touch, or the lack of it. Who does not at times question whether it is O.K. to put their arm around their teenage child or co-worker, or to initiate sex with their spouse, boyfriend or girlfriend, or how to say "no" to unsolicited and unwanted touch?

In my normal happy childhood, I was fortunate enough to be exposed to positive forms of touch as well. Beginning in my teenage years, with an intuitive awareness that there had to be an alternative to the middle-class, sheltered civilization of deadness to which I had belonged all my life, I began to seek out any excuse I could find to spend extensive periods of time in foreign countries. My first expeditions were spent with families in Colombia, South America and in small villages in the Yucatan Peninsula in Mexico. The seeming inconveniences of seven people living in one room, or sleeping in a hammock and taking cold showers out of a bucket, were negligible compared to what it felt like to live in an environment of intimacy, communion, love, and an overall sense of well being. In the effort to quench my enormous thirst for understanding, I pursued a career as a professional traveler, becoming a cultural anthropologist and immersing myself in cultures that were both full of, as well as devoid of, touch. Still dissatisfied with the education my heart was receiving, I turned to the study of psychology—delving into an investigation of both my own psyche, as well as the psyches of my clients. Yet my knowledge remained incomplete. Much work was occurring on the level of mind, but my clients would continue to come in with body postures of pride, insecurity or terror. Thus, I sought balance by studying a particular form of bodywork that gave specific attention to the relationship between the body and the emotions.

Both at home and out of the country, I began to immerse myself in environments in which people were attempting to live another way—places in which touch and the need for touch is carefully and consciously considered. For example, in the community of my teacher, Lee Lozowick, children are never hit, and are instead given plenty of safe and loving touch according to their own wishes and needs. There is also a sensitivity to the needs of adults who suffer the wound of unlove, and attention is given to providing them with supportive touch in their adulthood, in the hope of allowing even part of the missed process of bonding that should have happened in early life to take place. My travels, adventures and experiments in community have been far-reaching and at times radical, but not because I am unusual or eccentric. Normal just like everybody else, I am driven by an instinctual knowledge that there is another way—a way of greater sanity.

I do not claim to be the holder of this "other way." This book does not lay out a revolutionary plan as to how a contemporary Western culture full of touch and intimacy and generosity and caring will look. Instead, it points in a specific direction, and it is for us to look that way to discover just how that touch will show up within ourselves, our families and our communities.

This book includes many examples of other cultures who seem to have an inherent understanding of the importance of touch. The purpose of this is not to idealize these cultures, nor to encourage people to become Third World wannabes—for these cultures have their own problems. We don't have to start dressing in bright African gowns, or taking our prayers out of the chapel and into the Native American sweat lodge in order to rediscover touch in our lives. We live in the West—whether it be America, Canada, France or England—and we are products of the Western world. There is not a chance that families will sleep together on woven palm mats, or that mothers will strap their babies onto their backs while they go out into the rice fields, or that extended families including older siblings, grandparents, aunts, and neighbors alike will all assume responsibility in caring for a young infant.

However, we can integrate the best of the *essence* of other cultures into our own. We have certainly not hesitated in integrating ourselves into the politics, economy, and customs of other cultures—as evidenced by the Domino's Pizza sign painted on the side of a building in a Mexican village where many cannot even afford to eat; by "U.S. Army" camouflage gear being sold outside of an ancient temple in southern India; by a growing colonization of Western ideals throughout the world. If we intend to maintain any semblance of balance in our world, we must also be willing to embrace and include in our own culture the best qualities of those cultures that we have come to dominate.

The values I refer to are not indigenous only to foreign cultures. They once belonged to our own culture and are aspects of all cultures that live even remotely close to the earth, cultures in which the essential aspects of community are still intact.

The issue of touch in the present day is not a question of blame. In an effort to deepen our understanding, the origins of this issue will be examined and the perpetrators named. This is not to blame any one individual. When we come to understand the gravity of the situation, and how it wreaks havoc on us moment to moment, we know that there is no value in pointing a finger, except perhaps at ourselves. For although we are the victims of touch crimes, we are also the perpetrators. We are also the only ones who have the capacity to create change. This is just what I am proposing that we consider together.

The very small gestures we begin to make, as a result of a clearer understanding of the lack of touch in our lives, are received by others as marked and significant. Though we cannot heal the soul-wound by an affectionate pat on the back, for those who have felt unloved all of their lives, a small act of kindness can shake their whole perspective about who they are in the world. Touch, when done with heart, is always healing—period. Whether given by a trained nurse or a nervous friend, it heals.

On the most basic level, I will consider the need for simple, well-intentioned, physical touch. Everybody, and particularly young children whose innocence is still intact, needs this touch. However, touch is much more that skin contacting skin.

Touching has to do with the acknowledgment of our shared humanness. It has to do with the recognition of the inherent vulnerability and intense wish for contact that is present in each of us. Touching results from an acceptance of the separateness of each individual, and the knowledge that it is only through contact that union and communion can come about. Beyond this, the possibility of fulfillment through the medium of touch—whether it be physical touch or not—is far beyond what most people have ever known or considered. And this possibility belongs to all of us.

When people feel loved as a result of the abundance of touch and affection in their lives, they naturally extend themselves to touch others—be it by a simple pat on the shoulder or a touch on the hand. Secure in themselves, they are open to the other's response, but not expecting it. Their sense of safety and inner stability does not depend upon how other people respond to them. They touch in order to express themselves, and so that others may feel cared for. They wake up in the morning feeling loved, and go to sleep feeling loved—no matter what particular circumstances arise in any given day. From this love, which is the result of genuine bonding, arises wholeness, commitment, loyalty, service.

Throughout the course of this book, I set forth a detailed description of the degree to which we as a race have lost touch. I am unabashed and uncompromising in my opinions about the pervasiveness of all forms of abuse, the terrifying ways that we birth our children into this increasingly maddening world and raise them to become unfeeling machines, and the dangerous state that we as a people are in.

The actual physical touch—if it is True Touch—is the end of the road. That is to say that by the time somebody is able to give or receive affection from another person, deep understanding and healing have already taken place. Just as one must look to the sky to fully understand why the ocean is blue, so this book addresses touch by revealing the cause, the foundation and the context of touch. This book does not explain "how to" touch, but instead unfolds *the way* of touch. The human being whose mind state has been revealed to him clearly, and who has understood the roots of his own suffering, will naturally and necessarily desire to change and to transform, the "how to" emerging of its own accord and becoming refined through a process of trial and error.

There are thousands of parents, massage therapists, health practitioners, teachers, priests and lovers who respect the value of touch. They consciously practice it because they feel the truth of it, yet many do not know why they touch, or how they know to touch. There are also many more hundreds of thousands who do not touch, do not think to touch, do not want to be touched. Similarly, most of these people do not know why they don't touch, and many believe they do not know how to touch, or that they are inherently not inclined to touch. This book takes the reader behind touch, behind the skin, behind the urge to touch or not to touch.

You, the reader, already know the underlying principles behind everything that you will read in this book. I write from the premise that the knowledge of all things that are essential for living a sane, balanced and loving life (as is touch, as is love) is alive in everyone, only it has been covered by years of conditioning, abuse, falsity and a cultural mind that is dictated by fear. The gold is in everyone, only many are not willing to go digging in the mines.

I would like to extend my empathy for the pain that will be felt by those who do not take offense at my words and instead allow themselves, perhaps for the first time, to be faced with the reality and the gravity of our present situation. If you allow me to, I will walk you through a shattering of an illusion—i.e., that the human race is progressing in terms of its understanding, and that people are living according to what it means to be human. It is my sincere wish that from this shattering will arise something that is genuine and whole—a way of being in the world that allows you to feel good about yourself and to know that you are fulfilling your rightful place.

Something happens in people when they hear what they know to be true, and something still deeper occurs when they take steps toward living that truth. The enormity of the challenges and heartbreak that often accompany facing one's reality without buffers is subsumed by the sense of "rightness" and integrity one finds within oneself and in one's life. It is my wish to draw this forth from you, the reader—the knowledge of what it means to really touch another, and the courage to throw down the reins and risk living it. For if we who care enough to consider this possibility do not allow ourselves to recognize this truth and to live accordingly, who will?

CHAPTER 1

A Touched-
Starved Nation

In our crowded and urban world, we have battled on in this way, further and further from a state of loving, personal intimacy, until the cracks have begun to show. Then, sucking our metaphorical thumbs and mouthing sophisticated philosophies to convince ourselves that all is well, we try to sit it out. We laugh at educated adults who pay large sums to go and play childish games of touch and hug in scientific institutes, and we fail to see the signs. How much easier it would all be if we could accept the fact that tender loving is not a weakly thing, only for infants and young lovers, if we could release our feelings, and indulge ourselves in an occasional, and magical, return to intimacy.[1]

– Ashley Montagu

If you have ever looked closely at the barnacles on the rocks at the edge of the sea, you will notice that they appear as thousands of tiny mouths that are attempting to eat, eat, eat...No matter what you place in front of them, their "mouths" continue to reach out for food. In this same way the skin and heart of the vast majority of people in the Western world are hungering for touch. We are famished for the most basic needs for human contact and closeness. We are living with a feeling of deep disconnection and fear. We sense that something has gone very wrong, but we have no idea what. We are dying and only vaguely conscious enough to know it. The madness we have created in our lives and in our world is our way of crying out to some imagined savior, just as the hungry infant will scream and cry until he is fed. We are the walking wounded. We are the out of touch. We are the touch-starved, love-starved products of the material world. Our very lives are the casualties of the modern way of television and computers, and we are the current survivors in the age of threats of nuclear, chemical, and biological warfare. We are both the children of parents who did not know how to love, as well as the struggling parents who are trying to raise our children sanely in an insane world. We are it—the starving attempting to feed the hungry, the wounded attempting to heal the sick. We are the ignorant looking for answers, the blind attempting to live out a vision. We are the hope in the hopeless situation, the possibility attempting the impossible.

ON COOKING FROGS

If you place a frog in a pot of boiling water, it will immediately jump out. However, if you place a frog in a pot of cold water, and then very slowly heat the water to a boil, you will end up with a dead, cooked frog.

I do not mean to be insulting by reducing the human condition to that of cooking frogs, but it is a precise parallel to the way in which present day society is slowly taking the life out of us, leaving us feeling increasingly deadened without even knowing why.

"But how can this be?" we want to know. "We are just going along with the times." "We are living in an age of unprecedented progress and prosperity." "We are just sitting in a pot of cool water with the other frogs enjoying the abundance."

The price of the so-called progress we have made is our present state. Of course we all say we're doing "fine," but what does it really mean to be doing fine? Yes, we go out to dinner, go on vacations, pursue interesting hobbies, get married, have children and live in nice houses with nice things if we're lucky, but all of these activities are simply measures of survival—frantic endeavors to put bandages over our collective wound in an effort to avoid the full impact of the underlying depression and fear that we all feel; an attempt to somehow convince ourselves that living in a pot of boiling water is not dangerous.

When I looked for an example of healthy touch within contemporary culture as a model for this book—some group of people who were really *in touch* with themselves and their surroundings—I was unable to find one. Where were the people who could touch one another frequently and easily? For whom intimacy was natural, and who felt good about themselves? Where were the people who were genuinely content with their lives? (Not just a compromised position of, "Looking around, I seem to be doing as well as anybody.") What could I give my readers to relate to? To aspire to? I mentioned this problem to a friend of mine who responded by saying, "That's why you're writing the book."

I am not saying that there are absolutely no happy people in the Western world—land of the "We're in control and everything is fine." Of course there are some, and we all know who they are when we meet them. However, if we have to think about whether or not we ourselves or somebody we know is truly happy, we, or they, are not. "I guess I'm happy" is not happy. "He has a good job and a nice family, of course he's happy," is not happy. "I've got it all," is not happy. Such is the frog as it swims around in the small, warm pond on the stove, assuming that everything is fine. Perhaps it has a slight instinct that something is going wrong, but since it is in the company of other dying frogs, it is far too wrapped up in mating, having babies, and getting food to consider the possibility that it is being cooked alive. What would make it think that it was dying anyway?

It is not that somebody or something is specifically trying to kill us. It is more complex than that. This momentum is being driven by a combination of forces that are created from a context of fear, and are primarily motivated by a wish to gain power, money and control. A set of values has been locked into place that give precedence to thought over feeling, independence over connectedness and service, and quantity over quality. In order to sustain this wave of commercialism, consumerism and technological advancement, and to allow its momentum to increase still further, we must consume more, buy more, spend more, eat more. Much as the addict depends on his substance of choice, this momentum has become our cultural "substance of choice." We feed off of it, and it off of us. We find a kind of nourishment in it. It does not feed the soul, but it does feed the hole of loneliness and emptiness that so many people feel within themselves. That hole is fed by anything sugar-coated, caffeine-coated, stimulation-coated, get-me-away-from-reality-coated. This wave of consumerism provides us with an unending supply of numbing agents: gadgets, movies, foods, discoveries, escapes...all designed to ward off feeling. We nourish this wave in turn by keeping ourselves ignorant of it and at the effect of its force.

Fighting the wave of commercialism and consumerism is a very complex situation, really. It is as if this anti-life force has become so strong, so sophisticated and so seductive that it has swept us up in its wake. We must not underestimate, nor be naive about the power of this force. We are not unintelligent, but when everything in and around us—every advertisement, every emotion, every teacher, every politician, and every ideology is saying one thing...when all of this is washing across us with an unprecedented degree of uprooting force, it is nearly impossible to not get carried away by it. Standing clear in one's own knowledge in

4

the face of this force can be likened to trying to swim out to sea while a tidal wave is heading to the shore. Who would try, unless they knew that the only option was sink or swim?

Such is the condition of the present state of the world—almost entirely void of contact, intimacy and aliveness. For those who have come face to face with this, it is a shattering contemplation.

> *The nuclear man is a man who has lost naive faith in the possibilities of technology and is painfully aware that the same powers that enable man to create new lifestyles carry the potential for self-destruction...He sees that in this nuclear age vast new industrial complexes enable men to produce in one hour that which he labored over for years in the past, but he also realizes that these same industries have disturbed the ecological balance and, through air and noise pollution, have contaminated his own milieu...He suffers from the inevitable knowledge that his time is a time in which it has become possible for man to destroy not only life but the possibility of rebirth, not only man but also of mankind, not only periods of existence but also history itself. For the nuclear man, the future has become an option.*[2]
> – Henry Nouwen

12 STEPS TO AVOID HUMAN TOUCH AND INTIMACY

In a roundabout fashion, we in the Western world actually practice how *not to touch,* not to feel, and not to care too much. The sum total of the following twelve principles are a description of contemporary life in Western culture. Granted, not all of them apply to everybody. And granted, most people would never consciously aspire to such a state, but if you examine these principles closely and honestly, you are likely to find that at least a few of them are guiding factors in your life.[3]

1. Eat, exercise and dress in a way that will make you feel and appear strong, hard and invulnerable. If you are a woman, starve yourself and wear a lot of make-up and fancy clothes. Live according to an image of who you think you should be and not as you are. (Plastic surgery is recommended.)

2. Find a job in which you will be overworked and stressed out. Find a mate who has a job in which he or she will be overworked and stressed out. Become too busy to have time for anyone or anything else. Become too busy even to spend time with yourself, so that you won't have to acknowledge your present state.

3. Pursue a profession in which it is considered normal and even desirable to manipulate, swindle and gain the upper hand in the matter, any matter. Enter a field that causes direct or indirect harm to others such as the alcohol or tobacco industry, oil production, the armed services, etc. All of this will help to desensitize you to the depth of human need and sensitivity.

4. Avoid exercise, fresh air, and nourishing foods so that your body will feel weak, toxic and unworthy of touch.

5. Spend as much time as possible in front of the television, computers and the like, filling your mind with images of murder, rape and unrealistic relationships so that you do not measure yourself by anything realistic or genuine.

6. Drink alcohol, smoke cigarettes, and take antidepressants and other socially acceptable or unacceptable intoxicants that will numb your mind and body, obscuring your ability to clearly perceive your present state.

7. Become part of a social circle in which people are pretentious, polite and/or superficial. Be sure to live in a culture in which, as a norm, people are generally unaffectionate with one another. Or, disengage yourself from social interaction entirely.

8. If you have children, be sure to place your own needs above their needs. Get babysitters every weekend. Buy them toy computers and allow them to watch as much television as they would like. This will help you to avoid the needs of your child,

the depth of your responsibility to future generations and facing the innocence you have lost.

9. Buy a dog or a cat and place all of your love, affection and intimacy needs into that animal, while you avoid giving your loved ones this same attention.

10. Make a general attempt to deny your own feelings and your own pain. In doing so you will not notice the feelings of others, and if you do come across painful feelings in others by chance, you can simply blow it off to, "That's life."

11. Avoid close relationships with members of the same sex. They can see beneath your cover and do understand you, and therefore may demand that you be real with them.

12. In sexual relationships, be aware only of your own needs and do everything you can to get them met. (Isn't that what the psychotherapist said?) In doing so, you can avoid placing attention on your partner and his or her feelings and needs. Be self-centered and selfish in relationships in general.

Unfortunately, the above twelve principles describes us pretty well. Western society advertises a "look" that demands people to dress in a highly specific way in order to create a particular image, and to gear their eating and exercise habits (as well as face lifts and liposuction treatments for the rich), to create a body that matches it. Women have either starved themselves into skinniness or aspire to, and cover their faces with make-up (there are now "permanent" cosmetics available, thus women will never have to be seen "without their face on" again). Many people are stressed out by their jobs—their 40-hour work weeks coming nearer to fifty or sixty hours after they have commuted and put in overtime. Almost half of these workers are also women who have full-time responsibilities to their families. Many people have jobs which at best do not contribute to their society, and at worst stand directly in contrast to their moral integrity. Many do not have time to exercise, or do not live in places in which they are exposed to fresh air, and everybody inevitably takes in a tremendous amount of chemicals and pesticides from their diet—even those who primarily eat vegetables and fresh fruits. Close to 100 percent of Americans own television sets, and a growing majority own computers. Though cigarette smoking is generally decreasing in spite of the recent resurgence of smoking as a fashion, alcohol consumption is rampant and Valium™ and Prozac™ are taken without a second thought. People often find themselves in social situations that do not allow them to be vulnerable, expressive and genuine. Whereas some have the good fortune of one or two genuine friends, many do not. Because of growing financial demands, most parents have increasingly less time to be with their children, and a growing majority of children attend some form of daycare and are placed at the mercy of devices such as televisions and computers to serve as their "baby-sitters." Meanwhile, millions of dollars are spent yearly on the purchase of dogs and cats—these pets becoming the recipients of the attention and affection that children long for. (In the United States, more than one billion dollars is spent on pets every year.[4]) Men tend to have few, if any, close relationships with other men, and sex is used far more frequently as a commodity, a drug or a habit, than it is to invoke states of communion and to express genuine love.

Fortunately, there is more to life than these twelve bad habits—people still continue to fall in love, mothers hug their children and teach them to swim, attempts are made to live honestly and with integrity. But generally speaking, the trend is heading in one direction and you can guess what direction that is!

The question becomes, "Could it be otherwise?"

I say yes—that with a great deal of conscious attention, something else could be created. There could exist a culture of people who take good care of themselves—eating well, living naturally, exercising regularly, and maintaining healthy bodies while not being obsessed by their outer appearance. They would be people who worked at a reasonable pace, and in sane environments.

They would be people who indulged in the use of computers, television and toxic distractions with moderation, and who entertained themselves with one another's company. Women would find support and friendship with other women, and men through men. People would not consume excessive alcohol and drugs, as the richness of their lives would not dictate the same need or desire for such substances. There would exist a set of values that would encourage mothers and fathers to learn to really *be* with their young children—for mothers to breast-feed and for both parents to nourish them with lots of touch and affection. People might have pets in order to bring greater enjoyment into the family environment, but not to unconsciously supplement or replace their need for affection from one another. Time to reflect, relax, pursue our spiritual longing, and to stay connected with oneself would be valued, and adults would aid one another in healing their own psychological wounds so that they would not pass them on to their children. Relationships would be based on giving instead of taking, and sexuality and the body would be considered sacred. It would be a generally wholesome, life-giving, touch-giving, love-giving environment—an environment of sanity. Need this possibility be so far away from where we presently stand?

An Increasingly Impersonal Society

We do not live in a deeply personal society. When we fail to touch one another, the society around us will reflect this by becoming equally impersonal.

I was not quite prepared for what the bank teller would tell me and two eight-year-old children on a homeschool field trip to the bank. We were studying money, and in response to one of the children questioning her about what a world without money would be like, the bank teller described to the children the concept of the debit card that will eventually make money obsolete.

She went on to fill their innocent minds with the likely proposition that individuals will have small computer chips surgically set into their arms. The chips will be connected to their debit card and will serve many other functions such as that of an identification card, a key to one's home, and so forth. Needless to say, the children's conversation on the ride home was not about the origins of money, but about what it would be like for everybody to get computer chips implanted inside of their arms!

I was similarly shocked by a visit to the Arizona State University library where I went to do some research on the field of touch. I entered the library and found a woman at the information desk. When I told her what I was looking for she responded, "Oh, you should be able to find that in the sociophile on the silver platter." When I laughed in response, believing she was telling me some sort of techno joke, she gave me a blank look. She then explained that this was the name of a specific research program on a specific kind of computer. Now wary of the success I would have on this expedition, I walked through corridors of computers until I came to the proper set. I spent the next two hours learning how to use the program in order to access the desired materials, and soon discovered 2064 listings for "touch" in various libraries throughout the state. After spending the following three hours searching through about 30% of the titles, I was exhausted. Next, I endeavored to learn another program that would inform me *where* these articles could be located. Hours later, after going up and down elevators, in and out of rooms, purchasing copy cards, and talking with still more computers, I collapsed on the steps in front of the library with two short articles as my trophies for the day's work, pondering the growing complexity, impersonalization and lack of human contact even in public facilities such as libraries. I ended up doing the majority of my research at the Prescott Public Library, where I could walk from one end to the other without getting lost and where the reference librarians were willing to talk to me instead of insisting that I communicate with a computer!

10

Western medicine has become yet another impersonal institution. A friend of mine who is a medical doctor in India was shocked to find out about the relationship (or lack of relationship) between most doctors and their patients in the West. In India, a doctor has an investment in his or her patient as a person. He diagnoses not only the symptoms of the illness, but familiarizes himself with the person behind it, his or her life circumstances, and his or her individual needs. When he takes on a patient with an illness, it is his personal and ethical responsibility to see this person through to its cure. He will not continue to charge a flat rate of $95 per fifteen minute slot for each follow-up visit, particularly if he knows that the patient can not afford it. Even so, Indian doctors are well off financially. Institutionalized medicine in the West stands in direct contrast to this.

You can guess with a fair degree of accuracy what you will find when you go into a standard, mainstream Western medicinal institution. The smell of sterilized gloves, antiseptics, deodorizers and sanitation chemicals fills the air. Here you will be greeted by a hopefully polite receptionist, given a clipboard of forms to fill out and be expected to wait—indefinitely, if need be. Perhaps if you have not stayed in a hospital for an extended period, you do not know that patients are not spoken of by name, but are instead regularly classified either by their illness or their room number. You may or may not be touched by your doctor or nurse, as the touch codes in hospitals are continually becoming stricter, and if you are touched it will probably be by a plastic surgical glove covering a hand. In the words of one physical therapist who works in a hospital setting, "We are so fragmented ourselves, so disconnected from our own bodies, that we don't hesitate to separate a person from his body part, and to treat him as a broken leg or a sprained wrist instead of as a human being."

And not only is our culture imprinting upon us in 1001 ways that touch is dangerous, that bodies are dirty and unsanitary...but we are buying the party line! We are so afraid of our own sweat,

11

blood, germs and minor imperfections (as evidenced in an excessive use of antiperspirants and deodorants, unneeded anesthetics, scented sanitary pads, etc.) that we don't want to touch, or be touched by others. I was quite surprised when I walked into the bathroom of a popular family restaurant chain and found it "touch-free"—no doors to open, a toilet that was automatically programmed to flush as the individual left the stall, soap that drips on one's hands when they are placed under the dispenser, water that mysteriously knows when to turn on and off, and a hand-dryer that starts automatically when hands are placed in its vicinity. I could not disagree with my friend when she supported this system, as it was certainly more germ-free, but I had recently returned from an Asian country in which everybody touches everything and everybody, and the whole thing struck me as baffling—not only impersonal, but simply strange. Although the population is exploding at unprecedented rates, we seem to be living more and more in a society without *people* in it.

I have walked in two worlds. Half of my adult life has been spent tromping around rain forests in knee-high boots, bathing at a well in the company of chickens and mosquitoes, lighting a candle so I could read before I went to bed, spending an hour just trying to get a letter mailed, and walking crowded streets with my eyes on the ground to avoid walking straight into animal shit! The other half has been spent in educational institutions, sitting thousands of hours in front of a computer, racing around in my car from appointment to appointment, trying to keep up with the rat race, playing the game of big business. *Quantity* of life does not equal quality of life, and the challenge remains about how to live lives full of presence and beingness in an increasingly impersonal world.

I think that human beings were placed here together both because we have some business to do together, and because we need each other. We cannot get the same physical nourishment from spending a Saturday evening on the Internet looking at

12

pictures of naked women as we can cuddling with our husband or wife, or by spending a quiet evening with close friends. It is simply not as satisfying to heat up a Lean Cuisine™ in the microwave after work as it is to have a home-cooked meal. It is not the same to drive into an automatic, credit card operated gas station without an attendant, as it is to drive up and pump our gas when somebody is washing windows, somebody is cleaning the cement, and somebody else is collecting the money. These small details of an impersonal world, in their sum total, take a significant toll on the overall quality of our lives.

Human beings thrive from the nourishment, comfort, encouragement and joy that they receive from their contact with others. They grow from being confronted with failures in communication, through acknowledging the difficulties in loving one another, and by getting direct and indirect feedback from their world and from those whom they come into relationship with. Almost all religions of the world agree that the purpose of human experience is to learn to love one another, to grow and to help others. People in the Western world have devoted massive amounts of creative energy, time and money into complex technological pursuits. How would it look if even a fraction of this energy was devoted to creating an environment that was full of touch, intimacy, affection and an overall livability that would provide nurturance and sanity to those who wish to sustain their humanness in a time of growing alienation and modernization?

THE UNTOUCHABLES

They know that the world does not much like them and they try hard to be good to one another.[5]
– Jonathan Kozol

The term *untouchability* commonly conjures mental images of poor, hungry, and dirty people in India

13

who belong to the illegal, but still existent, class of "untouch-ables." These people are relegated to the lowest jobs, if any jobs at all, such as toilet cleaning and street sweeping. They are con-sidered as dirt by their society—as less than others; almost as flies or stray dogs that can be cast off by the flick of a hand. Higher castes in India consider it contaminating to have any physical contact with an untouchable.

Yet untouchability is not only alive and active in India and the East, but is operating in full swing in our own backyards. Who are the untouchables of the civilized world? They are the gay peo-ple, the African Americans, the Hispanics, the Chinese, the poor, the homeless, immigrants, people with AIDS, the elderly, people with physical and mental disabilities, and people who live in communities, spiritual groups and other alternative lifestyles. They are the "have-nots" in any given society. They are all those whom we try to cast off into the corners of society where they will not be seen, such as ghettos, or into positions in which they can not be heard, thus keeping them out of spheres of public and political influence where they would have a voice. They are the people whom we would rather not think about (because they make us uncomfortable) and certainly not talk about, for to do so inspires feelings of dis-ease, guilt, fear and irreconcilability.

Terms such as racism, sexism and homophobia have become popular fronts for our widespread prejudice. "Politically correct" language has become incorporated into our vocabulary such that many people now use the term "woman" instead of "girl," "Afro-American" instead of "nigger," and "gay" instead of "fag," with-out even knowing why they are doing so. However, these names are often little more than superficial niceties that often serve to mask the underlying fact of socially sanctioned untouchability. Although there have been improvements in the last fifty years, racism is still breaking hearts and destroying lives every day; gay men and lesbian women are still being outcast by their families; the poor are waiting in the emergency room line for three and four days in order to simply see a doctor. Untouchability implies that there are entire factions of society that do not receive touch—both literal touch as well as the acknowledgment of being citizens worthy of all the privileges (e.g., welfare, housing, healthcare) extended to all other members of the culture.

The issue of untouchability is perhaps most poignantly illustrated in the AIDS crisis. Although it is most widespread among the gay population, AIDS has now extended into all corners of the modern world, as more and more movie stars, school teachers, friends, and other "ordinary" people die of this illness. Unfortunately, most people continue to link AIDS with homosexuality, and proceed to feel increasingly separate from, and prejudiced against, gay men and lesbian women. Furthermore, there are a great many widespread assumptions about AIDS that are incorrect, such as the belief that one can get AIDS simply by touching a door handle that a person with AIDS has touched, or by hugging someone who has AIDS. Oftentimes, even those who want to touch people with AIDS are blocked by their fears.

In contrast to this perprective stands Ma Jaya Bhagavati, a spiritual teacher whose Florida-based community runs a hospice for people with AIDS and regularly visits AIDS patients in hospitals. She tells the story of walking into a man's room and noting the immense sterility and de-personalized setting. The doctors who visited him were formal and distant, and the man was connected to a complex network of machinery. Using her connections to cut through some of the red tape, Ma Jaya Bhagavati was able to spend some time alone with this young man. She immediately climbed into bed beside him, and held and comforted him, giving him some of the only genuine human contact and affection he would receive in his last days.

Untouchability is a reality. Although we'd rather not admit to it, most people do not want to touch the hand of the homeless person, or hug the young mentally retarded child. As badly as we may feel about it, the majority of us do not want to spend time visiting with elderly people in a nursing home, or to serve food at the local soup kitchen. We do not want this skin-to-skin contact, and hope that somebody else will do it for us.

Do professional touchers exist? Are there people who are willing to do this work? There are a few. They are generally the underpaid workers of the government social welfare programs whose funding is constantly threatened. Most are so overworked, and so drained by their lack of ability to meet the needs of the people they are responsible for, that they often become burnt out, hardened and cynical. Many of these case workers are people whose own touch needs were never met, and who are knowingly or unknowingly trying to fill this void by "touching," i.e. helping others.

I am familiar with the life of the underpaid, overworked and burnt out social workers because I was one of them. I worked in an abortion clinic as a bilingual assistant to the medical doctors who performed abortion. I did blood tests and pregnancy tests, handed tools to the doctors, cleaned up after the abortions, and provided emotional support for the many women who were traumatized by the surgery. I worked for less than seven dollars an hour at the hardest job I have ever done in my life when I could have been making forty dollars an hour, and many times I asked myself what was motivating me to do it. It is years later, and I now see that my own touch needs were in some way fulfilled by serving those who were otherwise not receiving healing touch. I did not become a professional toucher because I was altruistic; I *needed* to do so in response to my own feelings of touch-starvation.

Professional touchers sustain the hospices, the hunger programs, the nursing homes and the drug treatment centers for teenagers. Many times in these places you will find one or two individuals—usually doing dishes, cleaning the toilets, or patiently holding one of their clients as they cry—who have very consciously dedicated themselves to the task of caring for those whom society has rejected, knowing that while their assistance will not

16

produce change on a large scale, that it is having a significant effect on the few people with whom they come into contact.

In India, you cannot walk down the street without being met by several "untouchables." How then, in contemporary industrialized nations, do we hide our untouchables away?

Author and social critic Jonathan Kozol reports standing on a highway overpass looking at the New York city ghettos and being confronted with murals showing interiors of pretty rooms, window shades, curtains and pots of pretty flowers—all painted on the sides of buildings that face the highway. These pictures were "done so well that when you look the first time, you imagine that you're seeing into people's homes—pleasant looking homes... that have a distinctly middle-class appearance." The social worker he was with commented that the city had these murals painted on the wall "not for the people in the neighborhood—because they're facing the wrong way—but for tourists and commuters... The idea is that they mustn't be upset by knowing too much about the population here. It isn't enough that these people are sequestered. It's also important that their presence be disguised or 'sweetened.'"[6]

We hide from our untouchables with the numbness we have created in ourselves. We hide from the untouchables in our false hopes that our governments are taking care of them, in our ideals of democracy and freedom, in our prayers that "God" will tend to them, and in our wish not to see. We hide them from ourselves in nursing homes and in housing units in neighborhoods we do not drive by. We pretend that they are not there. We are too afraid of how we would feel if we did not hide.

Instead of exposing ourselves to this type of discomfort; instead of touching the untouchables with our own hands, we drop off our old clothes to the Salvation Army, we give a dollar to the homeless person, we smile at the retarded child once in awhile, and we carry on, figuring that there is nothing we can do, while a part of us dies with them.

The Hope

Mahatma Gandhi, the revolutionary Indian leader and perhaps the most admirable advocate of social change in the twentieth century, spent a lifetime working for the improvement of India's untouchable class, often visiting them and performing tasks with them such as cleaning latrines, which was unheard of for a man of Gandhi's social class. He encouraged people to change the term "untouchable" to *harijan,* which means "child of God."

A Christian couple in New England adopted over a dozen refugee children of the Vietnam war—many of them severely emotionally traumatized—and integrated them with their own children. They now operate their "House of Hope" according to a combination of traditional Christian and Vietnamese Buddhist religious beliefs and practices.

An influential and popular spiritual leader in India recently allowed an intercaste marriage to be conducted in his temple, much to the horror of many of his followers.

Are we willing to follow their example in our individual lives? Are we willing to simply admit to ourselves that there are large groups of people that we are afraid to think about and would rather not touch? In acknowledging our fear and prejudice honestly lies the seeds of change. Untouchability is yet another symptom of a culture that has been touch-starved and in which people no longer know how to relate with one another compassionately.

A LOSS OF TRUST

In 1995, Robert Putnam, a professor of International Affairs at Harvard University, released an article that caught the attention of the U.S. government and became the subject of widespread response and social concern. The article, entitled *Bowling Alone,*[7] spoke of the decline of what Putnam

18

called "social capital," which refers to an individual's network of social connections. He noted with statistical evidence that while individually centered activities (i.e., bowling alone, computer games, Virtual Reality) are on the rise, participation in community-based activities such as bowling leagues, PTA meetings, religious groups, Boy Scouts, civil and fraternal organizations, and voting are sharply declining. He quoted a poll in which Americans were asked if they could trust most people. In 1960, fifty-eight percent of Americans said that they did, whereas in 1993, only thirty-seven percent responded in favor of trust. What will this look like in another fifty years? At the current rate, nobody will be able to trust anybody.

A touch-starved nation very quickly becomes a trust-starved nation. The fact that Putnam's article caught the attention of the United States government, resulting in a series of talk shows and major magazine articles in response to it, is evidence of a real concern among the people. Suddenly a Harvard professor is telling us that people are out of touch with one another.

The more we cease to trust one another, the more violent we are likely to become. Throughout this book, you will read about the consequences of the failure to receive the necessary touch from birth onward. The result is that we simply don't trust ourselves. Most people have never trusted themselves, and regardless of where it originated, this climate of terror is now rooted *inside* of us. We are not unaware of how often we feel rageful toward our husbands and wives, our pets, and toward other drivers on the highway. We secretly note the small ways that we are scandalous and dishonest as we move through our days. Believing that we ourselves are untrustworthy, we do not bother to act in a manner that is worthy of trust, and we lose touch with what is most real in ourselves.

Trust is going to have to start at home. When somebody is expecting the worst of us, that is often what they get. On the other hand, when we know that somebody trusts us...when they show us by the way they relate to us that they are respecting our integrity, our maturity, and our ability to make decisions and to act wisely, we in turn begin to act trustworthy. Similarly, when we give someone else our trust and respect, the chances of that person acting in integrity with us increase dramatically.

There is no easy answer to the present predicament of distrust. It is not as though we can simply begin to trust everybody we meet—it is both impossible as a result of our conditioning, and impractical in terms of the state of the world. However, we can become aware of the profound lack of trust within ourselves and acknowledge the effects of this on a touch-starved nation.

THE FAST LANE TO NOWHERE

So what do we have to show for our lives as we pull up to death's gate driving seventy-five miles per hour in our Ford pick-up; having finally saved enough money to take our grandchildren to Disney World; having worked forty hours a week for forty-five years at the factory; having taken in two thousand pounds of hamburger, Swiss cheese and donuts; having failed to pay off our mortgage but receiving a small social security check; having smoked for thirty years without getting cancer; having watched our kids grow up and become just like ourselves; having watched "progress" sail by us, leaving us in its wake wondering what has happened; having *gotten by...?*

Is this the ticket to the heaven we were taught about as children—where the white angels open the gate and take us to a cloud-covered paradise? Or, as others believe, do we just explode into blank nothingness, and so what if the world is going to pieces and my plastic milk carton will be around for three generations and my great, great grandchild will feel isolated and depressed in her radiated world—unbonded herself because her mother, and mother's mother, did not know that breast-feeding and continual touch and affection is an absolute necessity for

20

raising a child who feels secure in the world? Is our touch-free, germ-free, computerized, God-free environment taking us to where we want to go? And more importantly, is it taking us to where our children's children want to go?

> *We wonder if we might not be making a very big mistake, missing that opportunity we have been waiting for all our lives. And even as we observe these things about ourselves, we feel the urge to defend them, to reassure ourselves that maybe it isn't as bad as all that.*[8]

There is a contract with fine print attached to the Western dream of wealth and prosperity. Even if we don't know it, we have signed on the dotted line. We have signed our lives over to an ideal that will not only never provide us with what we were really searching for, but one that promises to slowly consume our vitality and aliveness, just as the rising temperature of the water in the pot slowly takes the life from the frog.

Montagu says:

> *...The individual is gradually converted into a device with a built-in design for achievement in accordance with the prevailing requirements, entailing the suppression of emotion, the denial of love and friendship, the ability to trade with whatever serves one for a conscience, while conveying an unvarying appearance of rectitude.*[9]

Heaven or hell happens right here on this plane. In spite of the popular commentary on reincarnation, as far as most of us are concerned, this one life, and the conscious will to make of it what we can, is what we are given. And if we want to know how we are doing, all we have to do is look around. Joseph Chilton Pearce explains:

History doesn't necessarily repeat itself. Phenomena have appeared over the past fifty years that have no historical precedence, for which our genetic system can't compensate, and that have so altered our mental makeup that we are blinded to the obvious relation between cause and effect. [10]

The future of a nation that is either touch-starved or full of affection and aliveness, depends on one thing—our children. The child who experiences himself in his rightful place in the family, community and culture, will become an adult who will give more than he takes, and who will bestow affection freely. Feeling cared for, he *will* care for others. Touch begins right at the start.

CHAPTER 2

First Touch:
Birth and Childhood

Touching, yes, is the root...
We have to feed babies,
fill them both
inside and outside.
We must speak to their skins...
which thirst and hunger
and cry
as much as their bellies.
We must gorge them
with warmth and caresses
just as we do with milk.[1]

— Frederick Leboyer

Marasmus, stemming from the Greek root meaning to waste away, is a condition which results in physical death in infants when they are not given sufficient touch. Nearly fifty years ago, Dr. René Spitz discovered that more than thirty percent of infants raised in orphanages in which they did not receive contact, care and affection from a primary caretaker did not survive their first year of life, in spite of adequate food, materially hygienic surroundings and excellent medical care.[2]

On the most basic, instinctual level, physical contact is essential to sustain all human life—a type of food that is as necessary to the infant's well-being as is the physical food he takes in. On a deeper level, the intimacy that is created through touch is what creates a feeling of "aliveness" in the individual—for touch brings us to life.

The contact that transpires in the first moments, hours and months of a child's life will be largely responsible for the difference between a human life characterized by a persistent undercurrent of lack and desperation, and one that is based on a sense of security and belonging. Essentially, first touch—not only the first moment of physical touch, but the touch that the infant receives at the beginning of his or her life—is the single most influential factor that will determine a future life of love, or one of unlove. Although it is true that children are unlikely to remember their births and early childhoods in later life, the impressions they receive and how their parents treat them in their formative years is literally who they will become in later life. First touch is *that* important.

Parents have an utter responsibility to the life they have created. In one way, the child is separate and independent from her parents—existing as her own entity. But, at the same time, the child is very much interconnected with her parents, and is wholly affected by the attitudes and behaviors that they enact, both toward her as well as toward each other in her proximity. All a child's relationships, for the rest of her life, as well as her good and bad habits, her attitudes toward others, her sense of belonging or alienation, emptiness or fullness, are given by the parent, and will be either the child's sentence or blessing to live out. (Of course a person can always choose a path of self-transformation

24

in adulthood, but in unloved and unbonded children this consideration often never even arises.) If parents fully understood the implications of their influence on their child, especially in the beginning of his or her life, the necessity for abundant touch, nurturance, and affection, would never even need to be considered.

> *A baby deprived of the experience necessary to give him the basis for full flowering of his innate potential will perhaps never know a moment of the unconditional rightness that has been natural to his kind for 99.99 percent of its history. Deprivation, in the degree to which he has suffered its discomfort and limitations in infancy, will be maintained indiscriminately as part of his development...*[3]
>
> – Jean Liedloff

KNOWLEDGE LIES IN WOMEN'S BODIES

To the fault of no individual, women are systematically drained of their knowledge and intelligence. These powers, if allowed to express themselves freely, would provide the woman with all she needs to know to raise a child who, in turn, would be able to manifest his or her full capacity as an adult, uninhibited by feelings of shame and low self-esteem, and free from seeking other's validation of his or her basic "all-rightness." By instinct, such an "empowered" woman would raise a child whose natural state was happiness, health, intelligence and equanimity, instead of mediocrity, suppressed depression and a desire for power over others.

The knowledge of how to touch their infants is part of every woman's knowing—programmed into her very cells, stimulated by the process of pregnancy and birth, and always available. The only reason that this knowledge is unknown to so many women is that contemporary Western culture—with its emphasis on a highly developed intellect at the cost of the knowledge of body and heart—has placed a greater value on the mind of modern medicine than on the mind of the body. Concerning the process of birth and early intimacy, the past century has shown a 180-degree turn away from the knowledge inherent in a woman's body, and an equally strong movement toward a technological method of producing children.

In the 1920s, world renowned behaviorist John B. Watson wrote his classic book, *Psychological Care of Infant and Child*— a book that was to "revolutionize" child raising practices for decades to come. In an effort to bring up a child "as free as possible of sensitivities to people," he suggested the following:

> *Treat them as though they were young adults...Never hug and kiss them, never let them sit on your lap. If you must, kiss them once on the forehead when they say good night. Shake hands with them in the morning. Give them a pat on the head if they have made an extraordinarily good job of a difficult task. Try it out. In a week's time...you will be utterly ashamed of the mawkish, sentimental way you have been handling it.*[4]

Popular misconceptions about child raising support the idea that if parents satisfy all of the infant's needs, they are somehow indulging the child and setting up a system of dependency that the child will be locked into forever more. As a result, many mothers have lost access to their instinctual knowledge that would *never* allow them to treat their child this way, or to follow advice such as Watson's, to the letter. However, contrary to this mistaken belief, when the child's dependency needs are adequately tended to (not only the physical needs but emotional and psychological needs as well), they fall away naturally as the child matures and becomes capable of taking care of his own needs, paradoxically resulting in a *more* independent child. Montagu has noted that, "Anthropologists, looking at cultures where a baby's comfort needs are quickly and tenderly indulged—even before it cries—have found that by the third month of life these babies cry less than Western infants."[5]

BONDING

Given a choice of life companions, I would take any number of brain-damaged people, rather than one unbonded person, for we are flexible beyond measure and can compensate for extensive physical damage, but lack of bonding finds no compensation.[6]
– Joseph Chilton Pearce

In order to fully grasp the lifelong significance of touch on the child's life it is essential to understand the process of bonding, for it is the basis of all the birth and child raising practices that will be discussed throughout the chapter.

A contemporary thinker who deeply understands bonding, and articulates it clearly, is popular author and lecturer Joseph Chilton Pearce. Of this he says:

Bonding gives an intuitive, extrasensory kind of relationship between mother and child. Bonding is a felt process, not available to discursive thought, language, or intellect...[7]

And:

Bonding occurs when the infant is met on both physical and subtle levels by his caretaker. Anchored in the power of the subtle heart system, the infant is always anchored in the core of his life. He is rooted within the great subtle intuitive energies that power physical life, no matter how his physical situation shifts and changes.[8]

27

Bonding is the most profound measure of touch. It is a fusing of hearts, a tacit connection to somebody outside of oneself, an intermingling of life-forces that allows communion to occur far beneath the level of conscious awareness and external circumstances. It is a process that occurs *between* mother and child, by which two separate entities become linked with one another and operate as one unit.

One father explained:

The whole term "bonding" really means passing along caring— a sense of love, where affection is obvious, where the child just feels it. The way you do that is in every single interface with them, no matter how they show up. You are love—not hippie love, not lustful love, but simple care and compassion.

Mamatoto is a Swahili term for "motherbaby."[9] In contrast to the idea of mother and infant as two separate, but connected, individuals, *mamatoto* suggests that mother and child are operating as one. Though the task of fully satisfying the infant's needs is a demanding one, at times seemingly impossible, when the mother-child organism is considered as one, there is an absence of the tension that would otherwise be present if the mother thinks, "I am serving *you*," "I am doing so much for *you*," "I am providing for *you*." When mother and child are as one, what needs to be done is done.

Parents can educate themselves, but what occurs on a deeper level in the bonding process cannot be learned in any book. Bonding is physiological, psychological, emotional and intuitive. Nature has created a perfected system that is intended to insure the optimal maturation of the human being on all levels, thereby revealing a possibility for the experience of communion, selflessness and exchange of self with other through the process of childbearing.

The Mother Bonds Too

> *It is clear that the mother needs her baby immediately after birth quite as much as the baby needs her. Each is primed to develop their own potentialities—the maternal role in the one case, that of developing human in the other.*[10]
>
> – Ashley Montagu

Bonding is not a one-way street. The mother must bond with the child so that the child will be able to bond with the mother. The demands of mothering are going to be extensive. She will need to hold her baby when she is all "held-out," to respond gently and quietly when she feels like screaming. Though much of mothering is joyful, her patience is going to be stretched to the limit. What gives her the ability to extend herself to her child in the way that is being considered here is the strength of her connection to him and her love for him. Depth of bonding will yield greater ease and less hesitation in her movement to fulfill her child's demands and wishes. It will not be easy, but she will be willing to act because her connection to her child is profound and she knows how much her child needs her.

Therefore, the bonding process that occurs creates a sense of security not only in the infant but in the mother as well. When she experiences milk coming from her own breast—milk that she knows is sustaining her infant—she feels herself a woman. When she sees that her presence and touch can turn a wailing child into a calm one, she knows that her touch is power. The more she gives of herself to her child, the more she allows bonding to take over. Thus she becomes naturally devoted. Many mothers describe this process of bonding as a "rite of passage," discovering depths of womanhood within themselves that they never knew before becoming mothers.

29

TO TOUCH IS TO LIVE

The Unbonded

> *We are never conscious of being bonded; we are conscious only of our acute disease when we are not bonded or when we are bonded to compulsion and material things.*[11]
>
> — Joseph Chilton Pearce

Although the term "bonding" is frequently thrown around amongst medical practitioners, psychologists and parents alike, we as a culture do not understand the implications of it.

The reason that bonding is not understood is because so few adults were ever given a sense of real belonging, of knowing in the cells of their bodies that they were loved. (Just because a person can say, "Of course my parents love me, I know they do," does not mean that person has bonded.) If bonding is not an experience we know in the core of our being—if it has no more meaning to us than any other intellectual concept—how can we understand the full value of it, thus giving it the absolute priority that it demands? Instead, we understand the importance of bonding primarily through our own sense of unbondedness within ourselves.

If we as a culture genuinely understood bonding, there is *no way*, except in dire circumstances, that mothers would be given the amounts of anesthesia that are commonly administered during birth. It would be impossible to place babies anywhere but on the mother's breast in the first moments and hours of life. The conscience of our medical professionals would not allow babies to be placed in incubators except when absolutely necessary, and in these instances would only do so in the direct proximity of the mother. Bottle-feeding would be considered an option only when the mother could not breast-feed.

If we understood in our gut what was at stake for our child concerning the unfolding of his future life, mothers would take a stand in hospitals and insist on holding their infants immediately after birth. If we truly respected the necessity of bonding, we would give our children absolutely everything—not in terms of toys and clothes and birthday parties, but in terms of affection and attention, knowing how desperately they need this.

> *A child needs love. Love is not a thing. Love is life. It means being alive and caring for life. Life creates needs. To fulfill them is to fulfill love. Love sustains life. All a child wants is to be loved.*[12]
>
> – J. Konrad Stettbacher

The unbonded child will adjust to her unbonded state by a type of psychic death— becoming numb and indifferent even to her sense of loss and disconnection. However, the child will pay the price for her unbondedness in ten thousand ways throughout her life.

> *...For a child whose attachment needs are chronically frustrated, anxiety and depression will diminish when attention to the needs diminishes. The cost, however, is exorbitant: loss of the ability to trust, loss of the capacity for intimacy, and a diminished ability to empathize with oneself and others.*[13]
>
> – Paul Klein

If our ignorance regarding the need to bond was not unconscious, we might find it cruel. But we were not educated in this matter, and the best we can do is acknowledge the fact that whatever degree of bonding that we, as members of a touch-deprived society, were given as infants was not good enough, and that we have thus far been unable to provide better. It is only through this acknowledgment that we can begin to look at our present systems for bringing children into this world, and ask ourselves what aspects of these systems are responsible for sustaining this broken state. In doing so, we begin to take charge of creating something different in our lives.

BONDING IS NOT JUST SWEET SENTIMENT, IT IS A MORAL-SCIENTIFIC IMPERATIVE

The easiest and quickest way to induce depression and alienation in an infant or child is not to touch it, hold it, or carry it on your body. Extensive scientific research has documented that this form of sensory stimulation (touch and movement) during the formative periods of brain development is absolutely essential for normal growth and development of the brain and behavior.[14]
— James Prescott

Although the need for bonding is easily understood on an intuitive, emotional level, bonding is, in fact, a psychophysiological process. Although the bonding process appears to the naked eye as mother-holding-breast-feeding-infant-with-lots-of-eye-contact-and-tender-caressing, these behaviors are a mirror for underlying sensory-psychophysiological processes that are essential for the normal growth and development of the brain. This sensory stimulation is provided through nearness and intimate body contact between mother and infant. Joseph Chilton Pearce has said, "The issue is not sweet sentiment. The issue is intelligence, the brain's ability to process sensory information, organize muscular responses, and interact with the environment."[15]

Perhaps nobody understands the scientific implications of bonding more clearly than developmental neuropsychologist Dr. James Prescott, who has devoted more than thirty years of his life to scientific research and writing about the necessity of tactile stimulation (touch) and body movement stimulation in the development of the functional, non-violent human being. (For more of Prescott's findings, see section entitled, "The Roots of Violence" in Chapter Four.)

Prescott's initiated brain studies were inspired by the research findings of the Harlows and their associates that began in the 1950s and which documented the abnormal behaviors of maternally-deprived monkeys. In one experiment, described by Ashley Montagu, five female monkeys, of an ordinarily affectionate species, were raised without their mothers. When these test monkeys matured and gave birth to their own infants, three of them turned out to be highly indifferent and unaffectionate as mothers, almost totally unresponsive to their infants, and the other two were brutal and abusive to their infants.[16]

His own extensive research on isolation-reared monkeys (those raised in solitary cages with no physical body contact between mother and other monkeys) led Prescott to rename the "Maternal-Social Deprivation Syndrome" the "Somato-Sensory Affectional Deprivation" (S-SAD), which refers specifically to infants who are raised without sufficient body contact stimulation with their mothers. He explains that SAD results in the abnormal development and function of the brain. "During formative periods of brain growth, certain kinds of sensory deprivation—such as lack of touching and rocking by the mother—result in incomplete or damaged development of the neuronal systems that mediate affection (for instance, a loss of the nerve-cell branches called dendrites)."[17]

The cerebellum is widely understood to be responsible for the regulation of motor functions of the body including the maintaining of body balance. Not so well known is the role of the cerebellum in the regulation of the autonomic nervous system and emotional-social behaviors. In fact, the cerebellum regulates both painful and pleasurable sensations and states. Infants who are not rocked and cuddled are at risk for incomplete development of the brain pathways and systems that mediate pleasure (limbic-frontal cortical-cerebellar complex). Adults who have difficulty experiencing pleasurable states are more easily frustrated, more prone to depression and violence, and more vulnerable to drug or alcohol abuse and addiction.[18]

Prescott noted that monkeys raised in social isolation without physical body contact with their mothers or other monkeys would experience abnormal development and functioning of those brain structures associated with emotional-social and sexual behaviors. A number of brain studies conducted by other scientists on mother-deprived adult monkeys who were pathologically violent, confirmed the existence of these brain abnormalities. Similar behavioral abnormalities have been seen in hospitalized children as well as those raised in institutions. In other words, "When we don't pick up our kids, this results in the incomplete development and functioning of the cerebellum and related brain structures."[19]

The developing brain—like the body—is very immature at birth and needs sensory stimulation for normal growth and development. For the cerebellum, this means continuous gentle movement stimulation. Therefore, handling the baby—rocking and carrying it—is necessary for its brain to develop properly. Babies who are raised in institutions that are overcrowded and understaffed often do not develop the same intellectual capacities as other children do because the caretakers in these places tend neither to touch them as much as their parents would, nor have the same personal and emotional investment in them.

An increasing number of biological studies on animals suggest that even though many other factors are important, a parent's caressing, cuddling and "coochie-cooing" play a significant role in maintaining proper brain development in the infant. A study published in the *Journal of Neuroscience* in 2000 shows that blocking the physical attention from a parent negatively changes the architecture of their baby's brain as well as changing certain memory abilities.[20]

Joseph Chilton Pearce has subsequently affirmed these basic principles from a different perspective:

This limbic structure must be activated during the bonding
period at birth. Unless it is activated, the relationship between
the heart and the midbrain area breaks down. From then on,
this heart-mind relationship is compensating rather than func-
tioning, and there is a serious dysfunction in the way the per-
son can relate to others.[21]

There is a substantial body of scientific data on how the early physical environment influences brain development, function and behavior. It has only been touched upon here to highlight the facts of the psychophysiological foundation in the bonding process, and to emphasize from a scientific perspective the necessity of body touch and body movement in the mother-infant relationship in order for bonding to take place.

HOW TO ENCOURAGE BONDING

Having understood the sheer necessity of bonding, the question then becomes, "How can a mother best ensure the likelihood of bonding to occur, thus fulfilling the touch requirements for her child?"

The answer is very practical. For although bonding cannot be measured on a scale or sold in a package, there are specific things a parent can do. It begins in the womb, continues into the birth chamber, and is sustained by what I will refer to later in the chapter as "The Three B's"—breast-feeding, backin' da baby, and bedtime.

In the Womb

The field of fetal awareness began to receive popular attention in the seventies. In addition to his own experiments and extensive experience, Dr. Thomas Verny took it upon himself to devote six years of life and travel to meet with the experts in this field across the globe. In his comprehensive book, *The Secret Life of the Unborn Child,*[22] he summarized the evidence of hundreds of scientific studies with the following facts:

- By the sixth month of life in utero, and perhaps even earlier, the child leads an active emotional life.
- The mature fetus can see, hear, experience, taste, and even learn in utero.
- What a child feels and perceives in utero begins to shape the attitudes and expectations of himself that he will maintain throughout his adult life. The main source of these messages is his mother—not necessarily every thought or feeling she has—but her general mood and feelings about her child.
- The father's feelings about his wife and the unborn child are an important influence on the unborn fetus.

Verny further quoted a study done by neuroscientist Dominick Purpura of New York's Albert Einstein Medical College that revealed that the child in the womb has already formed the brain structures necessary for learning, and even awareness, between the twenty-eighth and thirty-second weeks of development.[23]

Bonding begins in the womb. When it is understood and accepted that the infant is "conscious" in the womb—perhaps not alert and aware in the same way as adults are, but nonetheless conscious—the need for maternal love, touch and bonding, becomes increasingly clear. The physiological functioning of the womb is designed to respect the "consciousness" of the unborn child. If not impeded by a mother who abuses her unborn child in the womb by smoking, alcohol or drug abuse, by living in toxic and abusive environments, or by holding a deep resentment toward the unborn child—the womb itself will nurture the unborn fetus, encasing the child in the natural intelligence of the mother's body. On the flip side—the modern world into which the baby will be born *will not* respect the child's consciousness. In fact, it won't even acknowledge it.

In one study, Dr. Michael Lieberman showed that an unborn child will become agitated (as measured by rapid heartbeat) each time his mother even *thinks* of having a cigarette—she needn't even put it to her mouth. He suggested that while the fetus can not intellectually comprehend that his mother is smoking, he is sophisticated enough to react to the sensation that will be produced in him due to the drop in his oxygen supply from the blood that she will provide for him through the placenta.[24]

The question therefore becomes, "How, in pragmatic terms, can the mother be with her child in a way that respects the child's already conscious state?"

Beginning with the obvious, the mother refrains from indulging unhealthy eating habits and from the intake of any type of intoxicant. She receives prenatal care and follows the doctor's or midwife's recommendations. She exercises and practices breathing and relaxation.

In addition, the mother comes to appreciate that she is connected with her child not only through the obvious intimacy that exists between them, as well as the food that she provides for them both, but also through their shared hormones and the physiological changes that emotions produce in the body. Dr. William Sears, one of the fore-fathers of conscious child raising, explains:

> *Mother and baby are part of the same hormonal network. Those same hormones which produce stress reactions in the mother (increased heart rate, increased blood pressure, flushing, sweating, headaches, etc.) also pass through the placenta to the baby. So when mother feels upset, baby is upset. Researchers theorize that if an unborn baby is continually exposed to stress hormones from the mother and is continually producing his own stress hormones in response to an anxious environment, he has a higher risk of developing an overcharged nervous system.[25]*

From this example, it becomes apparent that depressed mothers most often give birth to depressed babies, anxious mothers give birth to anxious babies, happy mothers to happy babies, etc. If the mother does not want her baby, the baby will, on some level, know it.

A periodical entitled *Birth*, published a study conducted in 1995 showing that women who had extended and early contact with their newborns looked at, talked to and touched their infants more, watched less television and talked less on the telephone than mothers with minimal contact with their infants. These findings suggest that increased postpartum contact with infants leads not only to more interactions, but also to more touching.[26]

Touching the Unborn Child

The mother begins to touch the infant in utero. On one level, she is already touching the infant entirely from within her body. But since she cannot touch the infants' body with her hands or hold the child in her arms, her touch must become creative. Paula Matthew, practicing midwife for the past twenty-two years, explained, "Pregnant women who take the time to get alone with their babies and their bodies, and who enjoy the sensation of being pregnant, will usually develop a normal way of massaging their babies. The baby will push out, and the mother might push back, or playfully poke a bit, or rub a little foot, and in this way they develop a relationship." The infant feels the motions of her mother's hand, and begins to become familiar his mother's caress. Matthew said that when she doesn't see this happening—when she assists mothers who are uptight and excessively nervous about communicating with the baby in their womb, and who seem to feel very separate from it—that she becomes concerned about the future ability of the mother to parent her child well. Furthermore, through mother's touch on the outside of the womb, the infant is also touched by the mother's presence, interest and concern.

In addition, singing to the pre-born child, playing pleasant music for her, softly dancing with her, and taking long, relaxing baths "together" are only a few of the ways that mothers frequently get in touch with their infants before birth. Every mother-child relationship is unique, and thus it is up to each pair to explore together their new relationship in their own way. The mother who fears to risk this exploration may still give birth to a healthy, happy child, but she will miss out on the intimacy and joy of the love affair with her unborn child that is right at her own fingertips.

As vital as the mother's direct physical contact is with her unborn child, there remains an important aspect of "touch" that is less frequently acknowledged and understood among parents. This concerns the way the infant is "touched" by the environment that he is constantly exposed to, as well as the various impressions that he is at the effect of. To highlight this point, Dr. Sears points out a study revealing that some infants in utero show significant disturbance when their mothers attend loud rock concerts.[27] The same is true of violent movies. Similarly, if the mother has a habit of hanging out at bars where people drink, smoke and act in an aggressive manner, even if she herself is not drinking or smoking, the infant takes in not only the secondary smoke, but also the attitudes of the drunk and careless individuals in the bar. Given the fact that the individual adult's emotional network is largely at the effect of the impressions that he or she takes in from his or her surroundings, one can only surmise that the delicate and newly developing systems of the fetus are significantly more sensitive to this input.

Touch is more than skin-to-skin contact. Touch includes a whole range of interactions between parent and child. Attending to the full spectrum of the needs of the child in utero are all ways of touching a baby.

TO TOUCH IS TO LIVE

Father of the Womb

The importance of the father's touch of his child in utero should not be underestimated. In his book entitled *Keys to Becoming a Father,* Dr. Sears discusses the various ways that the father can become part of the pregnancy, and thereby get "in touch" with his baby at this stage. Aside from the obvious need to help the mother in any way he can, both practically (e.g., assisting with chores, cooking, etc.), as well as through providing emotional support and understanding, the father can bond with the baby too. Dr. Sears suggests that the father talk with the baby. Reporting on fetal awareness research findings, he suggests that the baby can hear sounds outside the womb by the sixth month of pregnancy, if not earlier, and that the child actually may be able to hear their father's low-pitched voice more easily than the mother's higher-pitched voice.[28] (I would further suggest that the infant can feel the attention and presence of the father when he speaks to it even long before its auditory capacities have developed.) Sears adds that when a father practices talking to the infant before birth, it is easier for him to talk with his son or daughter after birth.

Dr. Sears also suggests the "laying on of hands" for the unborn child. In other words, a father should touch the mother's pregnant belly, thus forming a relationship with his child. In doing so, a man expresses his affection and commitment to his partner as well as to their child. Paula Matthew has observed that infants in utero respond to the father's touch in different ways than they do to the mother's. She says that babies tend to calm more to a father's touch, whereas they respond more actively to a mother's touch.

Although these suggestions might seem silly at first, if the father, along with the mother, approaches this experiment with the attitude of "believing is seeing," he will soon discover for himself the delights of this new-found intimacy. When he touches his pre-born child, he imparts a small piece of life—his life—and that life is received.

40

The Birth Chamber

> *It is through our hands that we speak to the child, that we communicate.*
> *Touching is the primary language...*
> *The newborn baby's skin has an intelligence, a sensitivity that we can only begin to imagine.*
> *How, then, ought we to touch—to handle—a newborn baby?*
> *Very simply: by remembering what this infant has just left behind. By never forgetting that everything new and unknown might terrify and that everything recognizable and familiar is reassurance.*
> *To calm the infant in this strange, incomprehensible world into which it just emerged, it is necessary—and enough—that the hands holding him should speak in the language of the womb.*[29]
> – Frederick Leboyer

Many of today's children are born in large, busy and often impersonal hospital settings. Medicines, monitors and an array of doctors, interns and nurses assist the mother throughout the pregnancy and birth process, even though she inherently and intuitively knows what to do and how to do it. The mother's awareness of the importance that these first moments have for her infant, and her ability to trust this knowing and to place primary importance on the need to initiate the bonding process between herself and her child, is one of the most essential elements in the birth process. When this awareness is present—whether the child is delivered by a highly trained midwife, or born in an overcrowded hospital on the Lower East Side of New York City, is secondary. Primary to the child is his mother—her touch, her breast, her reassurance and her genuine welcoming of him into her life.

The core values and beliefs of both individual women and the society in which they live are condensed into visible, focused form in childbirth, where their perpetuation is either assured or denied. In the end—or the beginning—the salvation of the society that seeks to deny women their power as birth-givers will arise from the women who give that society birth. [30]

– Robbie Davis-Floyd

Whether the child is born in a hospital, a home or a swimming pool is not nearly as important to the child as is the attention, intention, and mood of the caretaker. The best the mother can give her baby is her body, her instinctual knowledge, her focus, her attention and her ability to touch. It is that which the infant will feel. In the following account, Sandra, a thirty-one-year-old mother, shares the story of her struggles to create a conscious and healthy birth environment for her child:

I had been talking to my baby since conception. Yes, at first I kind of had to fake it—not really believing that she could hear me or feel my words, but I did it anyway, eventually understanding clearly that she could hear me. There was also an instinctual movement to always be rubbing my belly. I think most mothers feel that, whether or not they allow themselves and their baby that kind of touch. It's not just the tactile sensation of skin-to-skin that the baby is feeling, or the sound of her voice that the baby hears, but the intention and the care of the mother. There was a longing and excitement for all of my senses to be with my unborn child—to touch her, to hear her cry, to smell her...

From a physiological perspective, Ashley Montagu says that the first thirty minutes are the most crucial in terms of bonding, as bonding at this time enhances the essential hormonal changes that will contribute to the child's optimal functioning. Whatever

42

environment parents choose, the consideration of bringing a midwife or a woman friend who is experienced with children into the birth chamber is a worthwhile one. (The father, of course, is a welcome and valuable presence, but what he provides is distinct from what the woman helper is able to provide.) A woman's intuition is never closer to the surface than at the birth of a child. Oftentimes, childbirth is induced by "force"—involving drugs and intrusive medical instruments that could otherwise be avoided. When possible, a natural birth is more gentle on the infant's delicate system, and is empowering to the mother as it allows her to be more fully present for the birth of her baby. An advantage of homebirths, but also possible during hospital births as well, is that there tends to be a more open attitude toward allowing women's knowing to play a key role in the birthing process. Rachel, a mother of two who has attended numerous births, shared this story:

A close friend invited me to be one of her birth attendants. I was delighted, like always, because there is a specific, raw, primal energy present at a birth that is almost addictive. Anyway, her labor was going on pretty smoothly, but the baby was not crowning. I asked the doctor what was going on and he said, "I think we'll need to use forceps." I communicated to the mom that this is what the doctor was planning. She asked me if there was anything she could do to avoid this. I said to her, "We need to get the baby out." I told her how to use her breath and a specific visualization, and within three breaths her daughter was crowning and came out shortly thereafter. The raw power of woman was evident to me during that birth—that by her will, whatever it was that was holding the child back, she was able to overcome and have the result be successful without medical intervention.

Many babies do not come out readily and it is common for babies to initially have difficulty with breathing. For this reason, doctors have a variety of methods at hand to encourage the first breath—ranging from turning babies upside down and hitting them, to suction machines to remove the mucous from their lungs. However, one of the most unrecognized and understated tools in the doctor's reach is physical touch. One female medical doctor who is aware of the value of touch suggested, "I've seen babies born who are blue or gray and as soon as they are touched there is a pinkness that emerges at the heart and spreads throughout the body." Another obstetrician-gynecologist who practices alternative women's healthcare added, "When we have babies that are slow to breathe, if we just rub them and touch them, almost always that's all that it takes." The following story exemplifies this point more immediately:

> I was a backup nurse midwife and called in late on the scene because it looked like the doctor wouldn't be there. When the baby was born, we went ahead and put her up on the mother, but the main doctor arrived and wanted to see if the child was doing okay so she took the baby from off the mother's abdomen and right away the baby stopped breathing. An assistant listened to the baby's heartbeat and reported that it had stopped, so the doctor started doing very aggressive CPR on the baby. I asked if she could stop for a minute, or if she could do the CPR while the baby was on the mother's body. She stopped, we put the baby on the mother, and the infant resumed breathing as normal. It seems so obvious, but I guess it's not.

In *Nurturing the Unborn Child*, Verny tells a similar story about a Seattle pediatrician who was treating a very ill baby in the intensive care unit of the hospital.

44

Hooked up to a battery of life-support machines, the baby was flooded with light and exposed to more sound than you might hear on Fifth Avenue at rush hour. The child was just not getting enough oxygen, and he was turning blue. The doctor decided the infant was going to die anyway, so he took him off life-support systems, shut off all the machines, and turned off the lights. Then he took the baby out of the crib and rocked him in his arms. Within a few minutes the baby turned pink, and his recovery was complete.[31]

Hospital Birth v. Homebirth

For those who are aware of the acute sensitivity of the newborn infant, its need for touch, and the tendency for hospital births to be highly impersonal, the consideration of hospital birth versus homebirth, and medical doctor versus midwife, is a valid one. To put the dilemma simply, doctors concerned about being sued for malpractice are very uncomfortable having their patients give birth outside of a hospital setting in which the baby cannot get immediate medical attention if any difficulties arise. They are also angry about the last minute complications that have come up in natural births—like when the baby is rushed to the hospital because of difficulties during the homebirth, and the doctor at the hospital is held accountable for the procedural difficulties, even if it is the first time he has met the mother and baby. Furthermore, most doctors are not well educated in the science of midwifery. Popular stereotypes dictate that midwifery is outdated, idealistic and irresponsible. Women who choose to have their babies birthed with the assistance of midwives are often not taken seriously by medical doctors.

Parents also struggle with what Vancouver gynecologist Dr. Karen Buhler calls, "the where question." The foremost concern of most parents in deciding whether to have a hospital birth or a homebirth is the safety of their child. In a hospital, the safety of

45

the birth is taken for granted. Technology, lifesaving treatments and highly trained personnel help to assure the parents of a safe birth. On the other hand, parents know that a hospital birth means the possibility of unnecessary intervention, and also a less personal environment where the parents have less control about the birthing process.

On the flip side there are midwives who have been irresponsible. There have been unforeseen situations that have arisen in home-births that required immediate medical attention. There are many instances in which a hospital birth is required. Still, the arguments against the practice of midwifery and homebirthing are question-able. In fact, some studies on the subject reveal that infants tend to have as good a chance, if not a better chance, of survival when birthed naturally than when born in a hospital. In her book, *Homebirth*, educator Sheila Kitzinger pointed out that in 1986, the perinatal mortality rate in the Netherlands was 13.9 per thousand in hospital births, compared to a mortality rate of 2.2 per thousand in homebirths.[32] Buhler further elaborated:

> *Contrary to popular belief, homebirth is safe under the right conditions. In fact, in a well-selected, low-risk population assisted by competent, experienced attendants with good access to hospital for transfer if necessary, home birth is as safe or safer than hospital birth.[33]*

In 1993, the British House of Commons Select Committee on Maternity Services, in a report called "Changing Childbirth," emphasized:

> *Women should be given unbiased information and an oppor-tunity for choice in the type of maternity care they receive, including the option—previously denied to them—of having their babies at home or in small maternity units...the policy of encouraging women to give birth in hospitals cannot be justi-fied on grounds of safety.[34]*

46

Natural births are safe. "Since the 1920s," reported Janet Issacs Ashford in *The History of Midwifery in the United States*, "nurse-midwifery services have achieved lower-than-average infant and maternal death rates...this holds true despite the fact that nurse-midwives have primarily served low-income women who, demographically, are at higher risk for complications." [35]

Can a young woman, seemingly psychologically unprepared for the immense responsibility of mothering, effectively take charge of her own labor? Paula Matthew, from her experience delivering over 950 infants, says yes.

When I was just beginning my career as a midwife, a neighbor called me in to assist with her daughter's birth as the mother had gotten very nervous. The girl was fifteen. It was a real eye-opener for me to see the control she had. She made all the decisions about what she would do and when; she called the shots about who would get to hold the baby, who would get to touch it, what it was going to wear, who would get to wash it—the kinds of things that to a medical practitioner would probably sound very meaningless, but to a mother and child can make all the difference in the world. This fifteen-year-old was there saying, "This is how we're going to do this, this is how we'll do that...Give me my baby now." Everybody was there to assist her with what she needed—she may have been fifteen, but she knew exactly what she wanted and exactly how to mother this child.

Matthew contrasted this to her own experience:

When I had my first baby at age eighteen, a nurse actually called me an abusive mother because I sat up wanting to hold my baby right after she was born and wanting to breast-feed her. They were telling me that I was too young to know how to take care of my child, that I would be an abusive mother because I wasn't together enough to know what to do.

47

A co-worker reported to me a startling example of unconscious birth that happened to a friend of hers:

> She was given an epidural (spinal anesthesia) for her delivery,
> which is a common practice today. The woman had a history
> of rapid deliveries, so the nurses had instructions to check on
> her every fifteen minutes. At one point they went in to check
> on her and noticed she was reading a magazine. However,
> when they looked again they saw that the baby was already out
> to its knees with the cord tight around its neck. She had deliv-
> ered and didn't even know it—she was reading her magazine.

Bear in mind, from what we have discussed in the beginning
of this chapter, that the infant who is going through this process
is totally conscious. He does not have a language for this experience, but is nonetheless fully aware of it, and will experience the
long-term effects of it throughout his lifetime.

For a peek at the other side, consider this scenario. The parents have planned for this child well in advance. They have
already formed a relationship with the infant in utero, and want
his first moments and hours of life to be full of gentleness, and
as welcoming as possible. They have chosen to have the birth at
home, and when the mother begins labor, the doctor or midwife
whom they have engaged for this purpose is called, and also a
special friend whom the mother has chosen for support. The
room has been prepared, and is warm, with dimmed lights.
Plenty of blankets are available so both the mother and the newborn baby will be warm and comfortable. Perhaps the parents
have chosen to have music playing softly in the background.
During her contractions, the mother is encouraged to relax and
follow her breath. Her pain is respected. She wants to be fully
present without anesthesia so that she can be there with her
child, in mind and in body, feeling the slightest movements of
birth. She has been taught well in advance that there are many

positions in which to give birth, and she changes positions as she desires.

The doctor or midwife delivers the baby and place the newborn immediately on the mother's abdomen covering him with a blanket. All in attendance are sensitive in allowing the child to be silent or to cry, to nurse or to simply lay there. They naturally touch the infant, massaging him gently. Eventually, the umbilical cord is cut, the vernix is rubbed into his skin, and then the infant is returned to his mother for rest.

Ultimately, the issue of home versus hospital birth is not a "good-bad" situation. It is a personal choice. Karen Buhler, M.D., suggests:

> *My advice as a doctor to parents considering the "where" question is that you first take some time to formulate what kind of birth experience you hope to have, what your philosophy of health is, and what services you prefer. Then choose a caregiver (or caregiving team) that you trust and feel good with who shares your beliefs and goals. The caregiver can assist you by providing information, assessing your risk factors, and describing the options and facilities in your area. She can visit your home and help you assess its suitability for a home birth.*[36]

Again, the issue is touch—touch being the mother's loving regard for the infant even while he is still in utero; touch being the intention of the mother and her attention on the child; and touch being the unselfish physical affection she adorns her child with throughout his childhood.

THE THREE B'S—BREAST-FEEDING, BACKIN' DA BABY AND BEDTIME

The life-giving body of the mother is already coded with everything it needs to know to care for her offspring. The enactment of the three principles described below catalyzes this organic knowledge in the mother, allowing her to provide fully for her child.

The First B—Breast-feeding

When a mother makes the choice to breast-feed her child she is acknowledging the perfection of nature—that she has been given the perfect substance with which to nourish her child: a substance far superior to any processed formula.[37] Whether or not she is able to justify it verbally, she knows that this is what her child wants, and *needs* from her. Thus, she takes a stand. She recognizes the societal bias against breast-feeding; a bias which is largely a function of the multi-billion dollar corporations which promote the production of baby formulas and bottles. She is aware of how contemporary culture often scorns the breast-feeding mother, and wants her out of public view. She decries all the advertisements showing healthy babies who drink only bottled milk. She knows her own body—how the milk flows naturally to her breasts—and how her child desires to suckle and mold himself into her. She knows her own desire to hold her child closely to her skin. A letter from *Mothering Magazine* reads:

> *Breast-feeding is more than pumping nourishment; it is a psychic bond, which is not disposable from nine to five.*[38]

It is apparent that breast-feeding offers the best possible beginning to a child's life. Some mothers, however, are unable to provide this for their child, due to a wide range of physical, circumstantial or psychological reasons. A dedicated, devoted mother who places primary importance on touch, will bond with her infant regardless of whether she bottle-feeds or breast-feeds. Montagu says:

50

In the bottle-feeding situation, which is the rule in America, the infant experiences the very minimum of reciprocal tactile stimulation. The deprivation of tactile stimulation experienced in this way by both infant and mother explains the institutionalization in American culture of the nonexpression of affection, especially between mother and baby, through close physical contact. Tactile contact between the American mother and child expresses caretaking and nurturance, rather than love and affection...[39]

Breast-feeding not only provides physical nourishment, but the opportunity for mother and child to bond. Leaving her womb, the closest the baby will ever come to his mother again is while nursing. When the mother is present with her nursing infant, the infant will often hold unwavering eye contact with her. The mother is there for her child, providing nourishment, fulfilling his hunger on so many levels. When she touches her infant in this way, both through her eyes and her body, she is communicating to him or her, "You are safe. You are wanted. You are fed. You are loved." She doesn't need to give him excessive toys or treats. *She* is what the baby most wants and needs.

Breast-feeding mothers are often startled to find that their child wishes to nurse far longer than they had imagined to be "normal." Although practically unheard of, and nearly taboo in American culture, it is common in many, many cultures throughout the world for the infant to continue to breast-feed for two, three, four or more years, or until a younger child is born. Although the modern mother may be fearful of breaking a societal taboo, given what the costs are for an unbonded infant, breast-feeding over an extended period of time is worth considering. Regardless, whether she nurses her child for one month or two years, however long a mother is willing to breast-feed her child will be felt throughout the child's life.

Beyond this, breast-feeding is a crucial factor in the development of intelligence. Pearce suggests that chemicals found in the mother's milk are actually necessary to stimulate mid-brain functions that regulate certain aspects of intelligence.[40] Some studies have revealed that breast-fed babies grow up to be more intelligent than those who are bottle-fed. In 1992, Alan Lucas from the Dunn Nutrition Unit in Cambridge, Massachusetts, published a study showing that pre-term infants who were tube-fed breast milk scored much higher on developmental tests than babies who were tube-fed formula."[41] Similarly, researchers at the National Institute of Health conducted a study in which they followed 855 children from birth to school age to measure the correlation between breast-feeding and intelligence. They found that the longer a child had been breast-fed, the smarter and more coordinated he or she was.[42]

The Second "B"—Backin' da Baby

Every nerve ending under his newly exposed skin craves the expected embrace, all his being, the character of all he is, leads to his being held in arms. For millions of years newborn babies have been held close to their mothers from the moment of birth. Some babies of the last few hundred generations may have been deprived of this all-important experience but that has not lessened each new baby's expectation that he will be held in his rightful place.[43]   – Jean Liedloff

When I initially began to befriend the Creole-speaking Jamaican immigrants who settled on the Atlantic Coast of Costa Rica (where I was working at the time), understanding their language, although a derivative of English, was nearly impossible. Often I would inquire as to the whereabouts of a child from a sibling or the child's father. "Oh da' mudda she backin' da baby," I would often be told. Timid to ask for a translation, I began to notice over time that infants were constantly held in a sling on the mother's back, or perhaps in her arms, for the first several months of their lives. At other times they would be sitting on her lap, crawling near to her, or in the arms or lap of the father, sibling or grandparent.

In all of my extended visits, as well as during the time I spent with the indigenous people of the forest who lived nearby, I never saw anything that resembled a crib, playpen, walker or stroller, much less a leash! (To imagine a BriBri Indian woman navigating the paths of the rain forest with her machete in one hand and pushing a baby stroller with the other would be absurd!) Children were raised "in arms," to use a term coined by Jean Liedloff in her revolutionary book (in terms of contemporary Western culture), *The Continuum Concept.* "In arms" means that the infant is constantly in contact with her mother's body or that of a primary caretaker's body for the first several months of life, if not longer.

This constant contact is the second essential aspect of the bonding process. Not only is the tactile stimulation from the constant movement of the mother's body enlivening to the growing infant, but the young child becomes bonded into the family, and becomes integrated into the world around her, simply by being there with the mother as she goes about her daily chores and interactions. The mother is aware of her child and attends to her needs, but is not excessively doting over her. Instead, she brings her into the full spectrum of life experience, allowing her to simply be a part of it.

This extensive contact in early life gives the child a sense of security, a certain feeling of "home" that will remain with her throughout her life. The child will automatically develop a sense of confidence in her own body. Liedloff explained, "If he (the baby) feels safe, wanted, and 'at home' in the midst of activity...his view of later experiences will be very distinct in character from those of a child who feels unwelcome, understimulated by the experiences he has missed, and accustomed to living in a state of want, though the later experiences of both may be identical."[44]

I was recently telling a four-year-old child about life in that particular village in the rain forest where I worked, and how each of the houses was a one to two hour walk apart from the next one. "But they have roads to drive around in?" he asked.

"No," I told him, "The growth in the forest is too thick and the people cannot afford cars."

"Then they must have good sidewalks so the moms can push the kids around in strollers," he pressed.

"No," I continued. "Until a child can walk, he or she is carried, and once able to walk well (occurring usually by age two to three), the child walks along with everybody else."

This child was baffled. He probably could not imagine such autonomy, capability and confidence on the part of a young child. What I did not mention is that not only do these young children walk, but I would often follow them from far behind, laughing at my own clumsiness as they ran, seeming to fly, down the mountain, avoiding roots, lizards, branches and even an occasional snake, with the precision of a hawk.

These children, held in arms and nursed until they were ready to move outward, were totally competent. At first I was surprised to find four- and five-year-old children from across the forest showing up at my doorstep without their parents, but I quickly understood that they were already knowledgeable of all the dangers of the forest, that they had memorized all of its windy paths, that they knew how to protect themselves and where to get food and water. These were very capable children who were trusted by their parents.

Author Barbara Aria and researcher Carroll Dunham came to a similar conclusion:

Studies in Uganda have shown that babies who are carried in upright positions are quicker to walk, and develop faster in other areas too; the upright position heightens a baby's visual alertness while developing muscles in the back and neck. Carried around all day, babies become familiar with their worlds as they watch from their secure vantage point. Because they're held close and upright they stay calmer—studies show that they even cry less than babies that aren't carried regularly.[45]

Backin' da baby does not suggest that the infant must be carried only on the back. Front, side, right, left...in hoods like Eskimos...the variety of positions and types of attachments are numerous. What the baby craves is contact. Mothers can learn to vacuum, cook, clean, shop and work with the baby in their arms, though it might take longer. Many mothers in the West are enjoying a rediscovery of the simple sling, which they can take on or off with ease, and in which a baby may sit or lie as they please. Furthermore, as the child matures month by month, she will naturally want to venture out from her mother's body. "In arms" naturally becomes "in view" as the child gains confidence and curiosity about her surroundings.

Prescott summarized years of statistics and scientific research on this subject in the following:

I have concluded that the single most important child rearing practice to be adopted for the development of emotionally and socially healthy infants and children is to carry the newborn/ infant on the body of the mother/caretaker all day long, where the continuous "backpacking"...becomes the best "behavioral vaccine" against depression, social alienation, violence and drug/alcohol abuse and addiction in later life.[46]

The Third "B"—Bedtime

...The room that filled with suspicion at night: you made it harmless; and out of the refuge of your heart you mixed a more

human space in with his night-space. And you set down the
lamp, not in that darkness, but in your own nearer presence,
and it glowed at him like a friend.[47] – Rainer Maria Rilke

"When I told my family that I didn't want
them to buy my two-year-old a crib because she was sleeping in
the bed with my husband and I, they were scandalized," began
one mother. "My brother and sister were shocked too—'You can't
be doing this!' they said."

All over the world parents and their infants sleep in close proximity with one another. In the Yucatan Peninsula of Mexico,
where people commonly sleep in hammocks, one can purchase a
"family-sized" hammock which will amply accommodate the parents as well as one or more children. In Tamil Nadu, India, the
whole family sleeps on large palm mats on the floor, or on several cots piled into one small room. Japanese infants share their parents' futons.

When I was a young child there was nothing as reassuring as
my mother's bed. Terrified of the night, I vividly remember lying
in bed hour after hour, watching the fluorescent blue lights of the
digital clock by my bed, thinking of my mother sleeping sound-
ly in the next room. When the sleeplessness went on too long, the
fear too much, I would quietly get out of bed, tip-toe down the
hallway, and slip in my mother's bedroom through the door that
was always left open a crack. As I crawled into bed next to her,
and she spooned me into her body, I would fall asleep instantly.

Coined "shared sleeping" by Dr. William Sears, and "the family bed" by Tine Thevenin, the concept of parents and their
infants sleeping together is far from novel. Yet in the West, this
concept is just beginning to be renewed. For the past several generations, if the family can afford it, the American baby is given
his or her own room from birth, complete with crib, hanging
mobiles and toys, and perhaps an intercom monitor connected to
a speaker in the parents' bedroom if it is too far away for the

mother to hear her baby's cry. Although parents might do a bedtime ritual with their young children, and children who are unable to sleep may occasionally crawl into their parents' bed late at night, to most people the idea of a "family bed" is preposterous.

The hours of sleep are very vulnerable times for all people, especially for children. Even while sleeping, people are aware of where they are and how safe or unsafe their surroundings are. For example, a couple who sleeps together is aware of one another's presence, and their sleep patterns often change in the partner's absence. Similarly, the child is aware when the parent is there, and for many children this awareness provides a much-desired sense of safety and security. The mother's touch provides a quality of soothing that nothing else can. When the child feels this security, he or she is freer to fall into deeper states of relaxation, rest and exploration of the dreamworld.

Peace of Mind

Many parents worry about a disorder in infants known as SIDS, or Sudden Infant Death Syndrome. Although 99.8 percent of all babies don't die of SIDS—the stories that parents have heard about infants under six months of age dying suddenly in their sleep, apparently having stopped breathing for an undiagnosable reason, has brought considerable concern to many. Pediatrician Dr. William Sears was initially confronted with this disease when the mother of one of his three-month-old patients called him crying that her baby was dead. When Sears found that he had no answers with which to console her, he took it upon himself to research a cure for this disease. After years of study, his firm hypothesis is as follows:

I believe that in most cases, SIDS is a sleep disorder, primarily a disorder of arousal and breathing control during sleep. All the elements of natural mothering, especially breast-feeding and sharing sleep, benefit the infant's breathing control and increase the mutual awareness between mother and infant so that their arousability is increased and the risk of SIDS decreased.[48]

Similarly, research conducted by James McKenna, an anthropologist at Pomona College in California, suggested that shared sleeping may reduce the chance of SIDS.[49] Once again, I believe that science will prove to us what our logic already knows: if the mother is deeply bonded with her infant, and is there for him body-to-body as he sleeps, the infant will breathe more easily and she will be more aware of his needs during the night should problems arise.

In planning their sleeping arrangements together, it is helpful for parents to pay attention to their children's needs. Some children want to sleep between both parents, whereas others prefer to sleep "spooned" into the mother. As children get older, they may wish to spend part of the night in their own bed or their own bedroom, and then come to sleep in their parents' arms for the remainder of the night.

Parents are often concerned that shared sleep will mean they won't get enough rest. Although there is an initial period of adjustment, preliminary studies have confirmed sleep-sharing mothers did not get less total deep sleep.[50] Furthermore, the peace of mind that parents long for more deeply than a peaceful night's sleep will arise when they become aligned to the genuine needs of their children, and are able to provide this for them.

Sears concluded, "Based upon my own research, 25 years of pediatric experience, and 17 years of sleeping with our babies, I have come to the conclusion that the safest place for babies to sleep is with their mothers."[51] As with the child who is breast-fed and the one who is carried, when the child feels sufficiently secure and ready to move on, he or she will request his or her own sleeping space.

58

INFANT MASSAGE

Another wonderful way that parents bond with their babies is through infant massage. Although not always called by name, this practice is engaged by mothers all over the world. It is natural for a mother to massage her baby, invigorating the child's skin and thereby stimulating the organs, and providing the child with comfort and pleasure.

Massage with infants serves many purposes—both physiological and psychological. In her article, *Massage Therapy for Infants and Children,* Tiffany Field suggests that infant massage has been documented to: 1) decrease the production of stress hormones, 2) reduce pain associated with teething and constipation, 3) reduce colic, and 4) help induce sleep.[52] It also serves many other functions including stimulating the baby's organs, helping the nervous and digestive system to function more optimally, increasing daily weight-gain in premature infants, and inducing more responsiveness and improved sociability. Some reports indicate that infants who are blind and/or deaf become more aware of their bodies and that infants with cerebral palsy also benefit by more organized motor activity.[53]

The greatest benefit of massage, however, is the unparalleled experience of soothing, nurturing, safety and pleasure that only loving touch can provide. The child's body is teeming with life and fully open to receiving its pleasures, untainted by the emotional blockages, environmental numbing and body shame that will inevitably accumulate throughout his or her lifetime, making receptivity to touch more difficult. The infant has not yet entered the world of concepts, ideas and protocol, and can best be communicated to through the means of touch.

Furthermore, massage is likely to nurture the parent as much or more than it does the infant. Some parents are afraid of their children—afraid of their young and vulnerable bodies. Other parents are afraid of their own sensual desires to touch their children because they fear that their touch is sexual. Some are afraid of allowing their babies the pleasure that they (the parents) may have suppressed in their own early experiences. Massaging their infant often helps both mothers and fathers to extend themselves to their children in ways they would otherwise be unable to, thus bringing them into *relationship* with their child through the vulnerable and deeply communicative means of touch. Massaging also allows parents to know their child's body better, to impart to the child that touch is good, and that there is safety in receptivity. Again, it is the touch that matters—feelings of inadequacy or fears due to a lack of training can be coaxed into the backseat as we place our primary attention on this natural, health-producing practice of massage.

Children *need* touch. Providing them with ample, nurturing touch in infancy sets the foundation for a future life that will be full of intimacy and self-confidence. Yet the child's need for touch does not end when infancy fades. Touch is important throughout the child's growing years—important for both child *and* parent. Throughout childhood, the vehicle of touch allows children and parents alike to demonstrate a sense of appreciation for one another that nothing besides genuine touch can provide.

CHAPTER 3

Second Touch:
Affection with Children

When my Scottish sister-in-law's father finished reading my first book, he put it down and said, "My mother never showed me any affection when I was a child so I spent the first ten years of my life thinking she didn't want me." Children don't stand a chance of sanity and peace of mind in adulthood if they are not given proper affection in infancy and childhood. Whereas the most critical period in terms of touch is the first moments, hours and years of the child's life, his or her affectional needs will continue throughout the formative years. The initial bonding is still vulnerable, not yet rooted and stabilized, and can therefore be undermined when touch is not consistent as the child matures.

For many years I wondered just what a bonded child would look and act like? I have attempted to observe the differences between those children whom I know have been raised with ample touch and affection, and those who have not (not because they have uncaring parents, but usually because the parents are rigid, controlling or simply too wounded themselves to be able to raise their child in a healthy, affectionate environment). What I have discovered—at least at first glance—is that the bonded child looks and acts like most other children. He or she eats, sleeps, plays, spends time with friends, cries, laughs...the whole human roller coaster of experiences and emotions. However, a closer study of the bonded individual reveals a quality of acceptance—both of himself as well as of others—that is very rare. His life is not based upon a search for approval and validation from some ambiguous source. His interactions with others are characterized by the absence of insecurity, fear and the wish to impress others that is so common. You sense that he does not put his personality on the bed table when he goes to sleep—that what you see is what you get, and that this is perfectly all right with him. Furthermore, the bonded individual tends to be kind and considerate of others. At his center he knows he is loved, and therefore has no fort to defend, and wears no suit of armor to protect himself. Basic sanity—this is the gift that awaits the bonded child.

HOW WE LEARN TO LOVE OUR CHILDREN

Children need affection, and lots of it. Everyone would agree that all children need love, but love is a concept that is overused and under-practiced in the modern world. We as a culture need to become more specific about what this "love" means and about how it shows up in our interactions with our children. It might serve us to temporarily forget about the notion of loving our children, suspend our belief that all the strong emotions we feel about our children are actually love, and begin to touch them, to hold them, to be there for them in ways deeper than words can express and basic caregiving can offer. "I am here for you and I respect and honor you," is what needs to be communicated to the child. To truly respect and honor our children and to give them the touch they need demands a great deal more from us than our commonly held notions of love do.

In 1999, in a cross-cultural study of preschool children, the journal *Early Child Development and Care* published an article comparing a high touch culture (France) and a low touch culture (USA). Researchers found that the preschool children in Paris were touched more by their mothers and touched each other more. They were also found to be less aggressive toward their peers than the children in the USA.[1]

Essentially, children learn what it means to be affectionate from their mother and father. They also learn true masculinity and femininity from them. Children come to trust or distrust all men and all women, and to relate compassionately or defensively with them, by how their mother and father touched or failed to touch them. Although nannies, baby-sitters, older siblings and staff workers at daycare centers can be important role models for children concerning how and when to touch others, and what it really means to be a man or a woman, nobody can model this for them as effectively as their own mother and father can.

We teach children to demonstrate spontaneous affection by modeling that in our own lives. Ironically, children learn more from the way that adults express themselves with one another than they do from how the adults express affection to children. When parents express affection and love to their children, but treat one another as less than the dirt on the bottom of their shoes, the children know that something is not right. These children cannot fully trust the affection that is given to them because they see that somebody else—who Mommy or Daddy supposedly "loves"—does not receive the same regard. The child concludes both that the affection they are receiving is not real (i.e., "Mommy isn't really a loving person, she is just nice to me because I'm her kid"), and also that affection can be withdrawn at any point—that it is conditional. When these children become adults, unless they have undergone a thorough process of self-examination, they will demonstrate affection in their lives in the way they saw their parents model it with one another.

Whereas some adults may feel that they do not need or even want touch, all children crave touch, and they experience a lack of touch as traumatic. In the rare instance when a child appears to have an aversion to his or her parent's touch, trauma has already occurred, if not during the initial period of bonding, than in the womb or through some other event in the child's early life.

Another function of the parent's touch is to help the child to process emotions and energy. When a child is upset, it is not necessary to "coo" over him or her. Simply by taking a shaking child into her arms, the mother imparts a steadiness that is reliable. The parent's non-smothering touch communicates to the child, "You're O.K. I am here for you." Such touch allows the natural cycle of pain to move through the child—neither encouraging it's indulgence by excessive pampering, nor discouraging it's expression by denying the child his right to cry. The child then realizes, "I can be hurt and feel pain and I am still O.K." Parents can't make their child's pain go away, much as they would like to. Instead, by example, they can convey to him how to respond to it. Ideally, parents should not be trying to shield their child from reality, but instead teaching him to accept and manage it.

Parents will at times find themselves reluctant or unable to give their children unconditional affection. Unconsciously, they are aware of the depth of their own wounds due to the lack of appropriate affection they received in childhood, and giving this affection to their children instantaneously draws remembrance of this void to the surface of awareness. However, the parent who is willing and able to face this pain without avoiding his or her child's needs for affection stands to gain a great deal. In the words of one family counselor:

Allowing your child the expression of true touch from birth can provide a profound healing for the parent. Providing this for your child will elicit severe pain and crises in the adult who has never felt that before. If you as a parent are willing to face and acknowledge this, your child in his or her own inimitable way will draw you out of your own underworld into relationship with him or her.

One child I know who has learned to give and receive affection freely recently turned to me with her arms open wide and a big smile on her face and said, "You know, I have so *many, many* friends!" It was obvious that from the inside out, this six-year-old child felt loved.

WITHHOLDING AFFECTION

The main argument against providing children with ample, consistent and ongoing affection is a concern about "spoiling them." Ironically, our present approach to raising children, designed to prepare them to face a "reality" that is in desperate need of change, is perpetuating the very "spoiling" it is attempting to prevent. There is a difference between spoiling a child and providing for him or her fully. We literally spoil a child—ignoring her ripening development while her innocence rots away—when we refuse to pick her up when she lies in her crib crying, when we insist that she say "please" and "thank-you" when she is four years old, when we place her in a daycare center to be raised, when we deny her the right to nurse.

Withholding affection from a child should never be used as a form of punishment or reprimand for the child, no matter what the child has said or done. This is one of the most important principles in providing the child with a "hands-on" education concerning the meaning of healthy touch. Conversely, the child should not be given excessive affection for having done something that is good or pleasing to the parent. Clearly, touch communicates on a level that exceeds the intellect. A child can understand when a parent says, "When you hit me that hurt." If his mother puts him down and walks away after a child has hit her, he is devastated far beyond the message that he has hurt his mother.

For parents who regularly show their love to their children through hugging them and other forms of affection, withholding that affection communicates clearly to the child that he is not loved. Of course, the parent does love the child, yet in the moment of rage, when the child is stubbornly acting out an uncontrollable tantrum, the last thing a parent may be feeling is love. Still, the parent does have a developed intellect and she is responsible to her knowledge. She is capable of understanding that while she may be feeling enormously frustrated at her child, the simultaneous underlying and far more important reality is that she loves him. Therefore, no matter what it takes to do so, she must turn to the child and hold him and love him, communicating through the child's skin that no matter what he did, that he has not lost love.

The child is innocent simply because he or she is a child. Although the child will lose this innocence as she grows up, becoming manipulative, controlling, aggressive or withholding at times, any and all of this behavior is learned. If we wish to sustain the innocence in children, we must treat them according to who they are essentially and not who society is teaching them to become. On the flip side, the parent is not innocent. The parent has had ample time to learn to control and manipulate circumstances to get what he or she wants (and children are only too ready to comply in order to secure their primary source of love). The parent knows (if only unconsciously) what he is doing when he refuses love to his child, or when he demands a show of affection in spite of the child's wishes. The parent knows when he is putting himself first, and has the cognitive capacity to chose to act otherwise.

66

AFFECTION ON DEMAND

If a child blatantly refuses affection, it is highly unlikely that it is her "natural disposition." However, as children mature, they will desire varying amounts of affection, as well as affection from some sources and not others. (At a certain point, parents will longingly wish that their children still wanted the attention and affection they craved in infancy!) *Affection should always be given on the child's terms.* There's no way around it—it is demeaning and patronizing for a parent to insist that a child give him or her a kiss goodnight, or for an aunt or uncle to demand that the child receive a hug from him or her in spite of the child's obvious displeasure. It is worthwhile and quite humbling to reflect upon how unwilling we are to allow children to decide when they wish to be affectionate.

Even though I consider myself to be open-minded and sensitive to children, I was surprised in visiting an alternative school to find how often I would reach out toward children or stroke their hair when this clearly wasn't their preference. As these children had not been trained in the dogma of, "A good girl or boy always gives Mommy's friend a hug," they would simply ignore me or push me away if they didn't want me to touch them, and I would be left to consider my motivations for seeking their affection. I saw within myself, as well as in many others, that much of our affection toward children is an effort to fill our own emptiness, and to appease our own insecurities about being loved by them.

I was settling down at a restaurant early one evening with my friend Shawna and her young daughter Jenny, when a stranger in a business suit walked over, grabbed Jenny's cheeks, and in a babyish voice said to her, "Aren't you just the sweetest little thing! Look at those chubby cheeks of yours, you're such a darling little sweetheart!" He left giving her a pat on the head. Jenny, who was bonded and knew one kind of touch from the other, turned to her mother and said, "I don't like that man. I don't like that man.

I don't want to stay here." We left. As soon as we got out the door, Jenny began to cry. Shawna held her and let her know that she understood her pain.

Some people will read this example and think, "What's the big deal?" "Why did her mother let her get away with that and ruin the whole dinner for everybody?" "Everybody does that with children." That's the problem. That is the way that children are commonly handled, and most have adapted to it. A child who had not bonded and was not taught her own boundaries would never have said anything in response to that man's unrequested intrusion. The ordinary child would have assumed that it was her duty to accept the way the businessman treated her, and say nothing, believing that she did not have a choice about who touched her and when. Perhaps she would even feel good about acquiescing to his intrusion, as the stranger's compliments might make her parents proud of her.

The bonded child, on the other hand, who is given affection according to her own wishes and not demanded to provide it by her parents and others, knows the difference between when touch is needed and when it is excessive. The bonded child can take care of herself, and in doing so helps her caretakers discriminate between a neurotic motivation to demand affection, and a genuine wish to be affectionate with children.

FATHER BONDING

I knew my son needed me, began Joe, a tool and dye maker, *and I was going to do anything I had to do to be with him. I used to take off work just to hang out with him. Fortunately, I was a good liar because I used to tell my boss all kinds of things just to spend time with him. I'd strap him on my back and we'd go hiking or walking or out fishing. I wasn't protecting him in the same way as his mom. I was loving him and touching him but I wanted him to know the world... When*

68

my wife and I got divorced I quit my job and found a way to be self-employed. He was with me all the time. I taught him to use all the equipment I was working with. He'd help me out when he wanted to, or just hang out. I was lucky though. For one, I knew enough to know that a young boy needs his father's touch, and secondly, I was a good enough worker to be able to make it on my own in business...He is grown now and there's a big difference between him and my other son whom I wasn't able to raise and who never had a man to spend time with.

Bonding with the father will provide the child with something they cannot get from the mother. If a child is deeply bonded to the mother, but not the father, he or she may still grow up feeling loved, but will feel one-sided and imbalanced, as though something is missing. Children need a role model of the opposite gender to balance the masculine and feminine energies contained within them. Bonding with the father—not just "the masculine" but with a man—may be the single most important determining factor in that child's relationship both with the masculine aspect of themselves, and with all of the men that they will encounter throughout the rest of their lives. Furthermore, the child's ability to live constructively and sympathetically in a masculine-based society will result from having had a positive reference point for the masculine that is constructive and active without being aggressive.

What takes place during the time of bonding becomes internalized in the child—it becomes a part of their own internal makeup, including their worldview and the way in which their experience is perceived. If father bonding has occurred, the male child is more likely to grow up to be productive, confident, clear and capable of seeking warmth and companionship from other men as well as from women. The female child who has bonded properly with her father will mature into the strength of her womanhood, able to be as strong as she is soft, and will come to relate to men with respect and honor instead of fear or condescension.

Again, it comes down to touch. Children need the loving touch of a man to feel secure, grounded and capable. This rarely happens in a world in which men are required to work eight to ten hours a day, and in which, on a cultural level, men have not been given the support and encouragement to touch their children...but it could.

There are stages of the child's life when they will draw more on a masculine source of support and stages in which they will need the feminine. During the first years of life, the child needs the mother—when possible—like nothing else. Yet when it is time for the child to move out of the mother's protective embrace and into the surrounding world—often occurring around the age of seven—a father or male presence is often needed to help release the safety valve and transition the child into the outer environment. When children have bonded with both mother and father, that bonding will serve as an anchor to support them through the various stage-specific needs that will arise.

Having said all this, the reality of our present culture dictates that there are many single-parent families in which one parent has died or there has been a divorce. There are gay families and growing numbers of people living in alternative settings. The mother cannot be a father, and the father cannot be a mother— and that doesn't have to be a problem. One option in such instances is to enlist the support of a male friend or relative who is willing to spend time with the child, and to serve as a mentor or role-model. This can be a mutually fulfilling situation for both the mentor and the child, and with the right person, can provide the child with the guidance he or she needs at this time.

SEXUALITY IN CHILDREN

Although rarely spoken of, sexuality is a touch-related issue that all parents will confront in raising their child from birth onward. Sexuality does not suddenly "develop" when a child hits age twelve or thirteen—it was there all along.

As will be discussed extensively in Chapter Six, sexuality is much more than sex. It is not something that is exclusive to the realm of adulthood and taboo in children. To children, the vagina or anus is just another hole; the penis is just another thing that sticks out. Sexuality is not a problem for children until we make it into one for them. As a culture, we are afraid of sexuality in children because we are uncomfortable with our own sexuality. If it is considered socially inappropriate for a mother to breast-feed in public—the most natural of events—how will the culture embrace the fact of children playing with their penis or vagina when it is right there and it simply feels nice to them? One father shared:

> *They're going to play with their genitals, and if you're like me and really repressed, you're going to think, "What should I do?" because they really play with them. They don't just touch them. They lie there feeling good. If you get uptight and brush their hand away, you're telling them it is bad. You just have to keep your mouth shut and your anxiety to yourself.*

Working in battered women's homes, private schooling situations, and even walking through grocery stores, I have often seen parents grab their young children's hands away from their genitals, or give them a whack on the back of the hand when they were playing with them. Sexuality only becomes bad, dirty, taboo and inappropriate when we teach children that it is so. Oftentimes, the less said to the child the better. The more attention drawn to it, the greater the energy, fear, interest, apprehension and bias that will be created in the child, instead of allowing sexuality to be a natural thing.

Similarly, sexual play among children is natural. If parents are attentive to their children, they will know what they are up to. Wise parents will set boundaries—for example, no placing of objects inside of themselves or anybody else (because it is

71

dangerous, not because it is bad), or no playing with themselves in public or when adult members of the opposite sex are around who are not their parents (only because in our culture there is an already-present state of sexual confusion and misconduct. In many other cultures this would be no problem). One man shared:

> When I was nine and had just learned about kissing, I took my sister into my room and told her I wanted to show here something. I kissed her on the lips and it was really fun. But soon after that, I started to get the idea about the incest taboo, though I didn't have the words for it, and for years afterward I felt guilty about it, thinking I may have had incest with her. What wasted guilt. It was spontaneous, natural and healthy child's play—that's all!

When children are allowed to be naked in their homes, and to see their parents naked, they come to understand nudity as natural and normal. On the other hand, when a two-year-old is constantly being made to cover her genitals, and when her parents are uncomfortable with the child's nudity, she forms an assumption that there is something that must be hidden. When young children are left to have their nudity as they please, as they grow up they naturally gravitate toward the wish to wear clothes in order to "fit in" and to integrate with the surrounding culture.

Children can be answered honestly and directly when they ask about sexuality—they are more capable of such understanding than we commonly imagine. Parents may choose to answer their children in language that is simple and straightforward, rather than confusing their already-alert minds with stories of birds and bees and storks—which is demeaning to their intelligence. An honest approach is best. Granted, many parents may feel uncomfortable in speaking about sexuality—this is understandable given that most of us have been raised in cultures that do not speak openly about sexuality. Such discomfort is normal because of our training, but despite this uneasiness, parents are learning to speak clearly and simply to their children, answering what is asked in a language that they can understand.

In most traditional cultures, there were rituals, ceremonies and stories that would be told in order to teach the child about sexuality, not leaving the burden on the child's parents themselves. But we do not have that luxury. If we want to change our culture from one that has a largely aberrant sexuality, to a culture with a healthy sexuality, we can begin to catalyze such change by developing a healthy approach toward discussing sexuality with our children. And in order to do that, we need to set our discomfort aside, and be willing to answer our children's questions honestly and clearly.

Children benefit from knowing not only about sex, but about masturbation, menstruation and so forth. I know a young girl who for a time was fascinated by menstruation. She would often wear her mother's sanitary pads in her underwear, or play with tampons. After awhile, the fascination wore off. When sexuality is not repressed in children, they will naturally cycle through the various stages of sexual development at their own pace.

It is more common than we imagine for parents to experience some degree of sexual feeling toward their children at various times—it is natural that they would. Whether parents admit to it or not, most will probably find their young child's body to be sensual and beautiful to watch—that's because it is! It amazes me that this appreciation is such an unspoken reality, and it can only be attributed to the major confusion prevalent in our society concerning sexuality. Since these sensual feelings are taboo, when they arise in parents they are immediately suppressed, put out of the mind, denied, and often result in the parent feeling guilt or shame. It is often not understood that these feelings are commonly indicative of a desire for contact and intimacy as opposed to a wish to have a sexual relationship. In a touch-starved nation, where sexual dysfunction runs rampant, many people cannot make the distinction between non-sexual intimacy and sex.

If a mother cannot acknowledge her "sensual" feelings toward her young son, and understand them for what they are, she is far more likely to subtly treat him as a lover or surrogate husband. She will probably not take him to bed with her or expect him to take her out to dinner, but the covert ways in which she expresses these feelings has left many a man confused about his sexuality in later life, feeling that he is betraying his mother by being with "another woman" when he gets into relationship, or feeling guilty for feeling angry at her "for no good reason," as she was always "a good mother." Similarly, the unacknowledged sexual feelings of a father toward his daughter (or son) is one factor that may lead a father to have an incestuous relationship with his child.

At first, sexual or sensual feelings towards one's children may be hard for parents' to admit, but such feelings are not uncommon in a sexually dysfunctional culture. Parents address this by beginning to clarify and understand these feelings in healthy ways, within themselves, instead of acting them out with their children, and thereby save their children many subsequent years of confusion and difficulty in their own intimate relationships.

Because some parents feel these feelings does not mean they should not touch their children, or that their touch is sexual. Parents who are honest and clear with these feelings, and willing to take responsibility for them, are the least likely to abuse their children. Fathers at the present time are often left in a difficult bind—if they don't touch their children they may be considered distant, and if they do touch them they may be suspect of abuse. It is an unfortunate situation, but when the father is able to examine himself honestly—free of his need to deny and repress the uncomfortable aspects of his own inner world—he knows exactly what is appropriate and what is not. The same is true of the mother. They simply need to act on what they know.

A friend of mine recently told me that one night after dinner her three-year-old daughter jumped up onto Daddy's lap and asked him to play with her genitals. The father responded calmly and lovingly that this was not how their relationship should be, and that later in life there would be a man who would fulfill this role. The child was not shamed, blamed, or criticized—just guided in the right direction.

On the flip side, a client of mine who came into therapy because of difficulties in her sex life with her husband later reported memories of standing in front of the mirror as an eight-year-old and hitting her vulva saying, "Bad. Bad." Already at eight years old her future had been determined—she had no hope of having a healthy adult sex life unless she were to do extensive healing work as an adult.

When childhood sexuality is denied, misunderstood or abused, and when children are not taught about their sexuality, they often enter into a period of excessive experimentation in their early teenage years. Teenage pregnancies are the sorry consequence—resulting either in far too many mothers and fathers who are totally unprepared to be parents, or in abortions that are often traumatic and could otherwise have been avoided.

When children are taught the beauty and naturalness of sexuality and of right relationship to sex from the very beginning, they grow up inherently understanding the difference between the two, and are less likely to take on the distorted attitudes of the surrounding society.

The gap between what needs to happen in our world in terms of touch, and the reality of where we are and the direction we are going should be increasingly apparent. A culture of unbonded children will grow up to become a culture of unbonded adults, and it is the unbonded adult who is the most likely candidate to become violent and abusive. Abuse—the greatest misuse of the power of touch—is an often misunderstood phenomenon in our culture. Whereas obvious manifestations of abuse are relatively easy to identify, less apparent are the subtle and invisible causes of such behavior. Chapter Four discusses the relationship between touch-starvation and what I refer to as a "culture of abuse," for it is only in the understanding of the roots of violence and abuse that we have any hope of remedying the present situation.

CHAPTER 4

The Wrong
Kind of Touch:
A Culture of Abuse

*Aggression is not strength. It is exactly the opposite... The advo-
cates of aggression...say: "Life has been hard for me. I've been
knocked around, and it's made me what I am. Let it be the
same for my children."*
*Really what they are saying, without admitting it, is, "I've suf-
fered. Why shouldn't others suffer too?"*[1]
– Frederick Leboyer

      I was eight years old and on a camping trip
with my parents. My older brothers and I were happily playing
with some new friends we had met from the next trailer, when
suddenly their mother's voice came roaring toward us, "Jeerremiee
David Hopkins, get your god-damn ass over here right now before
I drag you over here myself!" Immediately the boy's face went
pale, his jaw started trembling and we were all silenced. I remember thinking to myself, "What could he possibly have done that

was so terrible?" Jeremy was too terrified to budge. Sure enough, his mother came over, grabbed him by the collar, and dragged him back to their trailer. Apparently, eleven-year-old Jeremy had not washed the dishes from breakfast as he had promised to and now it was lunchtime and the dishes were still dirty. We all watched through the trees as his mother, still screaming at the top of her lungs about what a "good-for-nothing, irresponsible son" Jeremy was, took a huge wooden spoon and raised it above Jeremy's behind. I'll never forget the look on his face—sheer terror, like the kind you see in the movies when somebody has a gun held to their head. Both my older brother and I were crying in anticipation. The smack on the butt she gave him with that spoon wasn't so hard, but Jeremy was already traumatized. Then she laughed. "Ha! I hardly have to touch him and he's already crying." In that moment, all of us present hated that woman. In fact, beneath her own rage, she probably hated herself.

This type of scenario—an outright and unabashed abuse of the gift of touch—happens thousands and thousands of times a day throughout the world. In fact, in many places it is not even considered a problem. But the frequency of its occurrence does *nothing* to diminish the lasting damage that it has on the child's soul—the child who will grow up to be an adult who does the very same things that they once hated their parents for.

This chapter explores the issue of abuse on all levels—from abuse done by individuals to abuse enacted by the culture—so that the reader may understand what he or she is faced with in living in a touch-starved nation, and what the consequences are of our failure to touch and love one another appropriately.

As profound as the capacity is for loving touch to bring us closer to ourselves and to allow us to feel loved by and connected with others, such is the capacity for abusive touch to devastate the soul and alienate us from the world, resulting in feelings of despair and worthlessness. The power of the human touch—by birth contained within each of us—must be used, or not used, with intense sensitivity and consideration. Many people fail to recognize that their choice to touch or not touch their children, intimate partners and friends, as well as *how* they choose to touch or not touch them, is the difference between creating either an environment of love, or one of unlove.

To take an objective inventory of the state of abuse into which we as a culture have "evolved" can be extremely unpleasant, if not altogether heartbreaking. Yet in order to deeply understand the power of touch and the necessity for it, and to seriously intend to bring loving touch into our lives, we must be willing to look straight in the eye of what happens when this power is wielded unwisely, as is so often the case.

What is most disheartening is that abusive attitudes and behaviors have now penetrated our culture so deeply that they have become a cultural "norm." It is so common for adults to neglect their children, spank them, scream at one another, threaten and hit each other, as well as to abuse one another in a myriad of subtle, psychological ways, that many people don't think twice about it. Because this abuse has been "taught" to us by our parents, and was taught to them by their parents, and is enacted by so many people in the surrounding society, many do not stop to question if such ways of relating to one another are sane. Instead, a low-grade abusiveness becomes part of the larger cultural behavior, escaping our recognition of it as such.

Some years ago, a close friend of mine was the victim of a violent crime, the kind you read about on the front page of the paper—rape at gun point, kidnapping, robbery. She barely escaped with her life. This was my friend—the one I drank coffee and ate pancakes with on Sunday mornings; the woman I could call at any time of the day or night when I needed somebody to talk to. Violent crime was suddenly a stark reality for me. It wasn't something that happened to "those people out there." Still, the majority of abuse happens much closer to home—in the home. It happens in shockingly obvious forms as well as almost undetectable but equally damaging ways. The damage created by abuse cannot be measured by the type of abusive activity enacted, but by its impact on the individual who has been abused.

The purpose of exploring abuse here is not to indict or blame any person or persons, but to further our understanding of ourselves and our world. Therefore, defensive statements such as, "I only hit her once," or, "Yelling at somebody isn't *really* abuse," are irrelevant to this discussion. Abuse is in the body of the beholder. If we as a culture really *felt* how others are affected by our own abusive behaviors (felt it in our guts and in our broken hearts), abuse could never occur on the level, and to the degree that it does at the present.

WHAT IS ABUSE?

The US Advisory Board on Child Abuse and Neglect documented some 2,000 annual violent deaths of children four years old and younger due to child abuse and neglect. Another 18,000 have been permanently disabled, and 142,000 seriously injured due to violence.[2]   – Gerald Kreyche

Nobody lives in the twenty-first century and escapes confrontation with the issue of abuse—and it is not going out of style. Whether we are reacting to our own abuse, or responding to those who are reacting, we are all in a state of alert with no neutral or objective party to clarify what is what. What is all the drama about? What is agitating us so?

According to Webster's College Dictionary, abuse is defined as follows: *to treat in a harmful or injurious way....to speak insultingly or harshly to or about....to commit sexual assault upon....harshly or coarsely insulting language....bad or improper treatment....rape or sexual assault.*

Abuse is a very tricky term to apply. On one end of the spectrum, executives who make seductive comments to their secretaries

80

are being taken to court on the grounds of abuse; on the other end, people are getting away with literal murder on the grounds that they were temporarily "insane," (which implies that we live in a culture in which the norm is sanity). Nonetheless, it is important for us to continue to refine our understanding as to what constitutes abuse.

If people are honest with themselves (though most abusive people are not), they know when they have harmed another person. How an individual life is affected by abuse is really the issue. One parent might regularly yell at his child and whip him with a belt and that child may manage to grow up fairly well adjusted— at least superficially; whereas another child may be broken in two as a result of this same type of treatment, and pay for it throughout his adult life.

Sexual Abuse

Sexual abuse is probably the most insidious misuse of the power to touch that human beings inflict upon one another. It is comparable to murder, only it is the soul of the individual that is often killed and not the body. It may occur between parents and children, spouses, boyfriends and girl-friends, teachers and students, and strangers. The National Center for Child Abuse and Neglect defines sexual abuse as, "Contacts or interactions between a child and an adult when the child is being used for the sexual stimulation of that adult or of another person. Sexual abuse is any inappropriate suggestion or actual sexual exposing or touching between adult and child."[4] When sexual abuse occurs between members of the same family it is called *incest*.

When a mother fondles her eight-year-old son's genitals, it is incest. When a young woman refuses to have sex with a man whom she has spent the evening with, and he insists regardless, holding down her arms, it is sexual abuse. When a father gets in bed with his daughter every night to "tuck her in," but instead rubs his aroused body against hers, it is sexual abuse.

There are also other forms of sexual abuse that are much subtler but may result in similar forms of damage in the psyche. For example, the male child of a divorced woman who is treated by his mother as a surrogate husband will inevitably wind up confused about his sexuality. The young girl who is "raped" by her third-grade teacher's lustful eyes, and then called flirtatious when she speaks about this, will suffer at least some of the effects of sexual abuse. As discussed in the section entitled *Sexuality in Children* in Chapter Three, in a sexually dysfunctional culture, it is fairly common for children to have sensual or erotic feelings directed toward the parent of the opposite, or the same gender, or toward teachers and other elders. It is part of healthy sexual development. It is also common for some parents to have erotic or sensual feelings toward their maturing children. However, the responsibility rests entirely on the part of the parent to refrain from responding to their child's feelings or seductions and from acting on their own impulses—both literally, as well as in subtle ways.

Physical Abuse

A mother takes her son over her knee and spanks him with her hand.

A teacher whacks her student's fingers with a ruler.

As his wife runs out of the house to the car after a fight, her husband chases her and grabbing her arms, pins her against the car until she gives him the keys.

Physical abuse is touch backed by aggression and a desire to inflict pain—whether it be a so-called disciplinary measure, or an outright violent attack. Yet another gross form of the misuse of touch, it is a painful reminder of how little responsibility human beings are taking for their intelligence. Physical abuse is the

82

easiest form of abuse to recognize, and it is what most people think of when they hear the term "abuse." However, one needn't wind up with a black eye or a broken rib in order for a physical attack to constitute abuse. A slap across the face, chasing another person and threatening them, pinching someone until they cry, tickling someone until they are struggling to get away, digging one's nails into another person's skin—all are forms of physical abuse.

Verbal/Emotional Abuse

Verbal and emotional attacks are abuse. A man who degrades his wife in front of their friends is verbally and emotionally abusing her. A mother who returns home from work and upon seeing that her son has not cleaned up after himself screams at the top of her lungs at him, "You good-for-nothing slob. Go to your room and I don't want to see your ugly face again for the rest of the night," has literally taken her child's face and rubbed it in the dirt. Similarly, when a child watches her sibling being degraded and torn apart by their parent, that child suffers the abuse. A client who had been verbally abused continually throughout her childhood by her father, and watched her mother and siblings undergo the same, expressed the sentiment of countless other children in the following:

> *I always wished he would have hit me and scarred me and made me bleed so that he could have seen what he was doing to me. He often threatened to and I would turn right back to him and say, "Do it. Then maybe you'll be forced to see what you're doing to me all the time." But he never would. I actually used to pray that he would hit me so that others could see what was happening and maybe they would help. I was never afraid. No wound on the outside could be more painful than the ones I was already enduring on the inside.*

Neglect

Neglect is the failure to support another individual emotionally and to tend to their needs, often including the refusal to give nurturing physical touch. Children who from the age of six come home from school to an empty house and have no further human contact until evening, and whose baby-sitters are televisions and video games, will suffer neglect. The child whose parents are so absorbed in one another that they ignore their child, or who give a lot of touch to their spouse and little to their child, will suffer neglect. The child who is never held by his or her parents, because the parent finds it awkward or embarrassing, will suffer neglect. The consequences of neglect are the failure to bond and the subsequent difficulty in forming intimate relationships in adulthood. Neglected individuals grow up feeling unwanted by the world and often repulsed by touch and affection. They become hardened, and may harbor deep feelings of rage and resentment at their parents or the world. They develop an attitude of, "I don't care about anyone or anything," in order to disguise a much deeper pain about feeling unloved. Lee Lozowick explains:

> *Neglect is not just to throw your baby in the crib and walk out the door (to the bedroom). Leaving your child when he does not want to be left—that's neglect, too.*[5]

Subtle Forms of Abuse

There are numerous forms of subtle abuse. When a jealous husband does not permit his wife to talk to any other men—it is abuse. When a teacher shames a student for giving an incorrect answer and tells him she is doing it for his own good—she is abusing him. When a mother fails to defend her child when she knows her husband is abusing the child—it is abuse. And the issue becomes still subtler. A father who is exhausted and wishes for time alone confuses his wide-eyed and alert child by telling her that *she* is very tired and that is why he is putting her down for a nap. A boss who, frustrated by his difficult relationship with his wife, acts this out by being controlling and inconsiderate toward his employees, may be unknowingly creating an abusive work environment. Parents who point out everything that their child does wrong, but fail to acknowledge his or her gifts, skills and achievements, however small, are contributing to an inner environment of abuse within the child. Subtler still are the countless ways that we fail to respond to the needs of our spouses, children and friends because we are too absorbed in our own experience to notice what is happening for them, and the endless emotional "jabs" we give one another throughout the day in our wish to put another person down in order to gain the upper hand. Abuse is going on continually. The rare moments we are able to glimpse the pain that we cause others throughout the day reveal the bittersweet reality both of how easy it is to hurt another person, as well as the possibility of what it would mean to genuinely love one another.

Self-Abuse

I often ask clients, "How would you feel if your best friend talked to you the way you talk to yourself?" The response is usually one of shock and horror. For many people, their entire day consists of an endless dialogue of criticism and guilt that may go something like this:

> *When am I going to start exercising before work? Why did I drink two cups of coffee again when I am trying to cut back? Why do I let this traffic get to me so much? How did I spend the whole morning at the desk and get nothing done? I shouldn't have eaten so much at lunch. I wish I dressed like so-and-so.*

Will I ever get a better job? Why did I marry a woman who was going to spend my whole paycheck shopping? I wish I would stop spending the evening in front of the television set and get outside more. My wife isn't attracted to me. Why can't I ever get everything done in time to get a full night's sleep?

On and on this goes, throughout the dream state and into the next day. Many people are steeped in a climate of internal abuse, irrespective of their interactions with anybody outside of themselves. This dialogue is so incessant and has been going on so long that it is almost unnoticeable to the individual whose reality has become one of intense suffering. The person is convinced of their worthlessness and overall "badness." Underneath all the abuse they are really crying out, "What's wrong with me? If only I was perfect, or even better, I would be loved." And still more deeply hidden is the core pain of, "Why didn't they (my parents) love me?"

A climate of internal abuse will inevitably result in difficulties within all of one's relationships. There is a continual expectation that others hold the same judgments and criticisms as the individual has about himself or herself, leaving the individual afraid and constantly on the defense. This fear of abuse emanates from people and draws this reality to them, thus affirming their beliefs. For example, the woman who was abused as a child and is now terrified of being rejected and unloved may isolate herself as an adult, apprehensive of extending herself to others. When others don't respond to her, her belief in her overall "unlovablility" is affirmed.

Other forms of self-abuse include alcohol abuse, drug addiction, eating disorders, self-mutilating behaviors and repeatedly placing oneself in abusive relationships, friendships, work environments. Although in part designed to ward off hurtful feelings, these are all ways in which the already-hurting people inflict further pain onto themselves.

TWO WRONGS DON'T MAKE A RIGHT

In September 1996, six-year-old Jonathan Prevette, a first grade student in Southwest Elementary in Lexington, North Carolina, was accused of sexual harassment by a school bureaucrat, and barred from his class for a day. Jonathan had planted a kiss on his classmate's cheek. (His parents were offered $100,000 for movie rights.)

A "touch paranoia" has swept the nation. As a result of so much attention on the issue of abuse, combined with the multi-million dollar lawsuits that have followed, as well as people's insecurities concerning how to touch one another appropriately, many people have responded with a concrete decision to stop touching one another altogether in particular environments in order to prevent being misunderstood, as well as to protect their savings account should they be accused of touching another person inappropriately.

Unfortunately, two wrongs do not make a right, and individual decisions as well as laws that mandate groups of professionals to refrain from touching one another are going to have a boomerang effect, returning with an exponential blow to the individuals as well as the society which has taken this initiative. It is the individual who ultimately suffers the isolation and loneliness of a personal life or work life characterized by a lack of intimacy, and it is the society which has outlawed love and disregarded the basic goodness of its members that will be responsible for creating an increasingly impersonal world in which genuine affection is a precious commodity with a price tag attached to it.

A man who worked for Boy Scouts of America for many years stopped his work with them when, after several accounts of abuse within the Boy Scouts organization had gained national attention, a rule was instated that a male Boy Scout leader was not allowed to be alone with a young boy—that there must be two or more boys present for any interaction to occur. This man said that the great value he had found in the Boy Scout movement was that young boys who were having difficulty in their lives at home and who were unable to talk to their fathers, or who perhaps didn't even have fathers, had the opportunity to form a relationship with, and to confide in, another mature man, and that this intimacy was not possible to the same degree when two or more boys were present.

The schools are a primary target for anti-touch laws. More and more states are making it illegal for teachers to touch their students, and even in those states that have not outlawed touch in schools, it is increasingly risky for teachers to touch their students. The consequences of these laws alone will be devastating to thousands and thousands of young children across the country. How is it that a teacher who hugs a crying student can be suspect by law for touching him inappropriately, yet that very same legal system allows her to whack that student with a paddle?[6]

Many children do not receive affection at home—period. Abuse and neglect rates are high—much higher than most people dare to imagine. A caring teacher who is responsive to, and respectful of the child as an individual may be the sole source of genuine affection the child ever receives, as well as the only role model of healthy touch he or she is exposed to. If a child is being hit or neglected at home, and treated as though he has no human needs for affection by his teachers at school, how could he be expected to grow up knowing how to respond to his wife, or how to be a loving father to his children? Obviously, he can't. He is more likely to feel uncared for, angry and genuinely confused by his simultaneous urges to be affectionate with the people closest to him, combined with a great fear of touch due to the messages he received in childhood that touch is dangerous and is not available to him.

What is a teacher to do? According to Barrie Beth Hansen, a music teacher in Takoma Park, Maryland, touching a student for *any* reason means putting one's job on the line as a teacher, and is not worth the risk. She explains:

88

The days of the spontaneous hug, the firm disciplinary hand—the days when the school was an extension of the home—are long gone...We live in a litigious society, with schools and educators frequently a prime target of lawsuits. Almost daily, charges of abuse against adults who work with children are splattered all over the media...Public accusations of physical abuse of children on the part of adult caregivers to children have reached almost witch-hunt proportions—a level totally unknown in even the recent past.[7]

Hansen's rationale, that educators must protect their futures, is a valid one, and she encourages them to develop new ways of expressing their concern for students. But will a gold star, a piece of candy or the words, "it will all be all right" ever replace the comfort of a teacher's arms around a young child's shoulder when he or she is upset, or holding the child's hand when he or she is quivering from a sprained ankle or a scraped knee?

Mike McKay, a fifth grade teacher from Illinois, agrees that physical contact with students is risky, and that the teacher is subject to criticism, or worse, for engaging it, but maintains that for some students, their teachers' affection may be all the contact they ever receive. "As teachers," he explains, "we're confronted daily with students who need caring, understanding and expressions of support. We all know students who desperately require nurturing." He further emphasized that the key to touch with students is discretion—knowing oneself, one's students, their parents, and being accountable for one's own actions. He reflects:

If a hug, a pat on the back, or even a "high five" had even a little to do with that feeling (that I have made a difference in their lives), then I used good judgment, discretion, and my heart. I've learned to use my heart more. It's making me a better person and, therefore, a better teacher.[8]

Laws regarding touch exist not only for teachers, but new laws are being implemented for students as well. Says Kathy Seligman of the *San Francisco Examiner* Staff, "Labeled 'teasing' or 'mischief' since boys and girls first started going to school together, acts like these are being reclassified for a whole generation of California students. Now they have a legal name—sexual harassment."[9] Unfortunately, warned Nan Satein, a leading researcher on sexual harassment who works at the Center for Research on Women at Wellesley College, the new laws don't require the schools to teach about sexual harassment, although students from the fourth grade up can be held legally responsible for this.[10] What are the psychological implications for children when six-year-olds such as Jonathan Prevette are accused of sexually harassing their school classmates? It is worthwhile to consider what types of messages are being conveyed to children about the sacredness of their bodies when they are being taught about sexual harassment even before they can read, and before they become comfortable with the most basic boundaries concerning touch with their friends. It is also useful to look at what kind of role models children are learning from, that would result in fifty-four percent of young women at a California high school reporting that they had been harassed.[11]

Similar laws exist for psychotherapists and counselors. Imagine if, as a therapist, you decide to give your client a hug after a particularly moving therapy session, only to receive a court summons many months after the therapy has ended for having touched your client inappropriately.

In my training to become a Marriage, Family and Child Counselor in California, we were required to learn about the laws that prevent all state-approved psychiatrists, psychologists, counselors and trainees from touching their clients—we were even warned about the physical contact that inevitably occurs when payment is exchanged! I left that class with a terror of touching my clients, backed by the "no touch" rule at the counseling center where I worked, only to be subsequently faced with what it felt like not to be able to touch clients whom I deeply cared for and who were in a great deal of pain.

Medical doctors, nurses, social workers and daycare professionals alike are subject to an increasing number of these laws. Those whose job it is to help people in need are facing the greatest restrictions on their freedom to give it, and the most severe consequences when they choose to do so in spite of it. According to one counselor who facilitates a children's grief group at her local hospice, "I know there is a danger of lawsuits for touching these children, but I'm just not going to sit across the room from a six-year-old who is crying about her mother dying of cancer and say, 'I understand how you're feeling.' I made a decision: I touch the children and take the risk."

Others decide not to, and not because they are uncaring. They are often people who have their own families at home and who are unwilling to risk a lawsuit for touching a patient or client inappropriately, in spite of their best intentions. Professionals who are dedicated to their jobs are struggling with issues of how to do their jobs in a way that will make a difference to their clients without breaking the law.

To understand the complexity of the situation more clearly, it is worthwhile to consider why these new laws, such as the ones forbidding teachers to touch their students under any circumstances, are made. They are not made only to protect the child, the hospital patient, or the psychotherapy client, but are primarily created to protect the state governments and the large insurance companies who will have to pay the cost if their customers are accused of touching their clients, patients or students inappropriately. It is *business*. These laws are made because, having been raised in a culture whose moral integrity is full of holes, people have been willing to take advantage of the abuse scare for personal and economic benefits, irrespective of the cost to the therapist, doctor or baby-sitter. Again, I am not saying that *most* reports of abuse are not accurate. An eight-year-old girl has little to gain by telling the school counselor that her male gym teacher came into the locker room and was watching the young girls undress. A fourteen-year-old boy is hardly going to benefit from the rejection and vindictiveness he is likely to face when he tells a social worker that his father has been molesting him on their weekend camping trips since he was nine years old. Then again, a secretary who has repressed memories of childhood sexual abuse *is* going to gain something when instead of working through her memories she files a $20,000 harassment suit against her boss for pinching her arm.

We have gotten ourselves into a difficult bind, and there are no easy answers. There is undoubtedly a need for laws and regulations that will help protect the victims of abuse, yet at the same time, these regulations must allow people the freedom to express simple gestures of care and affection. On the one hand, we must take care of ourselves in pragmatic ways, thus refraining from touching others in situations that clearly present a risk to us, and on the other hand, we must take care of ourselves and others by initiating physical contact, or by bringing intimacy and realness into relationships when that is what is needed in terms of help and support.

We are called to cultivate our ability to use our capacity for discrimination in deciding when to touch and when not to touch, in our willingness to experiment—taking small risks, like offering a supportive touch on the arm to a crying child or client, while paying close attention to how our gestures are responded to. Meanwhile, if children are not going to receive affection from their teachers at school, if clients are not going to receive contact from their therapists, and if medical patients may never be touched by anything other than a sterile gown and a latex-covered hand when they go into the hospital for surgery, the responsibility to give affection and caring rests entirely and unequivocally on our own shoulders within our homes and among our families and friends. Insecure or not, vulnerable or not, fearful of risking or not, it is the ordinary man or woman—you and me—who, if we wish to be a part of the solution instead of part of the problem, are going to have to do the touching, supplying the genuine affection so necessary in an increasingly impersonal world.

THE ROOTS OF VIOLENCE

If it concerned only you
one might say
"What of it?"
But this sadness, this despair
which comes from your mother
who got it from her mother
who inherited it from your great-grandmother,
this mountain of sorrow which has been building up
from one generation to the next
since the beginning of time...[12]   – Frederick Leboyer

The abuse of children is due to feelings of unlove in the abuser, stemming directly back to the wounds of their infancy and childhood. The abusive adult is the man who as a child was left abandoned in his crib at night where he lay screaming for his mother who never came until morning. It is the woman who, as a young girl, was taught that her value lay in her beauty and sexuality; as an adult she will go from man to man, seducing them until they fall for her and then dropping them on the spot. It is the woman who as an infant was smacked by her mother when she reached for the breast to snuggle, because her mother found nursing disagreeable; she has become the embittered third-grade teacher who expects her students to have the intellectual capacity of thirteen-year-olds, and shames them when they do poorly on their examinations.

Abuse is Passed Down from Generation to Generation

"What I do to you is nothing compared to what my father (or mother) did to me," are the words often uttered either aloud or in the silent unconscious of the abuser as he lifts the belt or the hand that will turn him into his father, or as she turns up the television to drown out the sounds of her baby's cry in the next room, just as her mother did. They express the incomprehensible helplessness and devastation of childhood wounds that are passed down from generation to generation in the form of aggression.[13]

Many people know that abuse gets passed down from parent to child, but most people do not grasp that the family heirloom of abuse can often be traced back many generations.[14] Most mothers who have allowed their husbands to abuse their children while they stood by, or who have busied themselves in the next room while the abuse was occurring, might be surprised to find that their mothers and grandmothers had done the very same thing.

Most people fail to understand the sheer power of behavioral conditioning—that the precise traits that they inherited from their own parents will be directly responsible for the most infinitesimal aspects of their child's personality. Genes are only part of what parents pass on to their children. Thus, when there is abuse present in any given household, the children present, particularly the young ones, will not only feel the effects of the abusive act itself, but will breathe in and absorb through their skin the whole toxic environment in which it occurs.

Most of the people in prisons—and many of those in mental hospitals—are there because of the unspeakable, unloving conditions of their early lives.[15]   – Roderic Gorney

The origins of abuse can be dated back to the species' primary instinct for survival. When it comes down to it, most people would kill rather than be killed. Unless something deeper and more unconscious was prompting them, young men of clear minds could not willfully volunteer to go to war and murder other people in a Third World country that could never possibly harm their own country, nor would they beat up their wives for not having a hot dinner ready when they come home late from work after a visit to the local bar. Mothers would not try to convince themselves, just to save their marriage, that their husbands weren't abusing their children *"that badly."* Individuals act like this because a primal instinct for survival is triggered—the soldier thinks that Daddy-government is finally going to be proud of him if he stands up and fights like a man, and will shame him for being a wimp if he doesn't (and he desperately *needs* his father's approval). The woman who allows abuse to continue in her home is terrified that if she refuses to "be a good girl and keep your mouth shut," Daddy-husband will abandon her and that she and her kids would be left without food and a place to live. The adult is not thinking and feeling these things consciously. The unexamined life is run by these primal fears. The adult is acting this way because he or she unconsciously believes that if they do not, they will literally die.

It becomes increasingly obvious that, as adults, not only our failure to share touch and affection, but our tendencies toward violence, excessive control, depression, etc., are sustained by our unwillingness to fully feel the hemorrhaging wounds of our childhood. Innocent, essentially pure and good individuals are so fearful of their pain that they must scream at their children or train them to be passive and well-mannered automatons so that they do not have to see in their children the innocence and joy that they as parents have lost.

Abuse May Have a Chemical Component

There is no chromosome for abuse. It is not genetic. Still, abuse may have a chemical component. Recall from Chapter Two that a failure to bond in childhood inhibits the natural occurrence of certain chemical functions that are necessary for the normal developmental maturation of the brain. James Prescott says that the neuronal systems of the brain are responsible for mediating pleasure, and that in the unbonded individual, the development of these has been stunted, thus failing to regulate the chemical aspects of depression and rage, and to balance them through pleasure. "The failure to integrate pleasure into the higher brain centers associated with 'consciousness' (frontal lobes) is the principal neuropsychological condition for the expression of violence, particularly sexual violence."[16] It becomes a plausible hypothesis that among the chemical processes catalyzed by bonding is also that which is needed to form a mature conscience in the individual.

Perhaps the most interesting of Prescott's findings emerged from his cultural studies on violence. He documented statistical evidence to back the fact that the presence or absence of touch is not only the distinguishing factor between a healthy and well-adjusted individual or a violent one, but also how cultural practices regarding touch are responsible for creating either violent or non-violent societies. He developed the means to predict, with 100 percent accuracy, whether a culture would be violent or non-violent simply by looking at whether the infant was carried on the body of its mother or caretaker (this factor alone resulting in 80 percent accuracy), combined with whether or not adolescent sexual activity was permitted or punished.[17] He explained, "Those societies which give their infants the greatest amounts of physical affection were characterized by low theft, low infant physical pain...and negligible or absent killing, mutilating, or torture of the enemy...The warmth of human touch and security of body contact are without question the most effective way to reduce violence in our culture."[18]

Thus, there is a direct relationship between touch and violence. When an individual has been adequately nurtured in childhood, he or she is highly unlikely to act out aggression in his or her environment.

Most Children Would Rather Have Abusive Contact Than No Contact

Jonathan Kozol explained:

Children long for this—a voice, a way of being heard—but many sense that there is no one in the world to hear their words, so they are drawn to ways of malice. If they cannot sing, they scream. They are vessels of the spirit but the spirit sometimes is entombed; it can't get out, and so they smash it![19]

Ironically, most children would rather be abused than be neglected or abandoned. What they really want is to be loved, held and given affection and for their parents to take interest in them. They want their sexuality to be supported and respected. They want evidence of their parents' love in the form of their attention. But when it comes down to it, abusive contact is often preferred to isolation.

As mentioned throughout the book, tactile stimulation is necessary for the growing body to develop and for the developed body to stay in balance. A child who is raised in a touch-rich environment will naturally seek contact, but even the child who is abused or neglected will seek this contact. The child's body will naturally look for what it needs to stay chemically balanced. The child may not know why she jumped into her mother's lap, or suddenly found himself in a screaming battle with his father, but unbeknownst to the child, the body had signaled to the brain what it needed in order to maintain balance. Many children are accused by their parents of provoking abuse; perhaps this is so, but the child's underlying motive is a need for contact rather than a desire to be abused.

When there is abuse, there is hope, in an odd sort of way. When the parents are unaffectionate with the child or absorbed in adult-conversation or activities, the child is stuck in isolation, whereas when there is abuse, there is action. The child has a chance to make a stand for himself, to try to be heard, to make a point—even if it entails further abuse. When nobody else is noticing him, he at least stands to gain something in terms of self-esteem for his willingness to advocate himself.

French physician and psychologist Dr. Alfred Tomatis further suggests that stimulation is sought through sound. There is a strong correlation between touch and sound. The vibratory effects of sound travel through the ear and stimulate the same centers of the brain as does tactile sensation, thus accounting for why infants, even in utero, immediately relax to certain types of music (e.g., classical, lullabies), and show disturbance in response to harsher forms of music. The unbonded teenager still craves this same touch. Thus, according to Tomatis, he or she will seek out loud and highly stimulating music (e.g., the now-popular heavy metal and rave music) in order to get the stimulation that his now-undeveloped system is craving. His ideas offer a plausible theory as to why today's youth culture has turned to such harsh forms of stimulation in search of "entertainment."

On this point, psychologist Erich Fromm suggested that if children can't get their strokes from life-giving situations, they'll get them from life-taking situations. If people, and not only children but all people, are not being touched by life, they need to be touched regardless, so they'll cut themselves with razor blades or touch themselves with body piercings. Adults will touch themselves with gluttony, or tobacco, or drugs, or by hitting their spouses. They will touch themselves by hurting the people they love, as this is what gives them the strongest pain—and pain is at least a feeling in an otherwise numb body.

This principle—the need to get attention, even if abusive attention—applies to sexual abuse as well, whether it be father-daughter, uncle-niece, or teacher-student abuse. The perpetrator (often unconsciously) uses to his advantage the knowledge that the child is raised in a generally abusive and unhealthy environment (often of his own creation), and therefore craves affection, acknowledgment and attention. Therefore, if he plans his attack well, he can possibly get full consent from his victim. For example, a father tells his son, "You're such a beautiful young boy. More beautiful than any woman, and what I need from you I can't get from your Mommy." Or a teacher tells his fifth-grade student, whom he has "detained" after class, "You are the most attractive girl in the whole class. I want to show you just how special you are." Remember, a touch-starved, unbonded child is at the effect of an inner desperation. Although deep in the body they know that something is very wrong, they are finally hearing the words they have longed to hear, and then being touched, held, and made to feel pleasure. They feel special. They feel important. They feel touched. This does not happen in all cases, but is a poignant example of how someone in an already touch-starved state can become easily manipulated into further abuse.

"Evil" Exists, But So Does Conscience

In his book *People of the Lie*, best-selling author M. Scott Peck risks the radical proposal that evil lies at the base of many crimes of abuse. Whereas we normally associate the concept of "evil" with gross images of violent actions, Peck suggests that evil is a force dictated by a lack of conscience that can manifest in "ordinary" parent-child relationships, and in subtle but definitive ways.

As a child of nine, I recall seeing a news report on the trial of a mass murderer who had escaped from prison, and had subsequently murdered several more victims, many of them children. The news showed him waiting to receive his sentence, sitting in a courtroom packed full of people. When the judge asked him publicly if he had any regrets about the crimes he had committed, the murderer looked the judge straight in the eye and said, "None."

I had seen evil. Although this murderer was speaking his conscious reality, both then and now I do not believe that conscience did not exist somewhere inside of him, no matter how deeply hidden.

Supporting the aspect of Peck's theory that evil does exist, I would take this back one step and purport that *one is not born evil,* but that *evil is created.* It is highly unlikely that this murderer was born to a conscious mother and father, was nurtured in the womb, was welcomed into the world in a loving way, was breast-fed on demand, carried around in his first two years, allowed to share his parent's bed, and given lots of affection as a child. Touch, affection and honest care and consideration must be communicated from conception onward. The force of evil—capable of murder, incest, and even global destruction, as well as being responsible for the insidious ways we invisibly denigrate even those we love most—is the result of nothing more, or less, than the human failure to love properly.

In the initial version of James Prescott's 1996 letter to the editor of the *New York Times* (which was significantly edited before printing), he set forth the following challenge:

> *The legal-judicial and criminal justice system is challenged to find ONE murderer, rapist or drug addict who has been breast-fed for "two years and beyond"—the recommendation of the World Health Organization—in any prison, jail or correctional facility in the United States.*[20]

Abusive Tendencies Exist Within Each of Us

If you have ever been willing to be ruthlessly honest with yourself in the moment in which you have gained power over another individual (in a fist fight, an argument, or even a so-called friendly debate), you may have been surprised to find that you found a certain satisfaction, or even pleasure in it. The feeling is no different from what is felt in a football game, a tennis match or a game of bridge at the moment when you know your opponent doesn't have a chance, or from the thrill of thousands of spectators at a bullfight when the matador pierces the bull, or the look on the lion's face when he has caught a gazelle. There is satisfaction in the kill. We enjoy the power of dominance, the taste of blood. In it we feel strong and invincible. Our survival is vindicated—we have the illusory experience of momentarily conquering our death. Many people will do anything for this.

The abuser is not other. The capacity to abuse exists within each of us. If you are using this book as a tool to explore yourself, you will know as well as I do that nobody in contemporary Western culture—save perhaps the rarest of rare—escapes the reality of this collective human wound. Our capacity to abuse is the curse and the blessing of the human condition. This wound is the curse because of the suffering it creates, and the blessing because in the understanding of it lies the seed of True Compassion. The sooner we are able to recognize that abuse is inside of us, the sooner we will be able to see it for what it is, instead of running from it, fearing that it is something terrible about *us,* or that *we* are bad. When we stop judging ourselves for our potential abusiveness, we begin to understand how it works in us, and we begin to understand how it works in others. We can then cease to judge others, and cease to defend ourselves from the intimacy we so crave. Thus abuse loses its grip on us.

Abusive tendencies exist within each of us, but not everybody is an abuser. We cannot help but to unknowingly hurt people in small ways as we move about our daily lives, but abuse is a function of action, not feeling. The more unaware a person is of their abusive tendencies, the more likely they are to act them out. Becoming aware of these feelings does not mean acting them out. If you have to, you can paint them, write them, ride them out on your bike, or punch them into a punching bag, but generally you let the feeling be, allow the intensity of it to teach you not only about yourself, but about the greater human condition. When we understand that the problem is not "other," we simultaneously understand that the solution is not "other."

HOW WE COPE

Defense Mechanisms

The field of psychology uses the term "defense mechanisms" to describe the specific forms of thought and action that abused individuals adopt in order to keep the pain of trauma out of conscious awareness and to protect themselves from experiencing the full impact of the abuse. Understanding how defense mechanisms work allows us to come into a fuller appreciation of the consequences of the wrong kind of touch, and what an individual attempting to heal this abuse is faced with.

Dissociation

Commonly, when a child is being sexually abused, her consciousness will take leave of the body, traveling up onto the ceiling or across the room. She literally separates from her body, becomes identified with her mental consciousness, and thus affirms, "*I* am up here. The body that is getting abused is down there."

In order to sustain this belief in adulthood, such a person must remain disconnected from her body, for her body "knows" the abuse she suffered. As an adult, she is likely to not really be *at home* in her body. Of course she walks and talks and eats just like everybody else, but she will often appear to be spaced out, unfocused, and have an awkwardness in her movements. When I am with a client and begin to feel disoriented or spaced out, I look to see if she is present "behind her eyes," that is, to see if somebody is there. Nine out of ten times, I find nobody home. "The hitting, the screaming, and smothering affection made me want to go somewhere else," said one young woman, "so I created a bubble in which to live in my head." Unfortunately, greater than the pain of the abuse itself is the individual's lifelong loss of connection with her body, for in keeping herself detached from the pain in her body, she also removes herself from the pleasure and nurturing qualities of touch.

Numbing

In order to cut off unpleasant feelings and sensations, the child will hold his breath, suck in his belly, and immobilize his diaphragm. He will lie very still to avoid being afraid. In short, he will "deaden" his body in order not to feel pain, and by these means abandon reality.[21]   – Ashley Montagu

A boy may unconsciously numb the surface of his skin as a means of self protection because his father regularly whips him with a belt. That same child may be seen outside in winter in shorts with no shirt, commenting that he doesn't feel the cold. A girl who has been sexually abused may lose all sensation from the waist down. She is able to feel external stimulation on the skin, but cannot feel the life inside of her body. One of my massage clients said she always felt like she was "walking around on somebody else's legs"—that she knew her legs were attached and would carry her around, but that they didn't feel like a part of "her."

A more extreme example of body numbing is illustrated in a story told by a friend of mind who is a nurse. An obese thirty-two-year-old woman, complaining of intense stomach cramps, admitted herself to the hospital where my friend works. Within hours of entering the hospital, she gave birth to a baby boy. Utterly shocked, this woman had carried a baby in her body for nine months and had never felt it!

Fantasy

Fantasy is another way that victims of abuse cope. The environment they live in is too threatening, so they absorb themselves in their own make-believe world, or in fictional worlds created by others. Whereas in young children, fantasy is a normal and healthy aspect of development, adults who spend the majority of their time in front of a computer or a television set instead of with family and friends, or absorbed in trashy romance novels, are using these activities as a crutch.

Disavowal

Many children who have been abused *disavow* their desire for touch to protect themselves from being hurt again in the same way. They may lose their desire for contact altogether. Somewhere early on they make the vow, "If this is what it means to be touched, I don't want it again—*ever!*" Or, "Love hurts too much, I'm *never* going to let somebody come close to me again." Such vows made by children are more powerful than most people would imagine, and often have lasting effects. They become part of the individual's unconscious, but are lurking nearby and readily available whenever any possibility for contact arises. For example, a man who says, "I just don't like to be touched, it's as simple as that," it is probably not so simple. He was either neglected, emotionally smothered, or physically or sexually abused.

Fortunately, the soul, or Self, can also make vows. One man I know recalls the precise time at which his True Self went away because of the pain of the abuse he endured as a young boy. However, at the same time, he made the vow to himself, "I swear that when I grow up and finally get out of here that I'm going to do everything I can to get my real Self back." And he did. He is now a thriving thirty-five-year-old man with an excellent career and a wonderful family of his own.

The Multiple "I's"

In my own experience, I have found that aspects of the spiritual philosophy of Russian teacher G.I. Gurdjieff have very practical psychological use in understanding and healing the consequences of abuse, and therefore opening oneself to a life full of touch and affection. In particular, his notion of the "multiple I's," though originally intended as a description of the spiritual development of the human being, can be applied to the psychology of the abuse victim. He says:

> *It is the greatest mistake to think that man is always one and the same. A man is never the same for long. He is continually changing. He seldom remains the same even for half an hour. We think that if a man is called Ivan he is always Ivan. Nothing of the kind. Now he is Ivan, in another minute he is Peter, and a minute later he is Nicholas...You will be astonished when you realize what a multitude of these Ivans and Nicholases live in one man.*[22]

Many individuals, particularly those who have been traumatized, are not aware of the complexity of their personalities.

105

According to Gurdjieff, multiple "I's" exist within every individual—a series of distinct identities which together constitute that which the individual thinks of as "himself" or "herself."

An example of this is the man who makes a decision to start getting up early every morning to exercise. However, when his alarm goes off in the morning, he presses the snooze button and goes back to sleep. Frustrated, he restates his intention the following day, only to remain in bed once again. Why is this so? The "I" who made the decision to get up, and the "I" who woke up in the morning, were not one and the same. The "I" who decided to get up and exercise really would do that, and the "I" who wouldn't get up, really wouldn't! Factors such as clouds or sunshine, heat and cold, as well as emotionally threatening situations, can call up entirely different sets of "I's."

Though the reality of the multiple "I's" is not commonly recognized for what it is, it is a recurrent theme in the work of artists including painters, musicians and sculptors. The lyrics to the popular Eurythmics song, *This City Never Sleeps*, captures this multiple "I" phenomenon:

I can hear the sound of the underground train
Though it feels distant thunder...
You know there's so many people living in this house
And I don't even know their names.
You know there's so many people living in this house
And I don't even know their names...
Oh some days I can almost hear them breathe
If I listen then I hear my own heart beating...
Guess it's just a feeling...[23]

A similar dynamic occurs in relationship to touch. Let's use the example of a fairly new couple going out on a date. Perhaps the man picks the woman up and gives her a quick kiss, and the woman is slightly annoyed. Her "I" that answered the door was

106

not immediately open to touch. They go out to a nice dinner, have some wine, and walk out of the restaurant arm and arm—they are each operating under the auspices of an "I" that feels safe, comfortable and relaxed. Afterwards, at the movie, he reaches out to hold her hand, but the "I" whose hand he takes is already different, feeling self-conscious about the intimacy that was shared after dinner and afraid of what will happen if she gives into it, so she quickly excuses herself to go to the bathroom, and when she sits down again has her hands covered under the sleeves of a sweater she has put on. Yet, as the movie, a romantic drama, unfolds, an affectionate "I" appears and shyly she reaches for his arm. It is he who is taken aback now. In response to her previous clues, a defensive "I'm not interested / I don't need you", "I" has taken over in him. She retracts in reaction to his response, as her "if you don't want me I certainly don't want you 'I'" comes to her rescue. The movie ends with one of the lovers dying, making a tiny crack in the woman's protective "I", and a softer and more vulnerable "I" emerges in her. On the way to the cafe, she takes a risk and tells him how much she enjoyed their time together and that she hopes it continues into the future. His "I" immediately shifts into a softness complimentary to hers and they enter into a romantic mood together.

Among individuals who have been abused, the phenomenon of the multiple "I's" is particularly pronounced. Still, multiple personality *disorder* is the exception rather than the norm. When people do not understand that multiple "I's" exist within everyone, they are likely to believe that there is something very wrong with them when they do not understand the range of moods and feelings they experience within a given day. Such individuals often believe themselves to be "crazy," when instead they are experiencing a phenomenon common to all human beings to a greater or lesser degree.

Touch is the Integrating Factor

Touch is a common meeting ground for the many "I's." When a trusted individual is present, and the body understands that there is no imminent danger, the defenses can relax, and the dissociated, disintegrated and split off "I's" can begin to come together. What people call a feeling of openness is often simply a relaxation of the defenses that are ordinarily keeping the separative "I's" intact. Safe, intentional and conscious touch by caring individuals can provide this healing.

The touch that heals may not be physical touch initially. Remember that the abused or touch-starved person may not be ready to receive physical touch right away, even when she knows that is what she needs. Her early wish for contact was brutalized, shamed, and often turned against her, and she is still wary and uncertain. The person may need "talk touch," listening touch, the touch of attention, of a steady gaze or of shared silence and presence. She may be able to feel touched at some moments and not at others. She may ask for touch and then freeze up when it is given to her. She may need the touch of patience. Since the skin was the scene of the crime (particularly in cases of extreme violation of the body, or the neglect of its needs), only by returning to the skin—not only facing the terror of touch, but transforming it from a source of fear to a source of pleasure—will there be a transformative effect. When the person who once disavowed touch has not only learned to tolerate it but to again desire it, she has cleansed the wound and is well on her way to a sense of well being.

SEXUAL ABUSE—THE TWISTED TOUCH

The absence of loving touch and the abundance of sadistic sexual touch has badly wounded me. Man does not live by breath alone.[24]
          – Greg Campbell

When a person is sexually abused, his or her physical experience of pleasure often becomes directly linked to emotions of terror, betrayal and "badness," and thus the body begins to experience loving touch as anxiety-producing, and gestures of affection as warnings of betrayal. The body and brain operate by a system that can be likened to complex wiring, and for the victim of sexual abuse, it is as if somebody twisted the wires that hooked up the normal pain and pleasure responses, thus severely impairing the abused person's organic capacity to give and receive touch and pleasure. You will often find these individuals to be highly intelligent and competent in many arenas of life, while at the same time extremely self-deprecating and undeveloped in other ways.

> *I crave sex just like everybody,* began Sheri, a 32-year-old sculptor, *but when my body starts to feel good, I am overcome with a sudden exhaustion and can't even stay awake, or I have a sudden allergy attack, or I am overwhelmed with feelings of hatred and rage at my husband, even though I love him. Sometimes when we have sex, I feel like I am being raped, even though he is gentle and kind. The torment inside my mind at these times is indescribable.*

The sentiment expressed above is affirmed in the lives of countless other women and men. What is common to all of these individuals is that they coped with their childhood abuse by learning, in some way, how not to feel. Unfortunately, this defense becomes stabilized and automatic in the body, and when they reach adulthood, even if they are fortunate enough to find themselves in a completely non-abusive circumstance, the defense system will oftentimes still not be able to discern the difference between a healthy and an unhealthy environment, and will continue to operate as though it was still in an abusive situation.

These individuals have lost their capacity to receive touch, and being so removed from their bodies, lack the sensitivity needed to touch others with love and gentleness. Instead, they grow up and repeat the cycle—men who were sexually abused will usually abuse, and women will find someone to abuse them. That is, they repeat the cycle until they decide to break the cycle. It is the touch that was once used as a weapon to wound them that can now be turned into the medicine that heals them.

Many individuals find it extremely frustrating to discover within themselves many or all of the symptoms of abuse listed here, but with no memory of any kind of dramatic abuse. Their childhood may appear quite normal and mild compared to the kinds of abuses that are now so commonly spoken of. Perhaps their mother was depressed or their father was a closet drunk. Or maybe their parents were divorced and their mother struggled financially and could not afford to feed her child well. As mentioned early in this chapter, abuse is not being discussed here in terms of blame, but instead in terms of how it affects the individual's capacity to give and receive touch. Therefore, it is less important that a person know exactly *why* they have difficulties around touch, or *who* is responsible for it, than it is to acknowledge the fact of *what is true for them,* and to seek ways of returning to feeling.

We continually underestimate the sensitivity of the child and how deeply he or she is influenced by their environment. In many cases, simply being raised by a mother who, unbeknownst to the child, had been abused by her own mother, that child, by virtue of his attunement to his mother, can easily absorb her devastation and fear of others, thus becoming skin-wary himself without ever having an inkling as to why.

The Point of No Return

There is a *point of no return* when it comes to abuse. Many people have had the experience, in the midst of their attack on another, of suddenly meeting the terror in the victim's eyes—a look that shocks the attacker into the realization that they have gone too far, that something has been broken. Such a glimpse of reality can be shattering. The individual recognizes just how much he or she has hurt another person—for deeper than the damage to the skin, the sexual organs, the pain-pleasure circuits and the emotions, is the soul wound. The soul can be broken, and to repair a broken soul, if at all possible, often requires many years of hard work—all for a momentary lapse of consciousness or a selfish indulgence on the part of the abuser.

As a therapist, many clients have said to me, "My mother told me that I was a 'mistake' and that she wished I had never been born, but I know she didn't *really* mean it." Or, "My father got carried away and locked me in the closet—but it only happened once." Once can be more than enough, however, to bring someone to the point of no return. The soul is not broken every time (some escape irrevocable damage), but the fact remains that when an individual slips into an abusive moment, he or she does so with no guarantee or insurance that, "Everything will be O.K."

If you look closely, you can almost always tell when somebody has lost their soul. Soul loss manifests in the child who looks far too old for his years—not just mature, but tired, worn out and very serious. Or in the child who appears to have totally "checked out," as though he saw too much and could not bear to see any more. The adult who has been broken appears to have a hardened shell, or a suit of armor, surrounding him. You feel a heaviness and deep depression when you meet the person who has sold out. This is the consequence of the wrong kind of touch.

CULTURE OF ABUSE—CULTURE OF DENIAL

> *Cultures and societies—like parents—are not all equal in their ability to provide and receive love.*[25]   – Roderic Gorney

A "culture of abuse" suggests not only a culture in which abuse is rampant, but a culture in which the same elements and symptoms that characterize the abusive family system are manifest in the society as a whole. In the same way as the abused child becomes a part of the abusive family system that has molded him, so the individual members of a society become a part of, and cannot be separated from, the larger economic and social systems that are responsible for the culture in which they live. This "abusive system" will permeate all aspects of society from the very structure of the government that runs it, to the individual roles in the cultural system, to the values and ideals maintained by the people.[26] A culture of denial goes hand-in-hand with a culture of abuse, as abuse depends upon denial in order to sustain itself.

The System

In the same way that abused boys often grow up to be aggressive, angry, hurtful, disconnected and emotionally handicapped adults, a patriarchal culture (including patriarchal women!) in which abuse is pervasive will manifest these tendencies on the collective level. For example, in a culture of abuse there will be a "dog-eat-dog" ethic and a get-rich-quick obsession. (The abused boy or girl thinks: "When I make it to the top and become rich and powerful, my parents will see that I am smart and successful.") There will be a strong basis of military power and dominance. (The abused child decides: "I'm going to become so strong that nobody can ever touch me again—I'll show them who to be afraid of.") There will be high rates of crime. (The hurt child figures: "Nobody respected my boundaries, why should I respect theirs?") Rape and sexual crimes will run rampant. (The son who was either sexually abused by his father, or watched his father sexually abuse his mother or sisters thinks: "They fucked me up, now it's *my* turn.")

112

Drug and alcohol abuse rates will be high. (The wounded child looks for any possible way to cope with feelings of grief, betrayal, rage, abandonment.) And the society will think of only its own benefit and the fulfillment of its present desires, even if that entails sacrificing the very earth that is to provide for its grandchildren. (The abused child turns his attention to himself, often becoming exceedingly narcissistic and self-centered, as nobody else seems to be taking care of him.)

Meanwhile, the abused girl grows up to be passive, afraid, shamed-based, and has a low self-esteem. Thus, the feminine aspect of society allows this violent culture to sustain itself as the dominant force (as the once-abused girl marries an abusive man just like her father, though she swore she never would). In the same way that the oppressed woman feels powerless to do anything as her husband screams at her children, she finds herself equally helpless to act when the government cuts funding for education and welfare. (The abused girl, unable to fight back against her parents, gives up her power and her voice.) Because she never learned to speak up, she grew to believe that what she had to say was unimportant. Other abused girls cope with their pain by becoming so strong, so competent, and so "equal" to men that no man can have power over them again. (Thus, we now have a culture full of women in business suits or driving bulldozers while a daycare center raises their children.) And as the child who was sexually abused learns that she can get love and attention through drawing attention to her body, we now live in a culture that supports promiscuity, pornography and the objectification of women's bodies. And just as the abused girl never learned to stand on her own two feet, thus we have a culture full of skinny Barbie dolls in high heels who have lost a sense of their true femininity. Now a wealth of feminine wisdom and knowledge lies buried in the collective unconscious of the culture—its worth entirely denied.

These attitudes of abuse pervade all facets of society. It is socially acceptable to go into other countries and murder tens of thousands of people. Journalist Robert E. Fatham reports that the Humane Society can bring charges of cruelty to animals for the same behaviors that are sanctioned when directed against children in the public school system. According to the National Coalition to Abolish Corporal Punishment in Schools, the only developed countries still permitting teachers to hit students are the United States, South Africa, parts of Canada, and Australia. Most European countries began to outlaw this type of abuse in the 1800s.

A culture of abuse is one in which its members feel generally let down, uncared for and disregarded. (On the superficial level of society, everything may appear to be just great, just as the face of the abused child may show little or nothing, while her heart aches within.) The culture does not know True Touch, yet often is well acquainted with the horrors of abusive touch. And it is not only the physical touch that this culture misses, but the experience of being surrounded by trustworthy and generous people. A culture of abuse does not support the experience of living in a world that respects the individual, and in which there is an overall sense of belonging and well being.

Again, it is not that everyone within the culture is abused. Instead, the overall symptoms of abuse have begun to permeate the culture such that general feelings of aggression and helplessness, plus a fear-based drive to consume—as opposed to a feeling of generosity, balance and consideration—have come to dominate almost all arenas of modern life.

The People

> In civilized societies...the differences among people are largely expressions of the ways in which they have adapted to the distortions in their personalities caused by the qualities and quantities of deprivation they have experienced.[27]
> – Jean Liedloff

114

When abuse has become the norm of society, it is undetectable by its members, as there is nowhere it is not present in some form. People have no paradigm of wholeness and peace by which to perceive the contrast of their present state of devastation. For example, the child who was raised in a household of sheer psychic insanity knows no model of sanity, and therefore accepts his terrible condition as normal, as objective, and from birth (or before) automatically begins to adjust himself to these conditions. Similarly, children born into a culture in which the underlying mood is one of aggression, competition, fear and depression, and in which the whole economic and family system is built upon this foundation, will literally cramp themselves, closing their hearts or their higher minds, or whatever they must, in order to accommodate the norm. They quickly perceive the vast gully of separation between their own innocence and purity and the aggression that surrounds them. In order to believe that they will be taken care of, children tell themselves, "Mother and father know best, and would never do anything to hurt me." Projected onto the culture, this attitude later becomes, "It's a democracy, the President is of the people, and everybody has equal rights. If I pay my taxes and register for the draft, I will be taken care of." For the sake of its survival, the child concludes that mother, father, culture, family structure, president, bank, democracy, etc. must be right, must be good, and so he recreates himself to become a part of it. Montagu elaborates:

> ...Driven to armor himself against attachment and betrayal, he (the child) may have arrived at a state in which all contact seems repellent, where to touch or to be touched means to hurt or be hurt. This, in a sense, has become one of the greatest ailments of our time, a major social disease of modern society that we would do well to cure before it is too late. If the danger remains unheeded, then—like poisonous chemicals in our

food—it may increase from generation to generation until the damage has gone beyond repair.[28]

There are many roles that the members of an abusive culture take on. Family systems theory, a widely accepted psychological model of how families operate, can be applied to the larger family, i.e., society, as well. The theory dictates that the family—whether functional or dysfunctional—operates as a whole unit, each part dependent upon all other parts for its functioning. Like a body that depends upon the heart, lungs, kidney, brain, arteries, etc. to function, and which cannot sustain itself when missing any of these components, so the family system operates—the abuser cannot abuse without a victim, and those present who do not prevent the abuse are active in their passivity. It is a common family scenario for the "man of the house" (the abuser) to hit his children (the victims) while a mother (the passive witness) does the dishes or stands by whining softly, "Don't do that." When these children grow up, they tend to repeat the cycle by becoming abusers, victims or passive witnesses.

Similar patterns show up in the members of a culture of abuse. The abusers are the people who hold power and wield it (often unconsciously) for their own benefit. Many of the power-wielders who run the country and its systems fall into this category—often they will be presidents of large corporations, government officials in departments of war, financial officers, dishonest businessmen, brokers, soldiers, policemen, criminals, etc. They become the perpetrators in the culture of violence in lieu of becoming its victims (in the exact same way as most young boys who are abused cope with their feelings of helplessness by becoming abusers, giving them the illusion of finally having power over the other, even if "the other" happens to be their own four-year-old child). This common pattern is often expressed as, "Kill or be killed," or, "May the best man win."

116

The victims are those who are at the effect of the societal abuser. Their voice, power and rights have been taken from them by the forces of discrimination. Included in this category are those who are African American, gay/lesbian, Hispanic, poor, homeless, mentally ill or immigrants. These individuals are largely abandoned by society, and experience the same disregard and lack of acknowledgment that the child feels from his abuser. They feel violated and stepped on by racism and inequality— being increasingly denied their basic human needs while a small, white, wealthy majority continues to grow more prosperous. Of course in these victims' minds they can see that these attitudes are ridiculous and reflect the views of society (the cultural "parent") and not themselves, but if day in and day out this is their reality, it begins to seep in, just as the child internalizes the abusive attitudes of his parents. When a whole culture is telling you daily in a hundred different ways that you do not matter, that you are less-than others and undeserving of the privileges allotted to them—it is nearly impossible not to take this on to a greater or lesser degree.

The passive witnesses comprise the majority of the members of a culture of abuse. Abuse can only occur in a system that supports it, and thus, although the present system is terribly unjust, the impotent members of society are as much a part of it as are the leaders they elect. The passive witness is the general public. Their sentiment could be expressed as, "As long as it's not happening to me, I don't want to know about it," or, "I'm too scared that if I interfere I'm going to get beat up too, so I think I'll just stay off to the side." We are all passive witnesses to some degree, even if at times we take on other roles. We want to get on with our lives, we don't want to suffer, we feel overwhelmed by the atrocities around us, it hurts too much to care, we don't want to believe that we can make a difference and so we remain detached and uninvolved. The price of the passive witness is summarized in Martin Neimoeller's famous poem, *First They Came for the Jews*:

117

First they came for the Jews
and I did not speak out
because I was not a Jew.
Then they came for the communists
and I did not speak out
because I was not a communist.
Then they came for the trade unionists
and I did not speak out
because I was not a trade unionist.
Then they came for me
and there was no one left
to speak out for me.

Lastly, there are the "black sheep" of the family. They are those children who did not, who could not buy into the illusion that Mommy, Daddy, country, or president were omnipotent and would take care of them.

he seemed *protected...but inside: who could ward off,*
who could divert, the floods of origin inside him?[29]
                                                    – Rainer Maria Rilke

These children who cannot accept the myth have few options, none of them favorable from a societal perspective. At best, they become the artists—the painters, the poets, the writers, the sculptors, the musicians. If through their art they are able to give the public just enough reality—to touch the places of supreme beauty that people have forgotten about—then the artists are revered and honored, though they often remain poor.

Others, artists or not, look around and see little boys in adult bodies married to Miss America wannabe's, and are devastated by how they see their "happily married parents" treating each other, and by the overall emptiness and superficiality of their culture. So they paint it black, write it bold, or scream it loudly at their

118

heavy metal concerts. They wear it bluntly in the piercings on their eyebrows, lips and cheeks, and on their shaved heads and spiked leather jackets. Needless to say, the average person in an "everything-is-just-fine" society does not want to face the reality of this much pain (which is really a pain that belongs to all of us, only a very few individuals take it upon themselves to express it), and so their materials are not printed, their lives not portrayed (except as derelicts), their music not heard, and their pain not acknowledged. So they scream louder.

When the pain is unbearable—when mother and father beat on them too hard, when they are unable to buffer themselves against the horrors of the surrounding society, and the depth of wounding will not allow them to adjust to the surrounding culture—the criminals, drug addicts and murderers emerge. Or, they "check out" and become another statistic on the list of the mentally ill. They become psychotic, autistic, borderline or schizophrenic. They commit suicide.

Still others become the visionaries—they are living experimental lives on the frontiers, offering their bodies, minds and labor to alternative possibilities. They are living in non-traditional communities, exploring spiritual practices, practicing organic farming, leading self-help seminars, studying holistic health and so forth. Some of their experiments are working, others aren't. Some are naive idealists, others are brilliant and generous people willing to risk everything for their highest ideals, and still others are dubious of widespread change, but are propelled by their integrity to refrain from participating in a destructive system.

Overall, society rejects such people. The government takes the failed experiments and spreads pictures of them all over the media to instill fear and prejudice in the public against these groups in order to maintain the effects of the cultural anesthesia it has injected into its people to control them.

An honest and sincere search for truth puts you in danger of being accused, abused and ridiculed by society. Sooner or later we'll all be called to stand for what we feel to be the truth.[30]

Denial

...The first step to solving our problems in relating is to acknowledge that they exist. To do this we have to be willing to call into question both ourselves and the entire collective in order to discover the causes of our disturbed consciousness.[31]

— J. Konrad Stettbacher

If, as individuals, we were fully conscious of the pain that we bring to others by our ignorance of the aggression, defensiveness and pain that underlies our interactions with them...and if, as members of a nation, we understood the amount of death and destruction we participate in every day by way of our tax dollars and our refusal to act...if we were suddenly called to face this directly with no buffers—we would likely *die* of the pain. For this reason, we set up elaborate systems which serve to negate, or at least soften, the stark reality of our experience.

Is it possible for an entire culture to sustain a state of denial? Absolutely. How do soldiers go through military training in which they are taught to murder and torture other human beings, and then go into Third World countries and drop bombs on villages of thousands of innocent men, women and children? How do owners of multinational fruit companies in the Third World allow of thousands of workers to inhale chemicals that will result in impotency and other life-threatening diseases?

We don't consciously acknowledge the pain of such atrocities. It is deeply buried through *denial*—a brilliant and complex defense created by the mind of the child, and then incorporated into the collective "cultural mind" to help the individual or group of individuals cope with otherwise devastating circumstances.

120

But who is really making the choice to deny? *Born on the Fourth of July,* Oliver Stone's popular movie about the Vietnam war, opens with a powerful depiction of Tom Cruise as a young boy at a victory parade for the soldier's returning from World War II. The scene is brilliant—a sunny day, marching bands playing drums and horns, majorettes twirling batons, and young and old people alike cheering and screaming; a feeling of great victory in the air. The young boy is captivated by the glory of the parade, which makes such an impression on him that as a young man he enrolls in the army and goes to Vietnam where he fights and kills many people.

Who is to blame for the deaths of the people he kills? We could blame the young boy as it is he who is ultimately responsible for his actions. Yet he didn't grow up and think, "I want to go to a foreign country and murder people, and it is all right because they are of a different nationality." He could not, in his right conscience, think and act in this manner. He was a teenager when he went to the military training camps where minds more sophisticated than his own brainwashed him into thinking it was O.K. to kill. We could also blame the country—the nation who celebrated the explosion of an atomic weapon on a foreign country. But the nation is simply one of many such nations involved in a "kill or be killed dynamic." We could blame the culture that allows such activity to exist, but the cultural mind is the result of centuries of conditioning. What allows such activity to transpire is denial—it keeps us alive and sane in an often impersonal world.

How would it look if we were not in denial? Imagine what would happen if for one week an entire country—including all of the government officials, CEO's, criminals and children—went off of anti-depressants, cigarettes, coffee, alcohol and sugar, and turned off all of its television sets and video games, and the government placed a national ban on all forms of violence within or by any group—from the home to the army.

121

The whole country would go berserk—literally. The first thing that would probably happen is that anger and depression would temporarily increase. All the rage that is otherwise smoked away, taken out on video games, lived out through violent television shows and movies, stuffed with sugar and drowned in alcohol, would be seething at the surface of people's skins. Yet the ban on violence would prohibit the display of it, and people would be forced to stay at home in bed writhing and sobbing. They would be cornered into feeling the pain of the emptiness of their present lives, and before that, of their childhood, and before that, their birth, and before that...they would feel themselves being shattered by this pain, piece by piece—feel their whole identity falling apart, feel like everything they had ever thought they knew was a lie, feel like they were dying...ideally they would all come out the other side, and, having felt the pain that is so feared, the pain that is considered to be so awful and undesirable, they would be left with an emptiness and spaciousness unlike the static, merciless depression they have come to think of as emptiness. From this feeling, otherwise known as compassion, many would not be able to return to their present line of work, aware of its effects on others, and those who did go back to work would be different while doing it. False and pretentious aspects of relationship would start breaking down in every home, and people would be faced with their lack of love. Life as we know it would necessarily collapse, yet something new and wondrous would necessarily arise in its place.

I am not naively suggesting that such a plan could, or would ever be carried out. Instead, I am pointing to an entire system set up by wounded individuals designed solely for the purpose of defending itself against its pain.

Just as the child numbs his skin as not to feel his parents' blows, so a culture numbs the heart of its people to the violence it proudly entertains them with. And, as the mother looks the other way from the abuse occurring around her, so the culture diverts our attention from the atrocities it perpetuates by boasting images of the "white-picket-fence life" in commercials, advertising, television, magazines.

A respect for denial begins to dawn on the individual as he or she comes to understand the devastation which it was created to cover up. As the individual must eventually come to a point in which he chooses either to face himself honestly, or to live out a life of falsity, there comes a time when a nation and its members must ask themselves, "Is it worth it?" "Are we willing to live in a culture of superficiality, distraction, violence and depression—a culture that is fully equipped to destroy all life on the planet?" "Are we willing to sell the soul of the nation to avoid facing the damage we have already done and continue to perpetuate?" Thus far, the nation as a whole and the majority of its members are, by their actions and lifestyles, saying "Yes—we are willing to sacrifice ourselves and the heart of our country to keep from feeling this pain."

Wounds do not heal until we heal them. Wounds tend to fester and infect over time if not tended to, and thus the lives of both the individual and the collective will manifest stronger and stronger symptoms—calling our attention to the underlying wound in any way it can. Crime rates and child abuse statistics will continue to rise, depression will further cloud any remaining traces of national integrity, nuclear build-up will continue, reports of earthquakes, flooding and natural disasters will cover the front pages, and economies will collapse left and right. Eventually, we must break through our denial or die of our own stubbornness. The choice is ours.

CHAPTER 5

On Healing
Through Touch

Sometimes the longest journey we make is the sixteen inches from our heads to our hearts.

– Elena Avila

The healing science of homeopathy is based on the principle that "like cures like"—disease is healed by ingesting small amounts of the very elements that produced the original symptoms. Similarly, the same touch that was once used to inflict pain upon a person, now given with intention and in the proper dosage, is the very medicine that can heal him.

Unbonded children and adults may or may not experience complete healing of their unbonded condition. However, healing takes place on a continuum, and there are many ways to bring an increasing sense of bondedness and wholeness into ones life. This chapter will consider several techniques to help you heal yourself and those around you through touch. First and foremost, however, I believe that it is enough to cease to be a part of the problem of touch-starvation. If you are unable to integrate touch, intimacy and affection into your life, if all you can manage to do is to cease to perpetuate the cycle of "untouched," you are doing your part.

CEASE TO BE A PART OF THE PROBLEM

The way to begin a life of touch is to bring a stop to the cycle of hurting other people on all levels, from the gross to the subtle. Violence ends first on the most obvious level—the cessation of the misuse of physical and sexual touch, the refusal to engage fist fights, hitting children, slapping, etc., and from no longer allowing others in our presence to be victims of this. Next, one ceases to scream and yell at others and to refrain from all hurtful language...then manipulative and controlling actions...then sly and hurtful remarks...and on down the line. When we get down to the recognition of the finer points of abuse, we realize it's in all of us. A friend of mine who is a prominent author and devoted advocate of ending abuse on all levels suggested:

> *When you wake up in the morning, you look in the mirror and say to yourself, "I am an abuser. I'm just going to try not to abuse anybody today." That's where we're starting from. By refraining from abusing one another, we are contributing to the solution.*

It is a radical approach, but we can acknowledge that "front and center" is the only place to put ourselves in terms of touch. Observing closely and honestly the ways we hurt others, we can say "no" to the abuser inside of us.

A useful approach in working toward ending violence in ourselves is to notice when we are feeling grouchy, angry, or irritated, and therefore more likely to be hurtful toward those around us. Instead of obsessing on all the things that are wrong with so-and-so or such-and-such, or all the reasons we rightfully have to be angry, we can experiment instead with asking ourselves, "What am *I* in pain about?" (even if we think we are not in pain), and wait for the answer. When we point the finger inward, we cease to victimize those around us.

From the moment we make a firm decision that abuse must end in our lives, our inner and outer worlds begin to change. Eventually, we must turn our touch inward, for there is nobody else who can stop the war within us, and nothing else that can stop it save this touch, this profound understanding, this compassion. We touch ourselves by allowing ourselves to breathe deeply, to keep the company of good people, to refrain from addictions. We cease to persecute ourselves and insist upon participating in activities or ways of life that do not require self-numbing. We let ourselves feel, and cease to judge ourselves. We allow others to love us.

HEALING THE UNBONDED CHILD

You may have raised, or be in the process of raising, an unbonded child and not even know it. Bonding, however, can happen at any age under the right conditions.

It is amazing to realize that with few exceptions, every child at every age loves their parents. Even children whose parents have abused them, even children who *hate* their parents still love them! Another amazing thing about children in relationship to their parents is their tremendous willingness to forgive. No matter how old the child is, when the parent starts to act differently, the child responds. I am not saying that when the parent calls the child or writes him or her a weepy note of insight and apology that the child responds immediately—that's not acting differently. The acknowledgment of having not loved a child well is important, but a change in *action* holds the capacity to heal the wounds of childhood.

Healing the bond with a child needn't be drastic. For example, many parents, especially fathers, are literally frozen with fear when it comes to touching their children. Parents who were not given touch in their own families think that they do not know how to touch their children. Healing can begin if one is willing to prioritize their desire to change their relationship with their child, placing this desire above and beyond their own insecurities about touching and loving him or her. We swallow our pride, acknowledge our fear, and *go for it* anyway. (An important note on this point is that a child may not immediately *want* touch at this time. He or she may be wary, angry, or just not want it for whatever reason.)

When children are older—whether they are teenagers or mature adults—the healing is different. Although the older child still looks to the parent for love, acknowledgment, and signs of change, when a child is no longer a child and is long past the stages of bonding, the most we can do for him or her is to be honest with ourselves. Parents and children are deeply connected—even in the most uncaring of circumstances—and thus when we begin to change, it is likely that our child will feel that, even before we say anything. There are numerous remarkable stories of people having insights or psychological breakthroughs in relationship to their children, after not seeing them for years, when suddenly the child will call them up out of the blue!

Beyond this, it is useful to share with our children what we are discovering about ourselves, if we are able to do so with sincerity and clarity. Our child will appreciate our vulnerability, respond how they respond, and hopefully allow for greater intimacy in their present relationships with their own husband, wife, friends, and/or children.

HEALING THE UNBONDED ADULT

As an adult attempting to remedy your own unbonded condition, the healing is different. You will not jump into your seventy-five-year-old mother's lap, and hopefully you won't try out some regressive therapeutic process that gives you a bottle to suck on and a teddy bear to sleep with. Your healing will take place within yourself, and with the help of other caring and experienced adults who share your intention to heal. The remainder of this chapter is an overview of some of the various healing processes and techniques that I have found effective in transforming a touch-starved life into a life full of touch, intimacy and wholeness.

Getting in the Body

The best way to heal any touch-wound is by "getting in" your body, turning toward the unkown "country" of our own physical, internal landcape. When *you* (as opposed to your wardrobe, your ideas of who you think you should be, etc.) are the full-time resident of your body, then you *are* touch, and you have nothing left to do except stay that way. To deeply embody our own experience is a tremendous task—most people have no idea how "disembodied" they are—but the fruit of such a labor are valuable beyond measure.

So, what does it mean to get in the body? That's certainly what I wanted to know when I first started hearing about this idea. People who are in their bodies—no matter the shape or size—have a certain radiance about them. It is as if consciousness is actively penetrating their skin, their bones, their energetic field. They are present—here! We are aware of being listened to when we speak with them. They seem to really show up wherever they go—not just as another body, but as a part of what is happening. They are energetic, attentive, involved. They feel the movement of their breath, their feelings and how they are affected by their environment.

When we are "in" touch with our bodies, we cannot help but notice the larger body—the earth—and what is happening to our environment. We start to pay attention to the kinds of chemicals in our foods, the quality (or lack of quality) of the air we are breathing and the water we are drinking. We receive a continual flow of feedback from our environment. Being "in" the body enlivens and animates the senses—we can smell lavender bushes from a distance, taste the sweetness of a carrot, or feel our whole body relaxing in response to the touch of a smile.

When I walked in the Costa Rican forests, I was always surprised when a friend would nudge me and point to a small, but poisonous snake hiding under a leaf ten feet in front of us, or draw my attention to a toucan sitting fifty feet away high in a treetop, or predict a coming rainstorm by looking at a cloudless sky. No prior thought or analysis, just instinct. The bodies of these native people (as opposed to their intellects) had been the source of their knowledge all their lives, and was sustained directly from the earth. All their senses were strong, alert, healthy— connected with the surrounding environment.

A further benefit of being "in" the body is that it allows us to gain access to a deeper level of feeling. Feeling is registered in the body. When we feel loving, there may be a tingle in the chest, an overall feeling of relaxation in our muscles, and a slow, relaxed pattern of breathing; whereas when we feel angry there may be a tightness in the jaw, tension in the chest, and a constriction or holding in the gut. Some people live in such an emotionally disturbed state all the time that their bodies always feel this constriction and tension. Hence we see chronic back problems, ulcers, and asthma.

Touch for Health

I was going in the hospital for my fourth spinal surgery and there was no guarantee I was going to come out of it alive, began Jake, a 52-year-old lawyer. *Although they never let spouses into the recovery room, I asked if they would make an exception in this circumstance and allow my wife, Susie, to come in. I knew what I needed...I had warned Susie that I was going to look terrible. I didn't even know if she'd want to touch me. But both Susie and the hospital staff agreed to my request. When I came out of the operating room, I was in a coma for days. Although I don't remember anything she said to me, I remember the distinct feeling of her touch. At the point where her hand touched my arm I could feel a sensation of warmth extending throughout my whole body. That warmth—the tangible feeling of being loved—is what carried me through.*

Many people actually become sick because they are touch-starved. Unconsciously seeking a similar type of attention and healing, their pain comes out in the form of physical illness. The memory of mother rubbing their forehead and bringing orange juice to them while they were sick in bed may be among their fondest memories of childhood.

Studies performed at the University of Miami Medical School's Touch Research Institute, indicate that physical touch reduces stress. Yet a 1993 U.S. Public Health survey estimated that 70%—80% of Americans who visit conventional physicians suffer from a stress-related disorder.[1] Modern medicine generally tends to treat the symptom and not the disease. Therefore, even if the individual is fortunate enough to have his or her symptoms cured, if the underlying causes, including touch-starvation, have not been addressed, then the disease will manifest sooner or later in another form.

Dr. Theresa Crenshaw, author of *The Alchemy of Love and Lust*, explains that touch alters the chemical composition of your body. "Lack of touch is just as detrimental to our health as a lack of Vitamin C," according to Crenshaw.[2] She tells us that the peptide oxytocin (a hormone-like chain of molecules that is naturally produced by the body) increases when an individual receives touch or nurturing physical contact. As oxytocin increases, the individual craves more and more touch. However, this touch "addiction" is far less hazardous than most common addictions, according to Crenshaw, as the estrogen-dependent chemical oxytocin relaxes the individual, promotes touch, encourages bonding, triggers milk let-down during breast-feeding and sets off the uterine contractions that accompany childbirth and orgasm.

Genuine and simple touch given in a safe and nurturing environment in which one can be held and allowed to feel the depth of the pain that he or she once endured, and continues to live with, is one of the best remedies available. Ideally such touch should be given by those who have been willing to explore their own pain, and who will not become frozen or uncomfortable when the other's pain is revealed. Receiving this type of touch allows one to learn to trust, over time, in environments that are loving and non-abusive—especially if the childhood environment was otherwise. While no other person can ever provide the "perfect" love that is longed for, and those helping us have been wounded too, it is still possible to receive nurturing touch from someone who is nonetheless trustworthy because of their commitment to us and their understanding of themselves.

Who are these people who can provide us with healing touch, and in what environments? Ideally, the "toucher" would be a husband, wife or trusted friend. A knowledgeable massage therapist may be the best alternative for many people. The most optimal environment is your own safe home, but might instead be a women's or men's support group. Eventually, this safe environment will be discovered in more of your surroundings—for as you heal and are able to give and receive love and nurturing touch, you will effortlessly transform your surrounding circumstances.

Your life will eventually change with the positive, ongoing benefits of healing touch, but it will take time—there is simply no instant way to affect such transformation. But isn't it worth it? You have suffered this wound for many years; wouldn't it be worth it to invest the next several years in healing it, so that you may come to live at least part of your life in the experience of love, touch, and intimacy? Wouldn't it be nice to know that you are capable of radically transforming your own pain into love? What price could be too high for that?

Holdings

Many of us simply need to practice being touched—letting the sensation penetrate the deep constriction of our conditioned defensiveness. An example of this is a practice we might call "holdings." To do a holding, one makes an agreement with a close friend to spend a specific amount of time together (ranging from twenty minutes to an hour, agreed upon in advanced), in which the friend will just hold them. This works best when there is a "holder" and a "holdee." In other words, one person is exclusively focused on holding, nurturing and paying attention to the other, and the "holdee" attempts to simply allow themselves to relax and be held, without having to "do" anything, just as they wished their parents had done for them in childhood. (Holder and holdee will often alternate turns over a period of days.)

Holdings are not a time for talking and analyzing, though a few words won't hurt anything. They are what the name suggests—a time to be held, and we should not underestimate the value of this. Many will find themselves uncomfortable, self-conscious or numb at first. Or their mind will wander, they will feel silly, or suddenly feel like they don't want to be there. Others will find that deep grief, tears and memories quickly arise. All of these are symptoms of the unbonded adult. Those who engage in holdings should realize that there is nothing wrong or right about any response, and no need to react or judge any emotional state that arises. Emotions and memories can just be noticed or felt. When we allow emotions to be processed through to completion, we will discover that feelings *do* change.

Counseling

Although it rarely involves direct touch, another path that people explore in their search toward wholeness is psychotherapy or counseling. In their minds, they may be turning to the therapist for help with their intimate relationship, or with personal problems at work, yet unconsciously many of these people are searching for someone to bond with in a genuine way—someone who is willing to "touch" them by listening to them and accepting them just as they are. Many of my clients have raved about how healing their therapy was, when sometimes all I did was sit there, with as much presence and as little judgment as possible, and listen to them, giving occasional feedback. Yet it is precisely this that so many children never received—no one listened to them, accepted them as who they were, and supported them in following their own dreams and aspirations.

Therapy is not a replacement for unbondedness, but it does serve to turn the client in the direction of self-healing. We are often blinded to the ways that we perpetuate our own woundedness, the ways that we block our own healing and deny ourselves affection. A good therapist can point out our blind spots to us and guide us in the right direction.[3]

Massage

Massage is another excellent avenue by which to seek out the benefits of touch. Several years ago, having just moved to a small village in England and looking to set up a local massage practice, I decided to test the waters at the popular Sunday morning flea market in the town square by setting up a chair beside which I had printed a large sign that read, *"Free! Ten-Minute Therapeutic Massage."* The responses were fascinating. Besides being confronted with peoples' extreme wariness of anybody who was going to give anything away for free (this insight alone made the day worthwhile), I was exposed to a wider range of responses concerning peoples' ideas about touch and massage than I ever had while giving therapeutic massage in a private-practice setting. "Why should I let you touch me?" or, "What's in it for you?" some asked accusingly. Several others, who had never been able to afford a professional massage, or who had been fearful, but secretly curious about it, sat down and allowed themselves to have this experience for the first time. Through a simple ten minute massage, many people were able to experience the nurturing qualities of touch that they had rarely known—I saw this when they got up from the chair relaxed, refreshed and happy.

The physical healing powers of touch—transmitted through the means of massage—allow for physical and chemical alterations (e.g., lower levels of cortisol and norepinephrine, which are anxiety and stress hormones) to occur in the body resulting not only in the prevention of illness and improved health, but in an overall sense of aliveness and well-being.

The benefits of massage are far-reaching. It is widely known that massage can heal sore and aching muscles, and release tension and anxiety, thus providing greater relaxation. But some of the other physical healing properties of massage are less widely recognized. Among adults, massage may aid in decreasing depression and lowering high blood pressure, as well as assist in the relief of symptoms associated with mental illness, stomach pain, spasms, heart disease and dysmenorrhea. It can help to restore movement in strained, fractured and wounded limbs, and it generally serves to improve circulation, help eliminate waste and reduce swelling.[4] In adults with chronic fatigue syndrome, which is believed to be related to depression, massage has proved to significantly reduce emotional stress and somatic symptoms, as well as depression and difficulty with sleeping.[5]

Children like massage too. Massage has been shown to improve health in diabetic children, and to decrease anxiety and depression in children with post traumatic stress disorder.[6] In children and adolescent psychiatric patients, massage decreased depression, anxiety and stress hormone levels. Massage also improved their clinical progress.[7] The journal *Adolescence* in 1998 reported that teenagers with ADHD rated themselves as happier and were observed to fidget less after massage sessions, while their teachers rated them as less hyperactive and as spending more time on task.[8]

The elderly, who represent the most untouched population in the Western world, thrive on massage. Many of our elderly are widowed, and unless they have frequent contact with their grandchildren or have children who are aware of how much touch an older person needs, they have little or no means by which to be in physical contact with others. Seeing this in my ninety-one-year-old great aunt, I approached her shyly one afternoon and asked if she would allow me to massage her. She laughed embarrassedly, feeling flattered and disbelieving that I would wish to touch her aged and frail body, but agreed to a massage the following day. Given her character and her initial discomfort, I was amazed to feel and watch how her body drank up the contact like a desert plant drinks up moisture. In contrast to the child mentioned above, I worked very softly and gently with her bones and cartilage, paying careful attention to her body for any signs of feedback that she may have been too timid to speak of. Geriatric massage is a field of growing popularity, but still largely untapped as a resource for the elderly.

Lastly, massage is increasingly being incorporated into the field of preventive health care. Perhaps the most inspirational of the new possibilities for massage come from studies with AIDS patients carried forth by medical doctors and students at the Touch Research Institute in Miami, Florida. HIV-positive men were given forty-five-minute massages five times per week for a one month period. The results strongly suggest that massage has an effect on the improvement of the immune system, not only with AIDS patients but in general immune function as well. In addition to improved immunity, AIDS patients also showed a reduction in anxiety, stress, and distress levels—a type of relief much needed in a dying population.[9]

You don't have to be a massage therapist to give a good massage. Anybody (yes, even you) can do it! I remember agreeing to trade massages with a man who boasted his extensive training and abilities in massage. It was terrible! His touch was technically perfected, but was totally void of qualities of presence, nurturing and care. On the other hand, my favorite massages are given both by a woman-friend who insists she doesn't know what she's doing, and also by a friend's five-year-old daughter! In 1998, one of many studies published in JAMA provides evidence that therapeutic touch decreased the pain and increased the level of functioning in patients with osteoarthritis and postoperative pain.[10]

Therapeutic Touch

Therapeutic Touch (TT) is another popular practice through which both professionals and laypersons have learned to heal others through their hands. A contemporary interpretation of several ancient healing practices, Therapeutic Touch is based on the premise that it is the patient who heals himself, with the healer acting as a conduit for the necessary healing "energy." A form of healing that focuses on balancing the energy field of whole person rather than treating specific physical diseases, Therapeutic Touch usually does not involve any physical contact; instead, the healer's hands are placed about two inches above the patient's body. The main benefits of Therapeutic Touch can be divided into four categories: relaxation, pain reduction, accelerated healing and the alleviation of psychosomatic symptoms.

A non-traditional method of healing, Therapeutic Touch has earned its place in the field of traditional allopathic medicine. In 1975, co-founder Dr. Dolores Krieger published a landmark study in the *American Journal of Nursing,* documenting a significant increase in the mean hemoglobin level of a group of patients in New York City hospitals who received Therapeutic Touch over those who received routine nursing care.[11] Since that time, it has been taught to more than 70,000 nurses, in more than eighty colleges and universities in over seventy countries.

Developing Boundaries

Developing clear personal boundaries will not only bring more caring touch into your life, but will provide you with a sense of clarity and certitude about yourself. Boundaries are a hot topic in pop-psychology. People are running around left and right setting supposed "boundaries:" "I have to set a boundary that you must refer to me as a woman and not a girl." "I am making a boundary that you cannot put your arm around my shoulder unless I give you permission to." When people say, "I know how to set a boundary," what they often mean is, "I read in a pop-psychology book that I can control a situation by saying, 'I need to make a boundary.'" Although a step in the right direction, these types of boundaries are usually rigid and superficial. A person who is clear about boundaries within herself would never need to use the words, "I have to set a boundary." She is able to assert herself clearly and directly, but at the same time in a manner that is neither aggressive nor defensive.

Real boundaries come from the inside. They come from knowing where we end and another person begins, from knowing who we are and what we want, and from understanding the signals of our bodies. When we know ourselves from the inside out, we can create or relinquish boundaries at will depending upon the situation. For example, at a bar or on a crowded subway, one can, through the power of his or her attention, energetically place a boundary outside of themselves that will not be permeated by

138

any "dark" forces around them. On the other hand, in a sexual relationship, a person who knows himself well can intentionally allow his boundaries to dissipate.

Good boundaries around touch come from knowing your own motivations. They emerge from a conviction that says, "Here, in this circumstance, I know myself well enough to touch you." You are aware of why you are extending yourself to the other—be it as a gesture of friendship, reaching out from loneliness, a desire for pleasure, or a wish to comfort. Any of these are fine motivations for touch if your intention is clear. However, when your motivation to touch someone is one thing, and your actions suggests another, you will confuse people and are likely to feel dissatisfied by their response to you.

When you are "in" your body, and are able to express and receive touch in a healthy, consistent manner, boundaries fall into place naturally. When you have clear boundaries inside yourself, it is unlikely that others will shy away from your touch. You will instinctively know who to touch and who not to, as well as when and how to touch them. When your judgment errs, you do not fall apart or feel ashamed for being inappropriate, nor do you blame the other for their frigidity. You just bring your touch back into yourself and go about your day.

If you are a man or woman who tends to shy away from touch, you can experiment with boundaries by deliberately being more affectionate. On the other hand, if you consider yourself, or are considered by others, to be a "touchy-feely" person, you may want to experiment with refraining from touching others for a day or two, to see what happens. Bring uncompromising honesty and attention to who, when, and why you touch (many "touchy-feely" people are actually terrified of intimacy, and use their hands to hide their fears—even to themselves).

Sexual Healing

The process of healing our bodies from the inside out is as arduous as it is gratifying. In a very real way, when we heal our own body we simultaneously heal larger bodies—the body of our family, our community, and in a small way, the body of the earth. Learning to see the inherent sacredness of the body—the subject of the following chapter—is the key that unlocks not only our own psychological healing and inherent joy, but catalyzes a process of gradual evolutionary healing of the planet through releasing ancient negative patterning that is responsible for the present suffering of humanity.

CHAPTER 6

Sexuality and
Worship of the Body

Every desire of your body is holy;
Every desire of your body is
Holy.
Dear one,
Why wait until you are dying
To discover that divine
Truth?[1]
— Hafiz

       Honoring sexuality and the healing of the deep and sacred sexual self are essential components of reclaiming and expressing the power of touch in our lives. When we fail to live in a way that expresses our own divinity—which is true of the majority of human beings on this planet in the 21st century—we are denying our birthright not only to be "in touch" with ourselves, nature, one another, and all of life, but to celebrate that gift through the joy of openly giving and receiving touch.

This chapter is about sexual healing and an embracing of our sexuality that leads to a deep appreciation of our bodies and the power of the erotic, creative force within us. Sexuality is so different for each of us—both the ecstasy of it, as well as the means of sexual healing. Our wounds happened at different times in our development, and in different ways; our aspirations to know and live our sexuality vary from person to person; and the path to healing will come through many and unexpected channels. Therefore, in this chapter I would like to provide the *context* of sexual healing and the celebration of one's own sexuality, whether we are partnered or not. I offer a context of profound regard and respect for one's own body; an appreciation of the touch it needs, deserves, and enjoys; an acknowledgement that whereas sometimes sex is just raw and raunchy, it can also take one straight to Divinity; and a recognition that the life of the body is short, precious, and is best lived free of shame and honored and held as sacred. It is my conviction that as you learn to appreciate the generous and sacred gift of your own body, the specific secrets of your own healing process and the keys to a deeply satisfying sexuality will reveal themselves to you naturally.

Sexuality is an essential and readily accessible doorway to the healing of a badly wounded human condition. When we consider sexuality, it is important that we recognize that sexuality includes *everybody*—those who are celibate, single, mated, very young, very old, disabled, ill. Sexuality is about all of us, all the time, and it certainly includes, though is in no way limited to, the expression of physical, sexual intimacy between partners.

Sexuality is everywhere. It *is* the creative force. It is what has created each of us, including the variations among individuals, races, cultures. It is what makes flowers reproduce, as well as the force behind the existence of every type of animal, tree, plant, insect, bird, fish. Sexuality creates art, architecture, music, poetry. It is the universal catalyst for the mysterious occurrence of love. It is the process that unites masculine and feminine energies within us, thus allowing for the possibility of a deep inner unification and an enhanced connection to all of creation. It is behind everything that is beautiful. Yet, through some weighty historical and cultural forces stemming from unconsciousness and ignorance, sexuality has come to be associated with something sinful, something dirty, something to feel ashamed of.

Before we can initiate a radical shift in our fundamental attitude toward sexuality and the body, we must understand and appreciate the critical degree and scope of the crisis. For as problematic as the issue of sexuality is in the United States, England, and many European countries, the confusion and repression is equally devastating in a different way in most of Asia and Central America. In fact, there are few places in the world that are "untouched" by sexual dysfunction. The whole planet (with many cultural and individual exceptions, of course) is suffering an epidemic disease of alienation from the body and its creative capacity. If this is difficult to conceptualize, simply consider the state of the earth and our collective relationship to it. Our bodies are comprised of the same substances that make up the earth. The earth *is* our larger body. Many theorists believe that our alienated relationship to the earth and to its inhabitants closely parallels our relationship with our own bodies—that we are as distanced and out of relationship with one as we are with the other.

Western culture, in spite of what may be a superficial appearance of openness, is deeply repressed sexually. Repression, in this case, is not measured by how few or how tight are the clothes we wear, what we dare to do in bed, how freely we assert our right to orgasm, how "liberated" our use of language is. Repression is measured by the overriding sense of alienation from our bodies— from really *feeling* the touch of sex, intimacy, and eroticism. Repression is about our inability to know the value of our own sex and sexuality—its force, its capacity, its sanctity, and of how to honor that force in ourselves, in all others, and in all of life.

143

The overemphasis on sex in Western culture is combined with a stark lack of deep understanding about it. While sexual obsession runs us on one level, there is an immense amount of depth, ecstasy, and knowledge available in the human body that remains largely untapped. Many individuals are aware that they do not understand the mysteries of their own sexuality. Perhaps they have had experiences that have hinted at a vast territory as yet unexplored, but they lack the knowledge, the context, the circumstance, and the guidance by which to further explore this terrain.

If we do not *love* our bodies, knowing, honoring, and respecting our sex and sexuality, we often reveal that by being contracted, withdrawn, ashamed, and not allowing ourselves to be fully present and interactive with all of life. Or we do the opposite. We flaunt our sex in inappropriate ways and at incorrect times. Either way, our intimate relationships ultimately fall into mediocrity, if not disrepair. Our relationship with our own life force is thus diminished, leaving the creative possibility of our human experience as an incomplete canvas.

Whereas many of us intuit this unfulfilled potential of our own sexuality, we oftentimes cannot even name it. The immensity of what is possible simply feels too large, and too far away from where we are, for us to believe that we could actualize something so extraordinary and beautiful. I recently spoke with an Aztec healer who asserts that the whole destruction of the earth is linked to a disrespect, by both men *and* women, of the sanctity of the reproductive organs and the inherent capacity for creation within women. If this is true, and if we wish to do our part in healing a humanity that is speeding toward its own demise, we are called to bring sexual healing to our own lives. The work is hard, but the payoff is incalculable.

When Sex is Just Sex

Before proceeding into an exploration of the deeper aspects of sexuality and the body, it is important to appreciate the fact that sometimes sex is just sex. Nothing more, nothing less. You just do what you do, however holy or raunchy that might be, and it's totally fine. It can be playful, raw, edgy, soft, and just plain physical! Intimacy doesn't always have to require "work," and it doesn't always have to be holy or have a deep emotional component. That would be just too much pressure! When people make grandiose efforts to have profound and meaningful sex because that is what they *think* they should be doing, it is a formula for disaster.

There is a time and place for a more refined, esoteric sexual experience, but sometimes sex is just sex and you act like teenagers in the backseat of the car, or you roll around on the ground like animals. Animals don't verbally process their "needs" before, during, and after the act. They just jump on top of each other and hump—and sometimes that is just what is needed.

Having said that, if "sex as just sex" is the only way you understand sexuality, you may be missing out on certain extraordinary possibilities available through sex and sexuality—possibilities that allow the ordinary human being to experience qualities of feeling and emotion that border on what could be called "mystical." As these more esoteric aspects are discussed throughout the remainder of the chapter, bear in mind that the mystical and the mundane are not always as distinct from, or far away from, one another as most people imagine.

Living a Sexual Life with Ourselves

Since sex is not just intercourse, living a "sexual" life is a possibility for everybody. Whether we are single by circumstance or choice, or widowed, or separated from our partner for any number of reasons, we can still live a sexual life, creating a sensual connection with everything. We can experience a touch-filled, passion-filled life by *tasting* our food, by *looking* more closely at beauty, by *feeling* the warmth and contact and affection when people in our lives do extend physical touch. Even a light hand on one's back, or a brief hug, can be a source of physical and emotional nourishment when it is really taken in.

Many people find that taking an art class, a dance class, appreciating music or poetry, or caring for their body and their own living environment, or cooking meals for themselves as if they were cooking for a loved one, connects them with their innate sensuality and creativity. Whereas we may not be having physical sex during those periods, living in this way keeps us aware that we are juicy, sensual individuals.

Furthermore, mystics of various spiritual traditions have written of profoundly "sexual" relationships with God. The literal, physical eroticism they relate in relationship to their spirituality would put the sexuality of many couples to shame.

Shame and the Body

On a recent trip to India, I heard a remarkable story from a woman who visited the great South Indian saint Yogi Ramsuratkumar years ago. She had gone to him complaining of her marital difficulties. The saint, who himself had practiced celibacy for many years, asked her, "What do you think about sex? Dirty or clean?"

"Why of course it is dirty," she told him, trying to hide her embarrassment at having such an unsanctified conversation with a saint.

At that moment, the saint picked up a single piece of passion fruit—a delectable, seasonal favorite. He carefully cut the fruit in half, poured a glass of milk, and tenderly squeezed the juice of the passion fruit into the milk. He then drank half of it and asked the woman to drink the other half. The woman was twenty-five years old at the time of this interaction. In the thirty years since that event, she told me, she has progressively enjoyed an increasingly sensual, sexual, and fulfilling marriage.

The origins of body shame, and the resulting difficulties in relationship with others, likely date back to childhood and the attitudes and behaviors we learned at that time. According to University of California psychologist, Mary Main:

> *Researchers have found that the affectional touch climate in the subject's family of origin is the major psychosocial variable related to a person's current sexual attitude and behavior. Subjects who originated from physically affectionate families were more likely to enjoy pleasurable and more frequent experiences in the sexual-affectional aspects of their adult relationships. Adults who experienced rejection and touch deprivation in their childhood tend to treat their adult partners and their offspring in a similar manner.*[2]

We inherit our parents', our culture's, and our religion's attitudes toward the body and sex. We inherit the sex life of our collective environment. Part of this shame comes from the deeply ingrained, though often unconscious, notion of original sin—a pervasive conditioning that tells us there is good and bad, right and wrong, and that the body, especially the body of a woman, is bad, wrong, ugly, dirty. Most of the time, if we examine ourselves closely enough, we discover that our conditioning about sexuality includes, at some level, notions of secrecy, shame, embarrassment, confusion, or perhaps simply an uncertainty about whether our sexuality, or our expression of it, is all right. The fact of this unfortunate truth means that, for most of us, sexual healing and the lifting of the imposed shame of our conditioning will require significant efforts if we are to finally experience organic joy and freedom within the body.

How many moments, months, years do we waste feeling ashamed, if not hateful, of our own precious bodies, ever forgetting that the body is the treasured vehicle through which we are *all*, constantly, searching for God (or some ultimate truth), even if we do not know that? Sometimes the hatred is overt—we look in the mirror and allow ourselves to wield unruly insults at our physical form. Sometimes it is more subtle, as conveyed through an attitude of disguised, yet pervasive disregard of our bodies. Still, what remains is a subjective, limited, skewed, and enveloping attitude of disdain and criticism for our own sexuality.

By whatever means we are able, we need to lift the shame from the body itself in order to experience our own sexuality and sensuality, and to be able to share that with others. Mediocre lives of moderate passion and passable sex simply won't do!

Many people first choose to engage healing work through more conventional forms of "talk therapy." Whereas this approach can address *part* of the problem, deep sexual healing usually needs to involve the body itself. Many people find healing through asking their partners to help them to process deep emotions that come up *during* sex; asking their partner to share in the intention to heal sexuality through sex. In certain circumstances, if both people are deeply committed to this aim, such an approach can be very powerful.

Other people approach body healing through yoga, massage, meditation, exercise, acupuncture, and any other number of available healing modalities. Finding an effective means of healing is usually a matter of being willing to experiment and learn by trial and error. The point to remember here is that a wound that occurred at the level of the body will also need to be fixed at that same level.

When deep shame is lifted from the body, the body will undergo a process that may be experienced as anything from a lightening of psychic weight, to a total "revolution." Such a revolution in the body may leave us feeling that we are experiencing life inside our own skin for the very first time. Since the essential creative potential in humanity is largely contained within the sexual center, when shame is lifted, the whole world opens up. We know, then, that we not only have a right to be here, but that we *belong* in the world as an integral and unique aspect of it, no matter how small we feel. This process is likely to continue on and off over many years, as decades, if not centuries, of conditioned limitations are gradually opened and our creative potential is released.

Selling Sex Cheap

What seems to be open and "free" sex is often a disguised devaluation of the sanctity of sexuality and the body based upon ideals of how we would *like* to be, while ignoring the recognition of where we actually *are* in terms of our sexual development. We Westerners, by and large, remain sexually confused, if not patently repressed, whether we live in a more superficially expressive culture such as the United States, a more reserved culture like England, or a more affectionate, yet still codified Latino culture. If we wish the situation were otherwise, yet have not done the necessary healing to transform ourselves authentically, we may take on a set of actions that imitate what we imagine to be sexual liberation. We may thus fail to discover a more genuine liberation in the body, and further impede that discovery by fooling ourselves into thinking that we have already done the required work.

Several years ago I was invited to speak about touch at a conference on community building. Until I arrived at the event, I did not know that the group focused on "free love" and unconventional approaches to physical intimacy. (The event, believe it or not, was actually not in the state of California!) The environment was very "touchy-feely." People went around stroking and caressing each other, exchanging partners, and listening to the

149

various conference presenters while lying on pillows on the floor, intertwined with one another in a clothed, but semi-orgiastic manner that was referred to by participants as a "puppy pile."

At one point in my talk I suggested to the men and women clustered in front of me that the expression of excessive touch is often an expression of the same shame and confused boundaries that result in the repression of touch and sexuality. In our efforts to get over our inhibitions about physical contact, I said, we sometimes over express ourselves. Being able to *do* a lot of things sexually, being skilled technicians or affection-mongers, does not necessarily imply that we have liberated ourselves sexually. In fact, such activities may be a cleverly disguised shield that we hide behind in our unconscious effort to defend ourselves against the vulnerability needed for deep sexual healing.

We often "sell" our bodies far too cheaply, underestimating and thereby diminishing the sacred possibility inherent in the human form. Whether we are single and touch-hungry, lonely within our marriage, or even basically content in our lives but unable to satisfy a deeper longing, we often make compromises of conscience, as well as of our bodies, in order to satisfy a seemingly insatiable craving for touch and love. When we sell ourselves short like this, we not only drain ourselves of the very life force that is required for healing, but we disrespect our own inherent integrity, supporting the disposition of shame and disregard for the sanctity of the body.

Whether we are consciously aware of it or not, sexual energy, and particularly the physical act of sexual intercourse, binds and bonds us deeply to one another. In a universe in which everything is literally interconnected, that interconnection takes on an exponential measure in sexual intimacy, particularly when saliva and or genital fluids are exchanged. Many people are unaware of the power of the link that sexuality creates between individuals, thus treating sex as a far more casual "affair" than it is.

If we are able to heal to the extent that we become more deeply sensitized to our own bodies, we may discover that the exchange of sexual fluid actually transmits our life force into the body of the other person. Through this process we literally become each other, and in a very real way find ourselves "walking around" in each others' bodies. If we, or our partners, are engaged in sexual relationships with others, we also end up with all the other "bodies" that are being carried by the person we are intimate with. If we happen to know, are comfortable with, and have the desire to live with the other individuals and the psychological inheritance that accompanies them, this can be a workable situation. However, few people possess the knowledge of how to integrate these energies, and more often than not end up experiencing "side effects" of others that are confusing and baffling, having no idea that they are working with "foreign" toxins they have allowed into their bodies.

The call of conscious sexuality is to give careful consideration to the immediate, physical needs of our bodies at a basic, ordinary level, while keeping in mind the possibility for sex and sexuality to bring about much greater benefits, both on the level of psychological healing and in the spiritual domain. We must use our capacity for discernment to recognize which relationships will ultimately serve us, and which, though they might feel good in the short term, are likely to reinforce life-negative habits.

The Body Knows

The body contains all the knowledge it needs, not only about sex and sexuality, but even about mysteries of the human experience and universal processes we may never have imagined knowing about. The key, of course, is how to unlock that knowledge.

Often we need help—the help of each other. When two individuals "touch" through the sharing and blending of bodies, they offer each other a rare opportunity to know themselves. When, in the mysterious union of the sexual experience, we are able to let go to the degree that we allow the body to guide us, we stand at the brink of creation, of creativity, of innovation and of true spontaneity. We stand the chance to experience ourselves and our bodies in a way that few circumstances allow—perhaps even gain a glimpse of God. Isn't that why sex compels us so? We desperately long to finally release the shackles of shame and subjective conditioning that keep us stuck in the endless loop of thought and behavior patterns we have come to call "ourselves."

The wisdom of the body is Earth wisdom, organic wisdom. Whether this wisdom leads us to deep bliss, raw vulnerability, or sterling objectivity, the transformational value of such states should not be underestimated. If we treat these states with lusty aggression mixed with shame, as our culture has taught us, we may have yet another intense, fleeting, perhaps temporarily ecstatic, but nonetheless confusing, and semi-conscious experience. However, if we learn to regard the body as the sacred vessel it truly is—which *can* happen simply by placing our intention on this task (as will be discussed later in the chapter)—we may discover moods, insights, and growth that are new to us, even if we believe we have seen and done it all.

Real trust and safety are necessary to allow a deeper and enduring self-knowledge to emerge. A trusting intimate partnership can be a crucible from which body wisdom may emerge. Unfortunately, in our relationships we more likely fall into emotional and sexual patterns that fail to support the process of emerging body-based knowledge, and further reinforce the already-present sexual wounding and deep-seated shame that we have carried with us since before we can remember. A relationship of intimacy and sexuality in which an individual honors their own body and their partner's body, and in which personal modes of sexual expression are valued and respected as sacred, allows the emergence of profound and enduring bodily wisdom.

152

Partners in such a relationship practice patience, encouraging one another to experiment in opening up to and expressing greater freedom. They vigilantly guard against unconscious tendencies to shame and dismiss the other's experience, and restrain from judging each other in this process, remembering that they must cross barriers of discomfort, and at times even imagined "appropriateness," in order to discover just how far they are able to expand.

Once we become aware of a "letting go" in our experience, we can create an intention to bring a light, spacious, and non-judgmental conscious awareness to it. To "bookmark" it as a valuable passage in the encyclopedia of our body. We begin to use our bodies to retrain our minds, rather than allowing the mind to continually dominate and repress the emergence of body-based wisdom.

One "gift" we may discover through such experience is the imprint of essential Masculinity and Femininity. As we get more and more "in touch" with our bodies, either through deep sexual experience or through our commitment to living a life of deep sexuality and sensuality without a partner, there are often moments of profound awareness of what it means to be Man or Woman in the truest sense. For example, as a man, perhaps in a moment of leaving self-consciousness behind in the heat of passion, you discover a quality of strength that is raw, organic, and even more "you" than you ordinarily know yourself to be. As a woman, perhaps while dancing with female friends, you may touch upon a type of softness that you once feared as a sign of weakness in relationship, but now experience as a beautiful expression of the power of surrender. If we are attentive (again with easeful awareness) to these energies as they arise, we may discover qualities of essential Masculinity and Femininity that are more vast and authentic than those we have been commonly conditioned to perceive and express. Conscious awareness of our essential Masculinity *and* Femininity brings about greater

153

confidence, as we relax into a wider understanding and appreciation of who we are, and into a more essential expression of ourselves.

When we begin to discover the wisdom of the body, it is often so radical and extraordinary that it is tempting to give it higher status over other forms of wisdom, such as that of the mind or the heart. Yet, rather than favoring one channel of wisdom over the other, a greater possibility is to integrate body, heart, mind, soul—all only aspects of a greater whole. Through a commitment to our own sexual healing, we come to allow these apparently distinct parts of ourselves not only to inform each other, but to blend, join, and "marry" one another such that the whole being becomes reconditioned by the imprint of higher knowledge.

When Sexual Healing is Difficult

Sexual healing is possible, but it just may be difficult. The patterns of contraction caused by the wound of touch deprivation are locked into the body. Sexual healing comes to those who are willing to work for it, and it comes through many ways. Most importantly, we begin by *committing* to sexual healing in our own bodies and our own lives. We then seek out and avail ourselves of opportunities for healing. One simple way this happens is by becoming more conscious of how we touch, and are touched, by others. Another way is through awareness of how we touch ourselves—how we treat our body, both physically and by way of attitude.

A friend of mine who has difficult health issues once complained to me, "I have a *bad* body."

"You should never say that toward or about your body!" I quickly responded. "If you need to say something, say, 'My body has pain,' 'My body struggles,' 'My body hurts.' We can't afford to treat the precious gift of the body with disdain." She thanked me for the reminder.

Cultivating same-gender friendships is another powerful vehicle for sexual healing. Women *know* how to honor each other, adore and adorn each other. Women know how to see beauty in other women. Listening to, feeling, and letting in other women's visions of our sexuality can be enormously healing. Similarly, men know how to support other men—they understand men's vulnerability, and support each other's strength.

Sexual healing happens both within and outside of intimate and sexual relationships. When the body is regarded as sacred and is treated well, by oneself, by one's friends of the same gender, and/or by a lover, it begins to reveal its secret pleasures. Sexual healing is for all ages, all circumstances, all bodies.

Gratitude for the Body

The human body is a temple of consciousness, in a highly individualized form. It is *your* temple, the place that God chose for you to enact the practice and prayer of the life force.

Whereas many of us will faithfully attend religious services, or pray to the goddess, or practice meditation, we casually desecrate the sanctified apparatus that houses consciousness itself in a thousand ways. We do this through a mental-emotional attitude of hating our bodies because they are the wrong shape or proportion, or because they have some physical condition we disapprove of (which is like walking up to God and saying, "You're ugly"). We further desecrate God through feeding our bodies with damaging substances and intoxicants (which is like poisoning God), through placing the body in environmental and emotional circumstances that are toxic and/or overwhelming (which is like hosting God in your teenager's attic), by ignoring it (refusing God's grace), and by stressing it excessively through workaholism and sleep deprivation (which is like sending God to a concentration camp). Regarding our lack of appreciation for our

155

own Divinity, Hafiz, the great Persian poet asks, "My dear, please tell me, why do you still throw sticks at your heart and God?"[3]

Worship of God through humanity begins with worship of our own body. Far from a sentimental indulgence of pride and self-centeredness, to worship our own body is to refuse to demean its shape, size, weight, health, age, posture, muscle tone, physical capacity, and sexual functioning. To abolish that mentality by whatever means is effective. For some, this may be a gentle, therapeutic process—one that slowly uproots the ancient and unconscious forces of shame, and the ingrained familial and culturally-conditioned belief systems about our bodies and sexuality. For others, this abolition will be straightforward—an unshakable commitment to say No to those demons of self-denial that continually attempt to thwart our efforts to place the practice of body-love over the conditioned stance of body-hatred. Still for others, the healing will happen through the alchemy of sexual union embraced with reverence, respect, and love. Such an embrace encourages the body to experience its own glory; its own unashamed, unabashed beauty; its own inherent perfection and capacity to serve as a vehicle to channel Godliness, thus creating a literal experience of "heaven on earth."

The shift from body-hate (fear), to body-love (gratitude), may feel difficult, but it is completely possible. It simply requires effort. A friend of mine who was dying said to me, "Day after day I hear people complaining that their hair has turned gray, that they have new wrinkles around their eyes, that their breasts are sagging, or that they are simply getting old. Not me. I love every scar on my body. I take delight in watching the shape of my body mature. Every time I have a birthday, I praise and thank God that I was given another year more than the 'experts' said I would have."

When we wake up in the morning, we can train ourselves to immediately engage in conscious gratitude to and for the body. We recognize that we have shifted from the domain of sleep and

156

unconsciousness to that of waking consciousness. We have been given the gift of our breath. Our senses are operant and in most cases brilliantly functional. We can express gratitude for that. Our organs allow us to eat, digest, eliminate. There is at least somebody who either cares for us or whom we care about . . . and in most cases there are many. This is something to be grateful for. Our lives will inevitably have difficulties, but also gifts, including the possibility inherent in each of us to discover the Truth of our existence. Awakening each morning, we have once again been given the miraculous opportunity to engage in life's lessons, however difficult they may be, knowing that this opportunity will pass all too quickly. We can internally express our gratitude for this tremendous possibility.

When we find ourselves feeling out of balance throughout the day, we can sit down, breathe, and re-call gratitude, taking the necessary time to realign ourselves. Whether we call this practice meditation, or simply basic sanity, is irrelevant. We need only make some gesture, even if we do not feel it, to behold the sanctity of the body.

If gratitude and respect for the body remains difficult to cultivate, which is often the case, why not consider taking a training at hospice, or volunteering to help people with AIDS, or serving the elderly population in some way? Something to kick-start a process of gratitude for all that we do have. Such measures may feel like a great deal of effort just to shift our attitude toward body-gratitude, yet for most of us, whatever we have done until now to abolish shame and establish freedom within the body has not been complete. If we believe, to even a small degree, in the possibility of radical freedom in and through the body, we will more likely want to experiment to discover how to wake up to the sanctity of our own circumstance.

Whatever our beliefs about the future of our soul—whether it be heaven, annihilation, or reincarnation—for all practical purposes we have been given *this* body at *this* time, and we have no

157

idea how long this gift will continue to be given. The passing of each day brings us closer to our death. While alive, we have many different opportunities. We can simply tolerate and bear life; we can engage it reasonably well; or we can fully involve ourselves in its radical possibilities, infusing the very cells of our body with gratitude and fullness; permeating them with energies of purified consciousness. In this way, the otherwise ordinary body becomes a vehicle of praise, service, and appreciation of the Divine.

Sex as the Doorway to God

> *Praise to Vishnu his hands*
> *Fondle in secret*
> *The large breasts of Lakshmi*
> *As though looking there for*
> *His own lost heart*
> —Venidatta, 17th century C.E.

Sex is a doorway to God. Sex is one of the great physical vehicles give–to human beings in order to experience Union with God. When, through the grace of moments that hint at the possibility of union we intuit where sex can lead us, we find ourselves at the doorway to infinity. Most importantly, perhaps, in such moments we are gifted with the bodily insight that God exists *in, through,* and *as* the human body. We must appreciate these moments as real—a gift from the beyond—and attempt to shift our relationship to our own bodies, touch, and sexuality, accordingly. Such a shift allows us to perceive, from the inside out, the importance of sanctifying the human body, and of regarding sexual experience as a literal process in which to praise and worship God.

Sex is a means for adoring, worshipping, and praising Spirit in the human form, our own and that of the other. But it can also be used as a vehicle to gain understanding of spiritual principles, of the deeper dynamics that underlie the creative process through which human evolution takes place. Simply having sex, even good sex, does not ensure that this understanding will arise. Instead, such knowledge comes far more readily when intentional sexuality is placed in the context of spiritual study and practice.

Knowing and embracing our own sexuality not only allows for glimpses of (and even secrets about) God, Truth, and the creative process, but urges us to express that same Truth and God through our own bodies. Sacred sexuality has the potential to heal the wounds created by false conditioning, body shame, self-denial, and self-hatred, revealing within our bodies the sacred temple where God has always lived, albeit disregarded.

Tantra, a term that is largely misunderstood in Western culture, is a vast field of spiritual practice that involves sanctifying ordinary life, experience, substances, and events by learning how to harness their inherent elements and energies for the purposes of spiritual transformation.[4] Tantric practitioners intentionally use the sexual process to access higher knowledge, deeper surrender, and a wider comprehension of the possibilities of "Love" and "Union." At times this involves specific techniques, but more commonly this knowledge, surrender, and comprehension arise naturally. Through the practitioner's consistent intention toward transformation, their sexual experience becomes naturally rooted in, and informed by, the ground of ongoing, disciplined spiritual study and practice. For example, perhaps in the course of lovemaking one begins to feel completely out of control. For some people this might be terrifying. They then simply block the experience or reduce it to simple, genital pleasure. On the other hand, a spiritual practitioner who has learned to bear uncomfortably strong experiences in the body, and who has tasted the value of surrender, may use their conscious intention to expand it into the whole body. Such experiences (and the example above is only one of an infinite number of possibilities) mark the intersection between great sex and sex that takes us to God.

The body knowledge obtained through sacred sexuality familiarizes us with a force within ourselves that is stronger than our own mental calculations, manipulations, and perceptions. Through appreciating the wonder of the human body, shame lifts and is replaced by an organic pride, one that results from resting in the dignity of our own form. The ensuing confidence allows for our unique gifts to be expressed and exchanged with life. Quite naturally, we enhance our relationships with others, and find an increase in the depth and quality of our perception of Truth.

Furthermore, if sacred sexuality can produce union, it can dissolve the self-created boundary that continually keeps us trapped in the false perception of separation. It similarly dissolves our opposition to the energetic continuity that connects us with all of life. Individuals who may not otherwise have the inclination toward, or the confidence to pursue, higher wisdom and truth, suddenly find themselves experiencing something much vaster than what they imagined life to be. Whereas sexual union between individuals is indeed that beautiful, more beautiful is union with God, with Truth, as expressed *through* union with the other. Whereas initially this union may be accessed through sex, it may then become available in all other relationships in our lives. The quality of connection we learn to bring to all things will thus sanctify ordinary life.

We are all in the same boat. We find ourselves in the very peculiar experience of inhabiting a human body that we must care for, that we are fully responsible for day in and day out, but which we ultimately cannot control, and that will perish all too soon. It is a body that we find at times filled with anguish, at other times with desire, in other moments with the weight of planetary sorrow penetrating its bones, and then suddenly filled with joy and sheer, unexplained ecstasy. It is a body that since its inception has thirsted for love, hungered for touch, craved self-understanding. Reverence for the body, the practice of gratitude for the flow of consciousness and life force that moves through it, and the expression of that graciousness by the embrace of and respect for sexuality as the creative force that penetrates all aspects of our lives, is the secret but ever-present doorway to union that we have all been searching for. It is my deepest wish that you feel the very real possibility for this expression of sexuality from within your own body, and that your longing for healing guide you to the richest, most satisfying experience of your own body and sexuality that you have imagined, or have yet to imagine.

CHAPTER 7

The Touch of God

We are always being touched by God—whatever we perceive Him, Her, or It to be. Even if we are atheists, swearing off all notion of God, we are touched by the greater order of the Life Force, and whatever divinity is present within it.

your slightest look easily will unclose me
though i have closed myself as fingers,
you open always petal by petal myself as Spring opens
(touching skillfully, mysteriously) her first rose[1]
                                                    – E.E. Cummings

When I was writing the first edition of this book, struggling to find cultural models in the Western world of a people who were not touch-starved, I began to watch those individual around me who were most "in touch." One man in particular caught my attention. He seemed to draw others to his company simply by his presence, and would leave them feeling touched in an inimitable way. To my surprise, closer observation revealed that he was rarely physically demonstrative of his affection. When questioned about this, he said that he had not been raised in a climate of consistent touch, and simply wasn't accustomed to it. How then, did he touch others so? His touch came through his eyes, which were ready to meet yours whenever you dared to look up and allow yourself to be seen. He touched by the quality of his listening when you spoke to him; his perfect attentiveness. He touched you in that whenever you needed help—even small help—he would suddenly appear to open the door for you, or he would show up with the last needed ingredients for a meal. He touched with his words, reflecting your point when needed, and refraining from speaking when nothing was required, never drawing unnecessary attention to himself. He touched with his smile, because you knew he meant it when he showed it, and also with his disapproval, for this was a sure sign that you had overlooked something important that was making *your* life more difficult. He touched you by the way he was with children, treating them with full interest and respect—not just occasionally, but always. He touched you because you saw he knew how to take care of himself, not demanding this from others. He touched you because his presence was touch itself. He didn't *do* touch, he *was* touch, and because of that, you felt touch in yourself.

Men and women such as these are the saints of our time, whether recognized by millions or known only within their own families. Though some give touch freely, such as the Hindu saint Mata Amritanandamayi who takes each of her thousands of visitors into her arms, holding every one of them and pouring her love into each, others, like Thomas Merton, who lived for thirty years hidden away in a cloistered monastery, similarly touch millions without ever seeing them or laying a hand on them. It is the context of a life lived in touch that affects those around them so strongly.

164

TOUCH AS CONTEXT

Joseph Chilton Pearce explains that people tend to be contextually determined, the context from which they are operating determines their response to any given situation. Of this he says, "Our culture breeds us to react to our outside context and so when we are in misery and pain and unhappiness, we try to change the outside context because we think we are determined by that context."[2] Although we insist on holding out for happiness until we have found the right mate, the right job, the right home, real touch comes from inside ourselves. Real touch is based upon the recognition that what we are ultimately looking for as adults will never, can never, be found outside of ourselves, that the *only* possibility for lasting and abiding fulfillment lies within. It involves taking the elements that are already here, and using our conscious capacity as human beings to masterfully direct them in such a way that love is produced.

Real touch is nothing more—and nothing less—than an opening of the heart and a relaxation of the mechanisms of ego that keep us from loving and being loved. It is a willingness to allow the body to open, both on the surface and deep within the cells, and to partake of a source of love that is continually available— not only from one's mates, children, and loved ones, but from what could be called God, the Self, the Great Spirit, Jesus Christ, the Infinite, or any name we choose to call the intangible reality that is the source of our existence.

The context of touch, therefore, is a way of life that rests on the premise of the inherent goodness present in each individual, as well as upon the recognition of an abundant presence of love. It does not naively propose that with a single kiss toads will become princes, but it does suggest that if we continually strive to understand the underlying suffering of the individual that is at the basis of his faults, and are willing to extend our love to him in spite of these, that the context of touch will be present, and healing will occur. To live life in the context of touch is to live in continual contact and intimacy with others—not exclusively in physical contact. Rather, the whole of one's being stays open to constantly being touched by and touching everything in its environment.

Whereas the context is extraordinary, a life lived in touch is ordinary. The context of touch is a mood of openness and a desire to bring love to the other, hour by hour, minute by minute. This vulnerability brings us immediately into the present. As we allow ourselves to be touched, we are suddenly met with reality unfolding in front of our eyes. We find ourselves without buffers, face-to-face with our child, spouse or friend. When we allow ourselves to be touched in this way, we realize that there is only the present moment—that our only "power" in terms of our capacity to make an impact on the world lies in the situation directly before us. We are either in touch with the present moment, or we are not. Once the domain of the heart is open, we don't need to be told how to touch, where to touch or when. Others don't need to convince us of the importance of touch. We know to touch, and we know that to live in a way that our touch is felt by others is the only way to really live.

True touch is not something that can be acquired, as much as it is found by relaxing into it. It is more passive than it is active. The touch itself is an action, but what gives rise to the mood of touch is a letting go of tension, and an allowing of ease, softening, intimacy, elegance. For those who have never let go, however, this is not always easeful. Some of us have hung on so tightly with all of our might that we have no idea what it means to let go—to just let go.

If only the individual could know that the pain he or she spends a lifetime protecting themselves from cannot compare to the suffering that the heart and soul already endure under the strain of their unwillingness to feel. If only the fire of the heart would burn strongly enough to melt the chains of fear that enclose it so that the individual would know, beyond the shadow of a doubt, that the greatest source of human suffering is our resistance to feeling the pain of our own hearts and of humanity at large.

Some would call it *grace*—that force which gives the individual the desire, strength and courage to move through resistance, see falseness with clarity, and feel the underlying pain that one must feel in order to become truly human. Others refer to it as wisdom or an inner knowing. Regardless of what it is called or where it comes from, this force or power is what we all seek; and although it comes from within, it is most easily accessed by touching others. When we touch others (and I don't mean giving them a polite and unfeeling kiss on the cheek), when we genuinely extend ourselves to them, we feel our own love, the love that is ever-present within ourselves, but is accessed through our willingness to give of ourselves.

Still, a life lived from the context of touch does not happen automatically. Rather, it is an ongoing affair. We move in and out of touch, get tastes of it and then fall back into habit or fear. Finally we find ourselves back where we started from, perhaps able to touch with a bit more ease.

Poets through the ages have described the hundred flavors of love. Just as the Eskimos have over a hundred names for snow because it is so essential to their survival (each name elucidates a specific quality, texture, size, degree of moisture, quantity, etc.), and as the Hindus describe one God by thousands of names, so when one lives in the context of touch, in communion with his or her circumstance, love becomes not one thing but many. Limited by their own minds and hearts, most people confine love to the romantic type, or the motherly expression, or perhaps to loyalty or commitment. But love can have qualities of fierceness, sorrow, compassion, wildness, rage, longing. A life lived in the context of touch is a passionate life full of many shades of love. This does not mean that the person experiences a continual intensity of emotional highs and lows, or always eats exotic foods or dresses in extravagant clothing; instead, his or her ordinary experience is alive with richness and depth, even amidst what appears to be a mundane life.

When a person shifts to the context of touch, a profound bonding is reestablished within himself and he begins to take directions from within, as opposed to relying solely upon his external circumstances. This in no way implies withdrawal from the world on any level, as his internal life remains in steady relationship to the world around him, but it does suggest that the source of his actions arise from an attunement to his surroundings, instead of an automatic reaction to them. When touch is the context of one's life, the individual's interactions with people attract love and brightness into his life. It is a magnetic quality that is capable of transforming the environment in which the context of touch is present.

The fact that thousands of spiritual, environmental and self-help movements are springing up across the globe, points to the first step in a shift of context. It is true that many people are participating in these groups for reasons other than they might believe (i.e., people say, "I want God," but the unconscious motivation is often, "Bliss me out so I can get away from this pain!"), and it is also true that many of these groups are fooling themselves about the lasting transformative effects of their work, but the very existence of these groups is a statement of the growing awareness of the undeniable and unavoidable need for change.

The shift to a context of touch is the change that people are seeking. Everything else follows naturally from there. Therefore, we initiate that shift by touching one another in loving ways, and refraining from touching each other in unloving ways. We pay attention to our internal experience, accept our own bodies and our own humanity, and in doing so begin to understand touch. We come to appreciate that touch, or the lack of touch, is a constant in our lives, and that we are either taking responsibility for participating in it consciously or we are not. We touch and are touched and begin to perceive what the way of touch is. As we become more loving, others are naturally touched by the way we interact with them. People begin to enjoy our company without knowing why. We take interest in others, and we look for opportunities to serve and to touch them. To touch is to live, and through our touch we come alive.

THE ILLUSION OF SEPARATION AND THE REALITY OF INTERCONNECTEDNESS

A human being is a part of the whole that we call the universe, a part limited in time and space. He experiences himself, his thoughts and feelings, as something separated from the rest—a kind of optical illusion of his consciousness. This illusion is a prison for us, restricting us to our personal desires and to affection for only the few people nearest to us. Our task must be to free ourselves from this prison by widening our circle of compassion to embrace all living beings and all of nature.

–Albert Einstein

Most people believe that the human being is somehow other than, or separate from, what can be called God, Spirit, the creative force, etc. Just because somebody can say, "God is everywhere and in everything," or wears a fancy philosophy on her sleeve, does not necessarily free her from the deeply ingrained belief system that God is somewhere in the sky, and that human beings are down below, having somehow fallen from grace.

Notions of God as savior, of God as other, have been passed down from generation to generation, reflecting our alienation from truth, mirroring the mind-body split, and often being used as an excuse for the need to take responsibility for our lives (i.e., "If it's all 'God's will,' then I don't have to do anything.)" Whether spoken or unspoken, this separation from God is the underlying context of the human condition, its roots more ancient even than the failure to have bonded. When we feel ourselves separate, it is as if we have not bonded with our very source. This illusion of separation is the wound we all share. Even those individuals who had highly-conscious parents, and for whom the bonding process was never disrupted, also remain at the effect of this.

Believing we are somehow separate from or other than God, carries with it the implication that there is a force that is working against us, waiting to destroy us by death, and that we must therefore take care only of ourselves—defending ourselves, seeking to benefit ourselves, acquiring for ourselves everything we can get. If we are separate, then we have the "right" to destroy the environment, to do what it takes to make it to the top, to support a "survival of the fittest" mentality, to dump a partner who doesn't suit us, to sleep around, to work for companies that exploit their workers, and to take what we can get, regardless of the implications of our actions on others. If we believe we are separate from others, we do not go out of our way to touch others, as we are too busy protecting our own self interests.

This instinct for survival, based upon every individual's belief that he or she is separate from every other individual, underlies all forms of aggression and self-protection leading to isolation, loneliness, depression, withholding of touch and the other shared ailments of our time.

In this vacuum, people attempt to harness God's help by turning to popular religion. They want something, anything, to make them feel cared for, to make them feel loved and secure. Oftentimes, however, what they are actually following is man's mistaken interpretation of religion, instead of God or the Universal Law, and thus they fall into the trap of dogma and ritual while missing the point of *experience* entirely. Due to confusion, ignorance and the misunderstanding of "tradition," they turn to a false (or dead) God, never finding the salvation they seek

170

as they are looking in the wrong place. When God becomes a savior who is separate from us, instead of a living presence in the nooks and crannies of daily life, it is an indication that people have substituted the necessity of intimacy for an idea of salvation.

God does not live in the sky, and I would further suggest that God lives in the body—our bodies. If we believe that He, She or It exists as some form of the creative force from which the human condition arises, we can be assured "he" is not up there behind the Milky Way twiddling his thumbs and wondering what to do with this mess. "He" is here among us, intermingling with every aspect of life, even manifesting as all of life. Mystics from the beginning of time, including Jesus Christ himself, have been saying this, and evidence from the contemporary physicists is pouring in.

And the verdict is...

...Not Separate.

We have trained ourselves to believe that the mystery of life is as basic as getting up, making the morning coffee, sending the kids off to school or going to the office, watching TV, having occasional sex with our mate, and going back to sleep. However, at the same time, as science and technology are driving us deeper into the well of consumption and materialism, they are simultaneously revealing discoveries that if considered even in a cursory manner would destroy the very notions of separateness that allow us to indulge in these things. Some scientists say they can prove the existence of God.

Every human being is actually, literally and physically a part of everybody else—inextricably linked with one another not just through a sappy "heart connection," but through our cells, molecules and breath. Energy cannot be created or destroyed, and therefore everything that is here now—both animate and inanimate—has always been here, though in a constant state of flux and change, and will continue to remain long after we are gone.

Human beings are constantly exchanging atoms. You have the highest level of atomic interchange with the people you live with and the people you sleep with (hence married couples begin to look alike, and even think alike), but it is also true that every human being literally contains the atoms of Jesus and the Buddha. Nobody escapes this—even if you live on the top of a mountain, in the purest air, with nobody around for thousands of miles...maybe there is less contamination, but everything is present—matter is matter. Death, therefore, can be understood not as annihilation, but instead as a dissolution and rearranging of form.

How is it that for tens of thousands of years mystics have known and described in detail that which only the most advanced scientific equipment is now able to detect? If we are able to entertain the notion that every molecule within our bodies has existed since the beginning of time and has lived as endless configurations of life forms in the shape of plants, animals, humans and the invisible, it is plausible that knowledge of the whole universe lies within us. A popular saying in Eastern spiritual traditions says, "The microcosm is the macrocosm; the macrocosm is the microcosm." This means that the whole of the universe is contained within the smallest particle. Therefore, although much knowledge is not accessible to ordinary human perception, it is conceivable that a person who dedicates his life to studying the depths of his being can obtain data that only the most highly sophisticated laboratories are able to produce.

Understanding how interconnected we are, we can either embrace the context of touch in order to nourish the greater life we are a part of, or we can insist on our separateness and not take responsibility for the exchanging of life that we are participating in.

The Power of Thought

We touch each other through thought. In everyday terms, interconnectedness means that many people who have the experience of thinking of somebody they haven't seen or spoken to for a long time, will suddenly receive a letter or a

172

phone call from them. The first five or ten times this happens, we call it coincidence; after that, it usually starts to rub us a little more, though we still may attempt to deny it, terrified of our own potential greatness.

Every thought we have (each backed by an emotional charge—be it positive, negative, or neutral) sends out a measurable electromagnetic charge into the atmosphere, and if it is about a specific person or thing, it is projected in that direction. Thoughts are things! They touch other people whether we want them to or not, and have the power to either kill or heal—literally. Thoughts can be "picked up," "read," and "communicated with," depending upon how receptive one is. Even when one is convinced that he or she is dense and insensitive, they are nonetheless impacted by the thoughts of others. When we think our thoughts are a private affair—that just because we are not expressing the hatred or desire we are harboring for a person, he or she does not feel it (whether it is recognized by them consciously or not)—we are fooling ourselves. It is for this reason that if I pass you on the street and you are in a good mood, I feel that from you. Similarly, if you are in a horrible mood and I walk into the room, I also feel that, because you are actually radiating outward what you think is your private mood. This is why we find some people uplifting to be around and others draining.[3]

Sometimes we don't want to take responsibility for our thoughts and feelings. We often want a person who has hurt us to feel as badly as we do. Sometimes consciously and sometimes unconsciously, we seek revenge on others, telling ourselves that they deserve it.

Yet as easily as our thoughs hurt each other, they can also heal one another. This is how prayer works. Larry Dossey, medical doctor and internationally renowned speaker in the area of spirituality and medicine, has devoted many years to the study of how prayer affects healing. In his book, *Prayer is Good Medicine*, he elucidates that in the more than 130 scientific studies done in the area of healing, over half of these experiments strongly indicate that prayer works.[4] In a study done by cardiologist Randolph Byrd of the University of California General Hospital, groups of very ill people were divided into two groups. Far from the hospital setting, one group was prayed for by an anonymous group of strangers, and the other group was left alone—neither group aware of whom would be prayed for. The effect of prayer on their healing was noteworthy—those prayed for experienced a more rapid and effective recovery.[5]

When somebody lovingly says, "You'll be in my thoughts," if he or she means it, you are in good shape because no matter who they are or where they are, you will be helped. The energy and attention of the other enters into your physical body, exciting the immune system, activating the mental chemistry, and adding the extra elements to it that just may take you over the edge of a healing crisis. There's really no mystery to it.

If individual thoughts holds this much power, it follows that people tend to be joyful and relaxed in cultures where there is an overall feeling of connectedness, a positive attitude, and in which the individual is held in the light of his or her strengths instead of their weaknesses. This is one reason why people tend to be so attracted to tropical paradises such as the Caribbean Islands or Hawaii. Aside from the obvious physical beauty of the places, and although visitors may never interact with the islanders, the environments themselves radiate qualities of relaxation, affection, openness and non-aggression. Whether visitors are aware of it or not, they pick up on this energetic field which is stronger than their own personal field, and find themselves feeling similar qualities of ease and relaxation.

It likewise stands to reason that if a depressed, cynical and addictive person makes a commitment to stay in a nourishing and affectionate environment, he or she will eventually end up, lawfully and naturally, patterning off of the environment in which they have steeped themselves.

174

Science reports that the body is continually renewing itself. The skin replaces itself entirely every month, the stomach lining every five days, the liver every six weeks and the skeleton every three months. In fact, ninety-eight percent of the atoms in the human body are replaced every year, and the whole human body is renewed every seven years! Still, the body ends up in much the same form. This is in part due to genetics, but also because repetitive and habitual thought-forms keep our physiological systems operating in much the same way, therefore reproducing a similar make up, even if this includes imbalance and disease. In other words, much of what keeps ailments and physical dispositions locked into our bodies is our minds.

The purpose of considering the impact of thought is not to inspire worry, terror or guilt in the individual concerning his or her own thought processes. Rather, it is meant to help us rid ourselves of the illusion that we are separate, independent and unimportant, and also to bring us face to face with the responsibility we have as a result of our interconnectedness. Mother Teresa once said, "We ourselves feel that what we are doing is just a drop in the ocean. But if that drop was not in the ocean, I think the ocean would be less because of that drop."

When we see the situation of our interconnectedness clearly, there arises within us a responsibility to it. If we don't take responsibility for our vision, we suffer our own conscience. Our interconnectedness reminds us that we are not solid, static, "preservable" beings, and that things are not as they seem to be on the surface. Although this initially may give rise to feelings of existential insecurity and panic, when we recognize from the bottom of our being that nothing is stable and that nothing can be held onto—when we know through and through that we are a small, but necessary element of a continually changing universe, we cease to need to protect ourselves from annihilation in the same way. We start to show up and take our place in the world, however great or insignificant that place is.

Yet, many people prefer to play ignorant, their claims of "disbelief" serving to cover the reluctance they feel to face this responsibility. However, whether we accept responsibility for our actions or not, their impact is equal. The Eastern notion of *karma* is simply a name for the ever-present law of cause and effect. Whereas many consider karma as something to be feared, equating it with a system of reward or punishment which rests on the premise of a supreme and separate God who sits in judgment of human beings, Tibetan master Jigme Rinpoche suggested that this is a limited and misinterpreted view of karma. He said that when karma is instead considered from the perspective that positive actions and gestures can have helpful and live-giving results, as opposed to viewing karma entirely from the negative, it opens up an extraordinary domain of possibility.[6]

Interconnectedness and the Environment

Nowhere is our responsibility for our interconnectedness more evident than in the relationships that comprise our immediate environment. The urgent sense of responsibility that a mother has for her newborn child dissipates all too quickly, however, as situations arise when it is inconvenient for her to do what is needed; and when self-interest is threatened, many people fail to apply that urgent sense of responsibility to their mates and loved ones. The famous Sufi saying, "Have faith in God, but tie your camels first," could be better paraphrased in the modern day as, "Go to church on Sunday, the PTA meeting on Wednesday, and the movies on Friday night, but first make sure you're hugging your kid and not abusing your husband or wife." Our responsibility is not only to take our loved ones' spoken wishes into consideration, but their unspoken wishes as well.

As with family relationships, our relationship to the earth tends to be one of either separateness and disregard, or one of connectedness and consideration. In present times, everyone is a

176

part of global destruction in a superficial sense, given that any-one who drives a car is participating in an oil industry that not only taxes the earth, but that has violent, competitive and aggres-sive undertones in every aspect of its functioning, and that the chemically-processed foods that we all eat involve various types of exploitation of the earth in their production. On the other hand, the two hundred sheets of recycled toilet paper we use a week will hardly make a difference in terms of deforestation. However, what does happen when we make the choice to buy the recycled toilet paper, or organic carrots (or whatever other con-scious choices we make), is that the positive intention that moti-vates our action goes out into the atmosphere in the form of energy, and our intention to regard our environment with con-sideration is strengthened and purified.

We touch our environment by how we relate to it. Whether it is understood or not, the consequences of our present context in relationship to our environment will have a lasting impact on sub-tle, often unseen levels. If every aggressive and violent thought carries with it a destructive electromagnetic charge, every abusive act is like an electromagnetic "bullet," and acts of violence against the body of the earth are equivalent to exploding a nuclear bomb on its surface. There is a direct link between our thoughts, our immediate environment, the body of the earth and every action we take. Either we relate to the environment from the context of touch, or we cause indirect harm through our ignorance.

While at the well washing clothes one morning with my indigenous friends, I realized how "out of touch" I was with my environment. Juanita, the woman whose house I lived in, asked me where my family in America got its water. I was stumped, my mind quickly scanned the local reservoirs in my home town, try-ing to determine from where our water came, but I wound up with little more than a vision of the kitchen faucet. I responded with embarrassment that I didn't know. Surprised by my igno-rance, Juanita's mother, Doña Cataliña, who gathered wood every

177

morning for the fire, asked me if I knew where the heat in my house came from. I hadn't a clue. I could not avoid the realization of my complete disconnection with the most basic elements of my immediate environment. I saw that it didn't matter how many letters I had written to Greenpeace in my past. When I grab an apple from the fruit bowl and mindlessly remove the sticker with the apple's "identification number" on it, I am living out my ignorance.

When we stop cooking, we cease to be in touch with our food. When we stop growing it, we are, again, further away. Every step that we distance ourselves from our immediate environment is a step out of relationship and away from integrity. I'm not suggesting that we all go back to farm life, we never will. But there are practical steps we can take. We can go barefoot in our homes or in our yard, feeling the ground beneath us. We can make a small garden and grow a few vegetables, or grow our own herbs in a window box if we live in an apartment. We can learn how to knit a cap, or start a compost pile. To be in touch with our lives, we have to be in touch with all of the elements of it to some degree, however small. When we have reverence for our environment, we still may eat processed foods, or choose to buy commercial vegetables over organic ones, but we are aware that our actions are costing the environment. Instead of feeling guilty about it, we can simply be honest with ourselves and eat with gratitude—the toxic effect of our actions thereby lessened.

When we know that we are affecting our world, we give up the lie of separation and cynicism. Irina Tweedie says:

> The Realization that every act, every word, every thought of ours...influences our environment...If we only knew deeply, absolutely, that our smallest act, our smallest thought, has such far-reaching effects...how carefully we would act and speak and think. How precious life would become in its integral oneness. It is wonderful and frightening. The responsibility is terrifying

*and fascinating in its depth and completeness, containing as it
does the perplexing insecurity of being unique and the profound
consolation of forming part of the Eternal Undivided Whole.*[7]

IT'S JUST LIKE THE BUDDHA SAID

The Buddha, who was well aware of the
principle of interconnectedness, could be considered to be one of
the greatest psychologists of all time. Two thousand five hundred
years ago, after having sat under the famous Bodhi tree for seven
years, he proclaimed to his disciples that, "All life is suffering."
The Buddha, who was the most compassionate of humans, and
who also represents that place of perfect clarity and acceptance
that exists within each of us, was not being cynical or pessimistic
as is so often misinterpreted. Instead, he was speaking to the reality of our condition. He wanted to teach people what life is, so
that they would have the opportunity to come to terms with it.
He was letting people know that the fact that their minds were
tormented, that they had such difficulty with their relationships,
with food, with how to be a good parent, with feelings of rage
and depression—did not mean that they were in any way "bad"
or doing anything "wrong." He was asking people to look at the
human condition, to consider the ways that we both hurt others
and are hurt by them, to acknowledge our fear of sickness and
death, and to realize that all of this is included in the package of
being alive. This was the first of what are referred to as *The Four
Noble Truths.*

Next, the Buddha explained to those around him that there is
a cause for this suffering. He called it thirst, or craving. He was
not only referring to the attachment to sense pleasures, wealth
and power, but also the attachment to the masses of ideals and
ideas, points of view, concepts, theories and beliefs that constitute the relentless chatter of the mind—the chatter that is constantly telling us what is O.K., what is not, what we want to eat,

what we do not, whom we like, who will hurt us, why we're no good, why we're so great, etcetera! This chattering mind is the part of us that did not bond; the part that labors under the illusion of separation, that is always looking for something to fill an obscure and unnamed void within. It is the part of us that is terrified of the insecurity that is a fact of our lives, and instead has created fantasies about reality that, even if they are inaccurate or bring further suffering upon us, we would rather hang onto than face the vulnerability that is at the base of our humanness.

Much to the relief of those who sat by him, who were rapidly becoming depressed as he spoke, the Buddha then set forth *The Third Noble Truth*—that there is emancipation, liberation, freedom from this suffering, and that it is not found in a pint of Haagën Däz™ or in front of the television set. He explained that whereas it is impossible to escape the realities inherent in a human existence (such as illness, aging, death, and sorrow), it is possible to cease to allow these forces to run our life. In choosing to see clearly and accept the reality of our lives (realizing that whatever happened in our childhoods is no longer happening yet cannot be undone), accepting that what is *is*—we stop wanting things to be other than they are, and in doing so cease to live in fear and reactivity to the things that we cannot change, accepting that we cannot control our lives. He was telling the group that we are not victims of our lives—that there is a way we can learn to move in and out of our days with kindness and clarity.

Lastly, Buddha explained a systematic method that would enable people to find their way out of suffering, which he called *The Eightfold Path*. This consisted of: Right Understanding, Right Thought, Right Speech, Right Action, Right Livelihood, Right Effort, Right Mindfulness, and Right Concentration. Although there are fine points to each of these eight components, he was basically describing how human beings would naturally come to live if they were in touch with themselves. His way was called The Middle Path because it did not advocate seeking fulfillment through an indulgence of the senses, as is so common in the West, nor did it suggest a denial of the body or the senses. Instead, we passionately seek fulfillment in the ordinary world— the wonderful, the terrible and the boring.

I am not Buddhist, and am not suggesting that the only way to get in touch with ourselves is to sit under the magnolia tree on our front lawn for seven years. For parents with young children, or individuals who work forty hours a week, it is simply not plausible to make such extreme gestures. On the other hand, emancipation from our suffering, and the cultivation of an inner freedom that would allow our lives to be full of touch and intimacy, does not come easy. It requires a ruthless and honest examination of our present state of touch-starvation and touch-phobia, and the willingness to *act* rightly, again and again, until our lives evidence greater touch and intimacy.

Buddhist cosmology suggests that of the many realms of life that a human being can be born into—including hell realms, heaven realms, and realms of the gods—that the greatest opportunity exists in being born into the human realm, because here there is always a possibility to transform, to change course, to be different, to get in touch with who we really are.

The way out of this suffering is by beginning to get in touch with ourselves and with others. Getting in touch needn't be dramatic, but can begin in simple ways. You start by taking ten full seconds to give your wife your undivided attention while hugging her when you (or she) come home from work at the end of the day. You begin when, instead of saying "fuck you" (either silently or to her face) when your close friend snaps at you, you turn to her and touching her arm ask, "Are you having a hard day?" You catch yourself entertaining negative thoughts about somebody and instead turn your attention to what you are doing. The Buddha didn't have it easy, and neither will you, but every step you take is one step closer.

TOUCH IN DAILY LIFE

It is no use walking anywhere to preach unless our walking is our preaching.

–St. Francis of Assisi

It is possible to become a student of touch, to aspire to live one's life in the context of touch, and to take practical steps in this direction. The earnest student gets glimpses of this context, and is increasingly able to recognize and observe it in others when it is present, thereby developing a refined sense about how this can show up in his day-to-day life. When he is inspired by the context of touch he makes choices about how to lead his life, and uses discipline to follow through with this inspiration when he is not feeling it. While one cannot "make" true touch happen, he or she can act according to its principles. In other words, until the mood of touch comes on its own, one can keep touching regardless, ceasing to feel disempowered by the absence of it when it is not present, and living on the premise of the truth of it while waiting for it to surface within more fully. This next section considers pragmatic ways that touch can be practiced in the context of one's daily life, beginning with an overview of some specific ways the individual can get in touch with himself internally, then moving into a discussion about how one can touch others by extending his or her hospitality to them, and finally by a consideration of service, which is perhaps the highest form of touch.

Touch on the Inside—Breath, Meditation and Martial Arts

We can have no context for touch in our lives if we are not in touch with ourselves. I recently spoke with a young man named Ray who had psoriasis—a condition of the skin that results in times of extreme irritation and long periods

182

in which the individual cannot stand to be touched in any way. Although Ray was aware that psoriasis often has a psychosomatic component (meaning that it originates in the mind and manifests in the body), this did nothing to ease the feelings of intense isolation and loneliness that ensued from the lack of physical contact in his life.

Ray recognized that the traditional psychotherapy he had been participating in for the past two years was unable to reach the places where he was most hungry for contact, so he turned to meditation. As with most forms of meditation, his practice required a great deal of patience. However, through this process, Ray found that he was literally able to *touch* places within himself that he had been previously unable to access. Through breath and awareness, he could move into both wounds and pleasures that were hidden deep within his body and mind, and in doing so he discovered a strong sense of intimacy and relationship within himself. This was simultaneously accompanied by a remission of his rashes and irritation.

Unless we are able to feel inside of our own bodies, we cannot be in relationship with our surroundings. If we are not in relationship with ourselves, we do not feel at home in the world, as if we had somehow been abandoned and are now in a game of tug-of-war with the universe. Yet the body knows all, and we can use meditation to optimize our receptivity to the constant feedback and messages that the body provides. Meditation and other forms of internal practice help us polish and refine the receptors so that the messages we get are clear and accurate.

Furthermore, when we are sensitive to our inner life, we know when we are "off" or have gone astray. When people say, "I'm in such a fog," or, "My body feels like lead," they are expressing a blockage in the mind-body connection that is inhibiting their receptive capacities. Internal practice is yet another avenue to increased consciousness and awareness.

Years ago when I was leaving for a ten-day meditation retreat in late December, my mother called and asked how I planned to spend my holidays that year. When I told her what I was doing, her response was, "Why don't you just stare out the window for ten days?!" I laughed, and explained to her that although meditation practices are often very simple, they involve a subtle process of working with the mind and body such that we cease to be slaves to our minds, thus freeing up the natural energy flow of the body. My point was that although these practices may look like just sitting on a cushion (as meditation does), or doing very slow and intentional movements (as is often the case in the martial arts), when the wisdom of the body is invoked by practice, it catalyzes certain processes that cannot be compared to gazing out the window!

Bear in mind that none of these practices are meant to replace the need for basic touch and affection in relationship to those in our environment. It is worth noting, by way of precaution, that countless individuals in all religions have, in their terror of intimacy, turned to lives of celibacy and meditation in order to disguise, even to themselves, their fear of touch and their fear of others. In an ideal situation, touch of self and touch with others would optimally build upon and enhance one another, creating an overall deepening of intimacy based on the individual's increased sensitivity.

Breath

Of the breath, Frederick Leboyer says, "To live freely is to breath freely." Called *prana* in Sanskrit, *ruach* in Hebrew, and *pneuma* in Greek, it is the same breath, the same life force, that is constantly exchanging life with the environment around us—breathing out carbon dioxide to feed all plant life, and taking in the oxygen that it provides. (To think we already knew this in third grade!) The breath has tremendous healing properties which have been known to all spiritual traditions, and which are now being discussed routinely by medical doctors. For not only is the breath directly connected with states of anxiety and/or relaxation, but through the breath we can directly control our blood pressure, body temperature, heart rate and so forth. I guarantee that if you stop right now and take a few deep breaths that you will instantly feel differently—probably more relaxed, centered, present, and with a greater sense of perspective.

Breath also connects us to our feelings. You will notice in a person who appears to be "in his head," or who "thinks too much," that his breath is very shallow. Children who have been traumatized in any way will often automatically develop unnatural and constricted patterns of breathing in order to ward off the intensity of their underlying emotional pain. These children grow up to become anxious adults who are probably entirely unaware that their natural flow of breath is obstructed, much less that their breathing patterns are making their physical and emotional lives extremely difficult. When we breathe we enter into relationship with the body, the center of all feeling—both pleasurable and painful. Through breath alone we can access states of deep calmness, clarity and equanimity, as well as move through painful emotional blockages.

Practicing with the breath needn't be a big production. Many of the fancy postures and closed-eye, dramatic breathing exercises that have become so popular are little more than cosmic fluff. Simply be aware of your breath throughout the day—when you are eating, when you are hurrying, when you are relaxed. It is particularly useful to pay attention to the breath as you pass through the various stages of falling asleep and waking up, for at these times the body is usually more relaxed, breathing according to its own organic rhythms. From that experience you can gain a reference point in yourself as to what it would mean to breathe freely. Eventually you will develop a more conscious relationship with your breath.

Meditation

There are many forms of meditation—some aim to focus the mind and sharpen attention, some are a type of prayer, others are solely intended to bring about peace and relaxation. Regardless, they all share in common the aim of helping the individual to get more in touch with his or her inner self, to see behind the screens of the superficial.

I will not give meditation instructions here. The subject of meditation is vast and complex, and would require a book of its own.[8] Depending upon one's make-up, various practices are more or less suitable to the individual's needs. However, if meditation is a subject that interests you, one that you wish to pursue further, and you don't already have your own practice, there are some useful guidelines to keep in mind.

The New Age scene advertises an endless list of possibilities for "Instant Enlightenment," "Spiritual Awakening in Three Days at a Fifty Percent Discount," "Everlasting Peace of Mind for only $175," "Soul Retrieval," and on and on. The propaganda can be enticing and convincing, and for this reason it is helpful to be wary and to use discernment when choosing a practice. First of all, it is important to understand that meditation is not equivalent to psychic healing, psychotherapy, hatha yoga, body work or deep relaxation. Secondly, it is pointless, and even dangerous, for beginning meditators to engage in advanced practices. Any promises of instant anything in terms of meditation should be considered as a warning flag. Thirdly, learning meditation should not be a financially costly process. Many times it will be offered free of charge or by donation, or if you are learning in a retreat setting, the costs will generally not be excessive.

Many basic types of meditation are grounded, reliable and effective. Among these are Vipassana (also called Insight), Zen and Tibetan Buddhist meditation practices and Centering Prayer, which are taught in many larger and smaller cities and towns.

These forms of meditation generally consist of sitting on a cushion for thirty minutes to an hour, and using the breath or another point of focus in order to undertake a process of self-examination. The "success" of meditation practice depends primarily upon patience, persistence, dedication and consistency. When we recognize the degree to which we are out of touch with ourselves, we will come to appreciate that getting in touch with ourselves is a slow process that will occur gradually. Other types of spiritual practice can bring us into specifically defined aspects of development and growth, but grounding ourselves in a simple and safe meditation practice will give us discernment and a more clear picture of what lies beyond.

Martial Arts and Yoga

There are numerous types of martial arts and yogas. Some, like *aikido* and *judo,* involve direct relationship with others, and others, like *hatha yoga* and *chi kung,* are primarily practiced alone. Most forms of martial arts and yoga involve a relationship with a teacher, who can be a source of valuable feedback, as the subtleties and distinctions in body posture, breath, attention and attitude are important. The intention of martial arts and yoga is to activate the life force, the *chi*, the natural energy of the body, and like the other practices listed here, to aid the individual in getting in touch with the inner workings of his or her body, and to bring him or her into a more direct relationship with his or her environment.

Though commonly thought of as a means of self-defense, the underlying goal of martial arts training is the achievement of mental, physical and spiritual strength. Aikido master Morihei Ueshiba asserts that, "Aikido is the study of the spirit."[9] Although what is visible to the human eye is a series of physical techniques, such techniques are merely vehicles used to express spiritual principles that have deep roots in Eastern traditions.

Martial artists who study not only technique but who apprentice to the context of the form they study, become deeply intimate with the subtle energies of the body. When an individual is in touch with himself in this way, he becomes a wellspring of knowledge as to the necessity and practical applications of this touch in his own life.

The spirit of yoga is similar to that of the martial arts. The numerous somatic exercises consisting of postures and stretches (known as *asanas*) that are usually thought of as yoga itself, are actually a form of *hatha yoga,* and are one aspect of a greater spiritual discipline that is designed to bring an individual into a harmonious relationship with life itself. Yogic exercises not only bring awareness and strength to the body, but are a form of self-touch. The practitioner of yoga knows her own body, and because of this sensitivity is more "in touch" with her surroundings.

The other principle forms of yoga (which literally translates as "union") are *karma yoga,* the path to union through selfless service, and *bhakti yoga,* the path of union by way of devotion (to God, Jesus, Allah, etc., or to an awakened spiritual teacher). The following sections on hospitality and service could be considered as forms of karma yoga. Hospitality and service could also be considered expressions of basic goodness, integrity and the only sensible outcome of a life lived in touch! Essentially, all touch is about devotion to The One—the one Love, the one Truth,—the One Whatever! We touch because we love. We love because we have been touched.

Hospitality as Touch

Hospitality is the greatest law given to man. If he knew how to obey this one law he could overcome his imperfections.[10]

– E.J. Gold

188

The Hindu tradition in India proclaims that God lives within every being. When a guest comes to one's home, he or she is to be treated as though God has entered the house. By hosting their guest in this manner, the Hindu people practice reverence and consideration of all beings, irrespective of their personal biases and preferences. Like the mother who— whether she feels angry, annoyed, or adoring in relationship to her children—continually provides for them based upon her underlying love and commitment, so the host places the guest before himself, and in doing so offers himself to service of the other. Hospitality is clearly a subset of service, but is considered separately here to give it a special seat of honor among the many forms of service.

In Japan, the Tea Ceremony is a highly respected and refined practice of hospitality. In mastering the simple act of serving tea and receiving it with gratitude, a synthesis of the highest cultural ideals, including religion, morality, aesthetics, philosophy, discipline and social relationship, is expressed. In the offering of tea, the host offers the guest attention, presence and humility— exemplifying an optimum moment of contact between two people.

All traditions at one time were rooted in the recognition of hospitality, and many individuals and traditions still practice this hospitality very intentionally. But the faster we continue to move as a culture, the more fast food pick-up replaces dinner-table gatherings, and evenings on the Internet or in front of the television are substituted for quiet family time, hospitality and gestures of personal consideration fall rapidly to the wayside.

Whereas the subtleties that give hospitality its particular elegance show up in the details, the details are not the point. Hospitality may include offering food to a guest, preparing his or her room, initiating conversation at times and allowing for quiet at other times. It may be the extra care that was taken to dust thoroughly, to put a vase of flowers on the table, to make the bed in a flawless manner, but all of these "details" are actually ways of honoring the person before you. By placing positive attention on your guest, you allow him or her to feel cared for and nourished, making yourself available to him or her, and communicating a sense of welcome. When your guest feels touched, it is not *because* of the fresh sheets or the flowers, but because of the intention and care that lies behind these gestures. He is responding to the mood created by his host's attention.

Hospitality is touch. It is an external gesture of respect and regard that does not demand anything of the other, thereby allowing him or her the full space to receive the gesture of touch that is being offered. When you allow your guest space, while still being attentive to her, you are giving her the space to bring herself forward, and as a result will often receive the best of her.

Many people are extremely shut down, and physical touch is just too threatening to them. Another unique aspect of hospitality as touch is that it gives a person who is fearful of touch an opportunity to feel nourished in ways that they may not ordinarily allow themselves to receive. To these people we offer ourselves more subtly and indirectly. Sometimes people send greeting cards, love letters or gifts to this end. The warmth extended by such hospitality may provide just enough safety for the other to let the touch in. In a touch-starved world, the subtlest of gestures mean a lot.

When we intentionally extend our hospitality to somebody else, we are able to experience our own respect and regard. When we are carefully setting up a room for a guest, or preparing a special meal for him or her, or even making a cup of tea or offering them a comfortable chair, we often experience within ourselves qualities of nurturance and a genuine desire for the other's well being, and in doing so are touched by our own goodness. Hospitality is a practice of service to all beings, in spite of our biases and judgments. Remember, the paradox of touch is that the one who serves, receives the most. Even if the host ends up sleeping on the floor, or eating the leftovers, if they have served wholeheartedly, they will reap the fruits of their own giving.

Guests need to practice hospitality too. It is as important to be a good guest as it is to be a good host. On the surface, this may show up as cleanliness, appreciation and a gracious acceptance of whatever is given. But more importantly, the guest's receptivity allows the giver to give—to pour forth themselves into an open receptacle. When both host and guest are participating in their respective roles, hospitality becomes a form of reciprocal relationship. Gratitude for giving and gratitude for receiving come together to produce a mood of harmony and communion between the two.

I learned the hard way. Though the principle of hospitality is an extension of common sense and basic integrity, I had not yet understood it clearly at eighteen when I went to work in Dzidzilché, Mexico. To express the appreciation for the work my colleagues and I were doing in the village, a very poor family invited us over for a special dinner. When they proudly presented the chicken they had slaughtered freshly that day, my stomach turned over. Actually, it was my mind that probably turned first. I had been a strict vegetarian for some years at that point, and the idea of breaking my vow was devastating. I politely refused the chicken, and responded the best I could to their baffled questions about why I would not eat meat. No matter how clear my responses, I could not avoid the look of disappointment on their faces. Several months afterward, when I was able to gain perspective on the situation, I saw how inappropriately I had responded to the situation, and felt remorse because of it. The principles of gratitude and receptivity that underlie hospitality are far more important than any rigid morality concerning personal preferences.

We can also offer hospitality to ourselves. We do this by taking an attitude of authentic nurturance and consideration toward ourselves (which is distinct from selfishness). We keep

191

our personal spaces neat, our clothes clean, our bodies fed with nourishing food. When we communicate an attitude of self-care inwardly, we feel respected and cared for in the same way we wish our guests to feel. We locate a core of self-respect within, and are more free to allow intimacy to flow in our lives. Of this, Father Henri Nouwen, author of over thirty books and mentor to thousands of seminary students says, "When we have found the anchor places for our lives in our own center, we can be free to let others enter into the space created for them."[11]

Service: The Touch of God in the Flesh

> *I don't know what your destiny will be, but one thing I do know: the only ones among you who will be really happy are those who have sought and found how to serve.*
> —Albert Schweitzer

My grandfather used to tell me the famous story of a man who was drowning in the ocean and who turned to God for help. He called to God, "I am drowning and I need your help! I am a man of great faith and good deeds so you must save me!" The man waited, growing tired from treading water, but confident God would come at any moment because he was pious. Meanwhile, a fisherman came by and saw that the man was drowning, "Here! Let me help you," said the fisherman throwing him a life preserver from the boat. Sputtering for breath, the man answered, "No. I am waiting for God to save me, for I am a man of great faith." The fisherman tried to insist, but the drowning man would not hear of it. Shortly after, a water-skier happened to come by, and seeing the condition of the man, offered him his rope so that he could be towed back to safety. Again, the man stubbornly refused. The fisherman must have gone to shore and called the coastal police, because soon there was a helicopter above that dropped down a ladder. A voice called through a megaphone for the man to grab hold of the ladder. Though bloated and nearly dead by now, the man refused, calling up to the pilot through the roaring ocean, "I have faith. God will save me."

The man drowned, but apparently because of his faith was taken to the gates of heaven where God was waiting. The man shook his fist at God, "Why didn't you save me?! I am a man of great faith and merit." Half-laughing, God responded, "What are you talking about? First I sent you a fisherman. When you stubbornly refused his help I sent you a water skier, and I even went to the trouble of sending a helicopter!"

If God or Spirit—in whatever form we imagine it to be—is going to touch us with help and grace, it is going to happen here and now, through the people in our immediate vicinity. God does not live in the sky, and if we don't find Him (Her, It) in one another, nobody is going to be waiting for us at the pearly gates of some fairytale heaven. A few individuals may be able to experience the touch of a formless God, but for the rest of us, it's either each other or nobody.

Jesus and Buddha are Joe and Gertrude who live on the corner. The only thing that makes a saint a saint is that they have given their life over wholly to the service of all humankind. Saints don't just tithe ten percent of their income to the church, or work in a residential treatment center, or serve as the PTA president, although they may do any of those things, the saint tithes their own *being*, living for others. Any powers they have acquired are insignificant manifestations of their service, and are only considered to be of value if they can be used to benefit others. Whereas it is unreasonable to assume that the average person can find within themselves the willingness to serve others to this same degree, the depth of collective wounding that humanity as a whole is experiencing is also unreasonable, and what it will take to remedy the present situation is far beyond what our rational minds care to consider. In other words, even if we are not Mother

Mary or Mahatma Gandhi, it is not beyond our capacity in the least to touch others in large and small ways. Mother Teresa has said, "Holiness is not a luxury but a simple duty."[12]

Still, the lives of the saints serve to inspire us, particularly when we recognize their humanness—their deep concern, the pain they feel for others' suffering, their own weaknesses that they must continually confront in order to express a deeper wisdom, and the way they persist against all odds because of the love in their hearts. Appreciating their extraordinary ordinariness, we can then model our lives after those individuals who, in Emily Dickinson's words, "dwell in possibility," instead of looking to the models provided to us by a dying culture.

A striking illustration of this comes from the life of the present day Indian saint Mata Amritanandamayi (known by her disciples as "Ammachi"). A man named Dattan showed up at her temple one day. He had been inflicted by a severe case of leprosy, which often eats away at the limbs and skin of the infected individual, resulting in deformity. Upon the man's arrival, Ammachi's close disciples tried to get him to leave the building, and to keep him away from their teacher, fearful that he would infect her. But when Ammachi saw him, she immediately called him over, took him into her arms and hugged and kissed him. Much to the disapproval of those around her, she then proceeded to suck the pus out of his open wounds with her own mouth. In response to the shock of those around her, she said, "Mother doesn't see his external body. She sees only his heart. I cannot discard him. He is my son and I am his mother. Can a mother abandon her son?"[13]

Another extraordinary story about how we touch one another through service is of Russian Orthodox Saint Mother Maria Skobtsova who, after years of protesting the Nazi movement and aiding its victims, was then sent to the Ravensbruck concentration camp. For the two years of her confinement she gave large portions of her food to others, and spent her time boosting the morale and faith of other inmates. Finally, she voluntarily joined a group of anguished older French women who were condemned to die, hoping to inspire them to meet their fate with fearlessness and faith in God, as she did. Ironically, the day after the murder, all the French women prisoners of Ravensbruck were liberated through the auspices of the Red Cross. Mother Maria is quoted to have said, "The way to God lies through love of people; there is no other way."[14]

Sister Chan Khong, a Vietnamese nun who was exiled from her home country because of her political involvement in peace activities, describes her way of touching people:

> *Being a nun in the West, I do not carry undernourished babies in my arms, but teenagers and adults do cry silently as they share the stories of their childhood of sadness and abuse. By listening attentively to their pain and helping them renew themselves, I am able to help heal many of these wounded "children," and this is very close to my ideal of holding the village children in my arms. I am grateful to be able to help in this way...together on the path of love, we can try to make a small difference in someone's life. What else is there to do?[15]*

Then there are the ordinary people, who it is unnecessary to call saints, but who may be secretly revered as such by their grandchildren; people who touch others deeply by rendering their services anonymously, and those who, after a life of crime and selfishness, perform one saintly act. Of these individuals Victor Frankl says, "We who lived in concentration camps can remember the men who walked through the huts comforting others, giving away their last piece of bread...they offer sufficient proof that everything can be taken away from a man but one thing: the last of the human freedoms—to choose one's attitude in any given set of circumstances. To choose one's own way."

The woman in the following story is such a person:

We had just searched a small village that had been suspected of harboring Viet Cong, began one Vietnam vet. *We really tore the place up...just up the trail from the village we were ambushed. I got hit and I don't remember anything more until I woke up with a very old Vietnamese woman leaning over me. Before I passed out again I remembered seeing her in the village we had just destroyed, and I knew I was going to die. When I woke again, the hole in my left side had been cleaned and bandaged, and the woman was leaning over me again offering me a cup of warm tea. As I was drinking the tea and wondering why I was still alive, a helicopter landed nearby to take me back. The woman quietly got up and disappeared down the trail.*[16]

The young can touch through service as well, and they do. Erin, an eighth grader, shared the following:

I was going down the stairs after first period. Everyone was walking all over a fifth grader on the ground. I decided to help him pick up his books and when I was finished I told him I'm sorry everyone was stepping on him. I walked away feeling good about myself but I knew he was crying. I know how he felt. I was also a fifth grader once. I'm not telling you this so you think I'm a nice person. I'm telling you this because what I did made me feel good about myself. I hope you take that into consideration. I want other people to know that by helping one person it makes you feel like you helped the whole world.[17]

A friend of mine corresponded for years with a man on death row who had been convicted of multiple murders. In the last years of his life, the prison inmate was introduced to Mahatma Gandhi's theories of *ahimsa,* or non-violence, and was deeply moved by them. Though there was nothing he could do to save his own life, he began to teach these notions to the younger prisoners, inspiring them to change their attitudes. Before his execution, he had created a non-violent sector of the prison as well as many study groups.

Again, when we embrace the context of touch in our lives, our actions are felt by others *as* touch, whether or not there is any physical contact. In his book *Grace and Grit*, renowned author Ken Wilber beautifully describes a relationship based on the context of touch. His wife, Treya, was diagnosed with cancer ten days after their marriage and died five years later. Recounting their relationship in the final days of Treya's life, Ken said, "In the last six months of her life, it was as if Treya and I went into spiritual overdrive for each other, serving each other in every way that we could. I finally quit the bitching and moaning...just dropped all that. I had absolutely no regrets; I had only gratitude for her presence, and for the extraordinary grace of serving her...it was a profound choice...we simply and directly served each other, exchanging self for other, and *therefore* glimpsing that eternal Spirit which transcends both self and other, both 'me' and 'mine.'"[18]

Sometimes it takes confrontation with our own death or the death of a loved one to bring us to the touch of selfless service, but this "exchanging self for other," can happen at any time of any day, and is our only hope for true happiness.

We all know examples of how we are touched through service in our own lives—they happen all the time, and this is because service is constantly taking place in the realm of the ordinary. I remember walking out of my house in San Francisco one morning to go to the University. I passed my neighbor, whom I had never spoken to though we had lived alongside one another for many months. He was washing his car and in a good mood, and looking at my filthy white car I laughingly joked, "Hey, when you finish yours maybe you can do mine." When I came home that evening and saw my car brilliantly clean, my heart literally fell open. And it wasn't the car—it was my suspicious heart that my neighbor had cleaned!

There is a story of a simple village woman who went to a famous sage lamenting that she could not keep her attention on God, and that she feared she would not progress spiritually. The sage then asked her what it was that she loved the most, and the old woman told him that it was her young granddaughter whom she adored more then anything else. The sage then told her to forget about God altogether, and to serve her granddaughter wholly. The woman did so and rumor has it that she became enlightened sometime thereafter.

It is hard to want to live in a context of touch in a world that needs more than one could ever offer, a world that is ever anxious to take *everything* from whomever is willing to give. We fear being swallowed up in another person's needs; we fear the pain we will feel if we open up to their pain; we are concerned that everything we have will be drained from us, leaving us desolate and impoverished. Yet we know that taking just doesn't work. An attitude of scarcity doesn't work. Selfishness doesn't work.

If we have given a cursory glance about us, looking even a fraction of an inch beneath the superficial level of things, we have seen that the only choice is to touch and to give of ourselves. Still, we cannot, nor should we, force ourselves to give. As will be discussed in the section entitled *Heartbreak,* when we acknowledge the pain in our own hearts, this recognition invites compassion into our lives and becomes the starting point of our service.

When we touch others through service, we tend to think of all the benefits *they* will receive from our help, failing to realize that we ourselves are likely to the primary beneficiaries of our service. The saint Swami Vivekananda suggests that we owe a debt of gratitude to those who allow us to serve them:

We must remember that it is a privilege to help others. Do not stand on a high pedestal and take five cents in your hand and say, "Here, my poor man!" But be grateful that the poor man is there, so that by making a gift to him you are able to help yourself. It is not the receiver who is blessed, but it is the giver. Be thankful that you are allowed to exercise your power of benevolence and mercy in the world.[19]

INTENTION

Intention is a remaining piece in this great puzzle of touch that we have been carefully assembling, and is perhaps the most valuable tool that we as human beings have at our disposal. Intention is what turns a touch-starved existence into a life full of touch and intimacy. Intention is not just saying, "Oh, I'd *like* to be one of those people who is really able to touch others." While that wish is a fine place to begin, if we really want to use intention to our advantage, much more will be involved. Intention means defining a highly specified goal and then cultivating within ourselves a complete and thorough desire to achieve this—a full-bodied willingness to do whatever it takes to manifest our particular aim. Finally, we follow through with our intention by way of disciplined and consistent action.

An intention of the degree of clarity and strength that I am suggesting here doesn't usually arise overnight, though it can. Oftentimes, an individual consciously wants to do something— to start being more affectionate with his children, for example— but the unconscious forces within him are not aligned with this wish, since he is still receiving some kind of payoff from his habit (in this case, protecting himself from the pain that much intimacy might reveal), even if it is a destructive one.

Sometimes a clear intention arises from crisis or trauma. For example, an alcoholic man who frequently drives his car while drunk may cultivate a powerful and clear intention to stop drinking when he nearly kills his wife in an accident on the way home from a party. Or an ordinarily cold and distant woman may decide to create more touch and intimacy in her life when, during an extended stay in the hospital, nobody comes to visit her because she has not acted loving toward others in her life. Sometimes intention comes from seeing the price that living in a touch-starved nation continually extracts from our wholeness, such as the individual who is diagnosed with a terminal illness and realizes that he has never really *lived* his life.

Whereas we cannot force intention to work for us, it does become stronger each time we reassert it and refine it. Restating one's aim doesn't have to be done on fancy paper in the presence of several witnesses—intention is grounded in one's relationship with his own true self (or God if you prefer). Intention is a force of unfathomable power, with a life of its own. Once it has been directed, it is as if the goal has already been achieved, just as when a coin is dropped from a tall building, it is only a matter of time before it hits the ground!

The power of intention is illustrated vividly in an account I once heard told by Jack Kornfield, a Jewish American Buddhist teacher, about one of the monks whom he studied with in the forest monasteries of Thailand.

When one enters a monastery—be it Christian, Buddhist, or otherwise—there is a firm decree that one must obey the teacher at all costs in order to optimally progress spiritually. Therefore, when the teacher of a young English monk told him to return to England to start his own monastery, to continue to wear his monk's robe, keep his head shaved and to practice the form of beggary they had done for so many years in Thailand, the monk was determined to obey, irrespective of inevitable feelings of insecurity and uneasiness. As the story goes, this man went walking through one of the many elegant parks in downtown London in his orange robes and with his begging bowl in hand. A curious and unsuspecting jogger stopped when he saw this odd sight, and asked the man what on earth he was doing. The young monk then explained that he was practicing the art of begging he had learned while living in the forest monasteries of Thailand—that he had been sent to England to set up his own monastery under the direction of his teacher. The jogger responded, "Well it so happens that I have a forest which I have been wanting to donate to a good cause. Would you like to have this land to build your monastery on?" Just as the power of intention, against all odds, won this man a beautiful piece of land upon which now stands a thriving Buddhist center, so will it bring genuine affection into our own lives and the lives of those whom we love.

As human beings, we need to become aware of our own power, so that we can consciously harness it as a resource and utilize it to benefit others, instead of remaining helpless at the mercy of pervasive, but relatively unimportant psychological issues. When we turn our attention and power toward getting in touch with our lives, or toward making sure that our children are given ample affection and attention in their early years, or toward acting out of compassion instead of defensiveness, then we have taken hold of the reigns of this force. Until we have admitted our own individual woundedness, as well as humanity's shared ailment, and allowed this to break us open to the compassion that lies beneath, we will be uncontrollably motivated to continue to exploit our own power for selfish gain. It cannot be otherwise. Yet, when we finally allow our heart to be shared with those around us, we will be inwardly moved to sacrifice our own desires for the benefit of the greater good.

The importance of harnessing the resource of our own power as human beings cannot be stated more eloquently than Nelson Mandela did in his inaugural speech:

Our deepest fear is not that we are inadequate. Our deepest fear is that we are powerful beyond measure. It is our light, not our darkness that most frightens us. We ask ourselves, "Who am I to be brilliant, gorgeous, talented, fabulous?" Actually, who are you not to be? You are a child of God. Your playing small doesn't serve the world. There's nothing enlightened about shrinking so that other people won't feel insecure around you.

We were born to make manifest the glory of God that is within us. It's not just in some of us. It's in everyone, and, as we let our light shine, we unconsciously give other people permission to do the same. As we are liberated from our own fear, our presence automatically liberates others.

SACRIFICE

Through personal sacrifice we connect ourselves to others and to the greater whole. The individual who leads a life of sacrifice is constantly touching others and the surrounding environment because he is attentive to, and resonant with, needs greater than his own. Contemporary spiritual teacher E.J. Gold says, "Nothing can be accomplished without sacrifice."[20] But, sacrifice is hard—it means that we willfully give up something we personally hold dear (like time, energy, privacy, money, not to mention greed, vanity, selfishness, pride) in order to serve the greater good. While our conscience may speak to us, our mind and the voices of the world at large may say the opposite, making it difficult to do what we know we must.

Practically speaking, if we really want to be part of the solution, we have to be willing to make constant, daily sacrifices—taking the opportunities for sacrifice that are presented to us all day long. We would give up having two and three cars per family, and driving to work alone. We would give up excessive consumerism and buying things we don't need and will never use. We would give up investing in companies that we are aware exploit human and natural resources. Certainly we wouldn't need to give up all our pleasures, but we would give up the continuous indulgence in those things that are taxing to the environment.

Yet sacrifice runs still deeper. If we are serious about touching those around us, we would give up our alcoholism, our overindulgence in television, our gambling, or whatever addictions keep us so obsessed that we become blind to the needs of others.

202

And sacrifice must occur on still another level. If we want to break the illusion of separation that keeps us lonely and isolated, we will have to give up the pride and righteousness that keeps us from touching others. We will have to sacrifice our selfishness that demands that all of *our* needs be met before we are willing to give to others. We will give up allowing ourselves to be controlled by the fears that keep us hiding away in our separateness. We will give up controlling situations to suit our own desires, and rather surrender to the needs of the life around us.

In one of the most astounding stories of personal sacrifice, an Indian holy woman, Mother Krishnabai, reported to her guru, Swami Ramdas, about her work in overcoming her judgmentalism toward others:

> *When I visited the homes of certain devotees to converse with them about you [Swami Ramdas], if I found any fault in the persons I met there, I would mentally pray to them...to be gracious enough not to make me pick faults in them anymore. I would also, in the case of women, when I noticed defects, go to them when [they were] asleep and take the dust of their feet and pray to them to prevent me from seeing shortcomings in them. In the case of men, I would drink as Tirtha [holy water] the water that dripped down on the floor from their legs when they came out of the bathroom to go into the house...If I found this was not possible, I would drink as Tirtha the water flowing out of the gutter at the back of the bathroom while they were having a bath. At the same time I prayed to them not to make me see faults in them again. By this practice I arrived at a state in which I could not see any fault in anybody.*[21]

Having said all of this, realize that no sacrifice happens before its time. I am not suggesting that people give up any of the things mentioned above until they are ready. The intentions we create will reveal what needs to be given and when. And even though we may give up a great deal, it will never be more than we can afford. It is only through our sacrifice that we find true touch.

HEARTBREAK

I used to be a Prince,
  attended by a royal entourage
with all the trappings
  of such a position
Now I wander the streets
  crying as a fool.
I used to presume our Father
  in Heaven bestowed wealth
Now I see Poverty
  is His true Gift...[22]

— Lee Lozowick

There comes a time when we turn to touch because we see that we are suffering tremendously from the chasm of separation that keeps us isolated from both ourselves and the ones we love. We intentionally bring physical touch into our lives because we are suffering, and we have admitted it. Because we intuitively know that there is another option to isolation, we grasp, with often frightened and timid hands toward that other option. We get "in touch" because living "out of touch" condemns us to a life of emptiness. We touch others because, having seen our own suffering, their pain no longer eludes us, no matter how clever the guise. Although once propelled into touch by the awareness of a lack within ourselves or by the wish to heal a wound, slowly something else takes over.

There is a time when the wound is no longer the dominating factor in one's life, when the voice of the essential self speaks

204

louder and more often than voices of falseness and confusion, when one has ceased to be a victim of circumstances and instead has taken responsibility for one's life. Still, however, we find that the wound has not disappeared. Instead, it has changed, deepened. The wound stays because it is part of the human condition. The wound remains in order to keep us humble and to remind us of the suffering of those around us.

We even begin to feel gratitude for this wound, for its tender pain, because it has helped us to understand ourselves, and in doing so we have found that we understand others as well. The compassion we feel as a result brings us into genuine relationship with others. This ongoing work of relationship—sharing in our humanness, in our joy, and even in our suffering— becomes the bridge across the very suffering from which it stems. Our pain is what connects us to others, and somehow in the seeming hopelessness of the situation we feel hope because the force of our love has mysteriously grown this within us.

This is the wound of heartbreak.

The way of touch *is* the path of heartbreak and service. The way of touch is what emerges when you see the big picture: the vision of a nation of hungry ghosts...the underlying alarm in people, and the insanity of distraction that has been created in an effort to wield power and to create a fantasy-substitute for reality. You take your first steps on the way of touch when you begin to feel the poison and toxicity of the environment, and to understand the way you have been manipulated into believing it is good, or when the fact of *your* birth and infancy become alive in your mind—what you must have gone through as an infant and young child; what your needs must have been; how your mother and father because of their mother and their father, could not have possibly fulfilled those needs; how your parents' unconsciously broke your tender heart while they were just doing the best they could. You walk the way of touch when you realize the amount of affection and acknowledgment you needed as a child

205

just because you existed, and not because of your achievements or who you would become for your parents, or when you start to see that your essential self went underground, and that who you think you are is a series of personality traits that you took on in order to make life bearable, and how you deadened yourself to make this all right. You experience the way of touch when you grasp the rage and helplessness that this has left you with—the same helplessness that is in all the people in the society that surrounds you...the people who have suffered as much loss as you have but who have coped with it by wielding power over others, by acquiring, commanding, abusing. You progress on the path of touch when you see what all of this aggression leads to, and you admit that it is as much in you as anybody else, and when you feel the loneliness of the too-large gap between yourself and others—your apprehension of them, your feelings of inferiority, superiority, hatred even. The way of touch is revealed when denial finally makes sense—when you see the necessity of it and can comprehend how it is present in every individual and every institution because reality *is* often too much to bear...when you start to suspect that life isn't how you imagined it...when you grasp that it is truly nobody's fault, that there is nobody to blame...when you recognize that you are paying for this false sense of security with your life. You are living the way of touch when what once seemed to be solid ground becomes shifting sand...when you admit how much of your life is a lie...when you see the pain of the lie in other people's eyes.

Where does this path eventually lead? To heartbreak. Why then bother to walk it? Because with heartbreak comes a clear vision of reality.

Your heart breaks—not as it did when you were an infant, but instead breaks open. You want it to break open. Yet even when you have been wholly broken open, you remain right where you are, vulnerable and raw, realizing that all you want to do is help others with the suffering in their lives. You want to do everything you can to bring more love to them. You want to hold crying children, and make babies feel welcome and beautiful and important. You want to touch people with your presence and your concern. You want to be kind and to share your resources. You want to see the beauty in others and help them to see it for themselves. You want the food that you place into your body and that you serve to others to be prepared with love. You want to treat everything—animate and inanimate—with care and respect. You want to use every moment to do whatever is needed to help heal, to bring joy, to celebrate the beauty in the small things of life. You want to do no harm. You want to live in gratitude for your heartbreak because it has made you real. This is the life of service— the way of touch.

N O T E S

Chapter One

[1] Montagu, Ashley, *Touching: The Human Significance of the Skin*—Second Edition (New York: Harper and Row, 1978), pp. 243-244.

[2] Nouwen, Henri J.M., *The Wounded Healer* (New York: Doubleday, 1972), pp. 5-7.

[3] Note: if you are in a 12-step program or have any intention of engaging in one, I *do not* recommend these 12 steps!

[4] Morris, Desmond, *Intimate Behavior* (New York: Random House, 1971), p. 173.

[5] Kozol, Jonathan, *Amazing Grace* (New York: Crown Publishers Inc., 1995), p. 64.

[6] Ibid, p. 31.

[7] Putnam, Robert D., "Bowling Alone," *Current,* June, 1995.

[8] Editors, *Tawagoto,* Winter, 1988.

[9] Montagu, p. 315.

[10] Pearce, Joseph Chilton, *Evolution's End* (San Francisco, CA: HarperSan Francisco, 1992), p. 197.

Chapter Two

[1] Leboyer, Frederick, *Loving Hands* (New York: Alfred A. Knopf, 1976), p.16.

[2] Chang, Jolan, *The Tao of Love and Sex: The Ancient Chinese Way to Ecstasy* (New York: E.P. Dutton, 1977), p. 27.

[3] Liedloff, Jean, *The Continuum Concept* (Reading, MA: Addison-Wesley Publishing Co., 1977), p. 48.

[4] Watson, John B., *Psychological Care of Infant and Child* (New York: Arno Press, 1972), p. 81.

[5] Montagu, Ashley, *Touching: The Human Significance of the Skin—Second Edition* (New York: Harper and Row, 1978), p. 142.

[6] Pearce, Joseph Chilton, *Magical Child* (New York: Bantam, 1977), p. 72.

[7] Pearce, Joseph Chilton, *Magical Child Matures* (New York: E.P. Dutton, 1985), p. 25.

[8] Ibid., p.34.

[9] Dunham, Carroll, et. al., *Mamatoto* (New York: Penguin Books, 1991), p.4.

[10] Montagu, p.142.

[11] Pearce, *Magical Child,* p. 72.

[12] Stettbacher, J. Konrad, *Making Sense of Suffering* (New York: Dutton, 1991), p. 112.

[13] Klein, Paul F., "The Needs of Children," *Mothering,* Spring, 1995.

[14] Prescott, James, "Failure of Pleasure As a Cause of Drug/Alcohol Abuse and Addictions," *The Truth Seeker,* September/October 1989.

[15] Pearce, *Magical Child,* p. 61.

[16] Montagu, p. 176.

[17] Prescott, James, "Alienation of Affection," *Psychology Today,* December, 1979.

[18] Prescott, James, "Somatosensory Affectional Deprivation (SAD) Theory of drug and alcohol use," in *Theories On Drug Abuse: Selected Contemporary Perspectives,* 1980. Dan J. Lettieri, Mollie Sayers and Helen Wallenstien Pearson, Eds.) NIDA Research Monograph, March 30, 1980. National Institute on Drug Abuse, Department of Health and Human Services. Rockville, MD).

19 Prescott, James, Time Life Documentary, "Rock a Bye Baby," premiered at the 1970 White House Conference On Children.

20 Turhan, Carli, Zuo Zhao, James Brewer, John D.E. Gabrieli and Larry Cahill, "Event related activation in the human amygdala associates with later memory for individual emotional experience," *Journal of Neuroscience,* 2000/20: RC 99.

21 Pearce, Joseph Chilton, "Interview," *Mothering,* Spring, 1985.

22 Verny, Thomas, M.D. and John Kelly, *The Secret Life of the Unborn Child* (New York: Dell, 1981), pp.12-13.

23 Verny, Thomas, M.D. and Pamela Weintraub, *Nurturing the Unborn Child* (New York: Delcorte Press, Bantam Doubleday Dell Publishing Group, 1991), p.xxiii.

24 Ibid., p. 20-21.

25 Prodromidis, M., T. Field, R. Arendt, L. Singer, R. Yando and D. Bendell, "Mothers touching newborns: a comparison of rooming-in versus minimal contact," Birth, 1995, 22, 196-200.

26 Sears, William, *The Fussy Baby* (Franklin Park, IL: La Leche League International, 1985), p. 29.

27 Sears, p. 30.

28 Sears, William, *Keys to Becoming a Father* (New York: Barrons, 1991), p. 3.

29 Leboyer, Frederick, *Birth Without Violence* (New York: Alfred A. Knopf, 1984), pp. 59-60.

30 Davis-Floyd, Robbie, "Hospital Birth as a Technocratic Right of Passage," *Mothering,* Summer, 1993.

31 Verny, p.xxvi.

32 Kitzinger, Sheila, *Homebirth: The Essential Guide to Giving Birth Outside of the Hospital,* 1st *ed.* (New York: Dorling Kindersley, 1991), pp. 43-44.

33 Buhler, Karen, M.D., *Raising Issues.* Summer, 1997.

34 Department of Health, "Changing Childbirth Report of the Expert Maternity Group." London, England: HMSO, 1993.

35 Ashford, Janet Issacs, "The History of Midwifery in the United States," *Mothering,* Winter, 1990.

211

[36] Ibid.

[37] There was a worldwide boycott on Nestle™ baby formula when it became publicly recognized that infant mortality rates soared, particularly in the Third World, when infants were given baby formula over breast milk. (Palmer, Gabrielle. "The Politics of Infant Feeding," *Mothering,* Summer, 1991.)

[38] "Letter to the Editor," *Mothering,* Spring, 1994, p.15.

[39] Montagu, p. 264.

[40] Pearce, *Magical Child Matures,* p. 31.

[41] Excerpted from Glick, Daniel, "Rooting for Intelligence," *Newsweek,* Spring/Summer 97 Special Edition, p.32.

[42] Excerpted from "Breast Feeding and Intelligence," *Pediatrics for Parents,* July/August, 1993, p.12.

[43] Leidloff, pp. 36-37.

[44] Ibid, p. 37.

[45] Dunham, pp. 164-165.

[46] Prescott, James, "The Origins of Human Love and Violence," p. 8.

[47] Rilke, Rainer Maria, "The Third Elegy," *The Selected Poetry of Rainer Maria Rilke* (New York: Vintage International, 1982), p. 163.

[48] Sears, William, *SIDS: A Parent's Guide to Understanding and Preventing Sudden Infant Death Syndrome* (New York: Little, Brown and Company, 1995), p. 102.

[49] Excerpted from Gordon, David, "Preventing a Hard Day's Night," *Newsweek, Special Edition,* Spring/Summer 1997, p.56.

[50] Ibid, p. 125.

[51] Ibid, pp. 102-103.

[52] Field, Tiffany, "Massage Therapy for Infants and Children." *Developmental and Behavioral Pediatrics,* Vol. 16, No. 2., April, 1995.p. 106.

[53] Ibid., Research attributed to Auckett, A.D., *Baby Massage,* *NY:* Newmarket Press, 1981; McClure, VS, *Infant Massage,* NY: Bantam, 1989.

Chapter Three

[1] Field, T., "Preschoolers in America are touched less and are more aggressive than preschoolers in France," *Early Childhood Development and Care*, 1999, 151, 11-17.

Chapter Four

[1] Leboyer, Frederick, *Birth Without Violence* (New York: Alfred A. Knopf, 1984), pp. 110-111.

[2] Prescott, James. "Hollywood Violence . . First Do No Harm," *Imagine a World of Wanted Children*, August, 1995.

[3] *The American Heritage Dictionary of the English Language, Third Edition* copyright © 1992 by Houghton Mifflin Company, p.8

[4] Hyde, Margaret O., *Sexual Abuse—Let's Talk About It* (Philadelphia, PA: The Westminster Press, 1984), p.15.

[5] Lozowick, Lee, (cited in) *Hohm Sahaj Mandir Study Manual, Vol. 2* (Prescott, AZ: Hohm Press, 1996), p. 132.

[6] In the United States, 29 states still allow corporal punishment in their schools. Almost every European country has outlawed this practice beginning in the 1800s. (Fathman, Robert E., *Mothering*, Winter, 1991.)

[7] *NEA Today*, February, 1994.

[8] Ibid.

[9] Seligman, Katherine, "Sex Laws for Schools," *San Francisco Examiner*, May 30, 1993.

[10] Ibid.

[11] Ibid.

[12] Leboyer, Frederick, *The Art of Breathing* (Paris, France: Editions de Seuil), p. 135.

[13] The majority of blatant abuse is perpetrated by fathers and men, but women are accountable for many of the subtler, yet equally damaging forms of abuse including passive witnessing,

neglect, manipulation, failure to tend to the infants needs, etc.

[14] For further study in this area, see: Bradshaw, John, *Family Secrets* (New York: Bantam, 1995); and Sheldrake, Rupert, *The Presence of the Past* (New York: Random House, 1988).

[15] Gorney, Roderic, "Hope for Humankind," *The Humanist,* January/February,1996.

[16] Prescott, James, *NIH Violence Research Initiatives*, p. 8-9; *The Origins of Human Love and Violence,* p. 4.

[17] Ibid., "The Origins of Human Love and Violence, p.7.

[18] Ibid., p. 15.

[19] Kozol, Jonathan, *Amazing Grace* (New York: Crown Publishers Inc.), p. 239.

[20] The edited version is found in *The New York Times,* August 21, 1996; the unedited version can be found in Issue 38 of *Wellness Associates Journal,* 123 Wildwood Trail, Afton, VA, 22920.

[21] Montagu, Ashley, *Touching: The Human Significance of the Skin*—Second Edition (New York, Harper and Row, 1978), p. 206.

[22] Ospensky, P.D., (Quoting G.I. Gurdjieff), *In Search of the Miraculous* (New York: Harcourt Brace Jovanovich Inc., 1949), p. 54.

[23] Reprinted with permission from: Lenox, Annie and David Stewart. "This City Never Sleeps." D'N'A' Ltd., BMG Music Publishing, Ltd., 1983.

[24] Campbell, Greg, Interview in Germany, June, 1996.

[25] Gorney, Roderic, "Hope for Humankind," *The Humanist,* January/February, 1996.

[26] To do any justice to the complexity, intricacies, and consequences of this proposition would require a full volume, at least. For the purposes of understanding the consequences of the lack of touch in our lives, however, an overview is included here.

214

[27] Liedloff, Jean, *Continuum Concept* (Reading, MA: Addison-Wesley Publishing Co., 1977), p. 143.

[28] Montagu, pp. 243-244.

[29] Rilke, Rainer Maria, "The Third Elegy," *The Selected Poetry of Rainer Maria Rilke* (New York: Vintage International, 1983), p.165.

[30] Lozowick, Lee, Public Talk, May, 1996.

[31] Stettbacher, J. Konrad, *Making Sense of Suffering* (New York: Dutton, 1991), p. 11.

Chapter Five

[1] Referenced in: *Advanced Living Technologies,* 2442 Meade St., Denver, CO 88021-4440.

[2] Crenshaw, Theresa L. *The Alchemy of Love and Lust.* New York: Pocket Books (Simon & Schuster), 1996.

[3] It is important to be able to distinguish between a skilled therapist and an unskilled one. The chapter entitled "Sources of Help" in my first book, *When Sons and Daughters Choose Alternative Lifestyles* (Hohm Press, 1996), details the process of selecting a qualified therapist.

[4] Field, Tiffany, "Massage Therapy for Infants and Children," *Developmental and Behavioral Pediatrics,* Vol. 16, No. 2, April, 1995.

[5] Sunshine, W., Filed, T.M. et al. "Chronic fatigue syndrome: Massage therapy effects on depression and fatigue." *Journal of Chronic Fatigue Syndrome,* 4, 1997, pp. 43-51.

[6] Field, T., Delamanter, A.M. et al. "Diabetic children's adherence and glucose levels improve after touch therapy," *Diabetes Spectrum,* 1997; Field T., Seligman, S. et al. "Alleviating post-traumatic stress in children following Hurricane Andrew," *Journal of Applied Developmental Psychology,* 17, 1996, pp.37-50.

[7] Field, T., Morrow, C. et al. "Massage therapy reduces anxiety in child and adolescent psychiatric patients." *Journal of the*

American Academy of Child and Adolescent Psychiatry, 31 (1), 1992, pp. 125-131.

[8] Field, T., O. Quintino, M. Hernandez-Reif, and G. Koslovsky, "Adolescents with attention deficit hyperactivity disorder benefit from massage therapy," *Adolescence,* 1998, 33:103-8.

[9] Ironson, Gail and Tiffany Field et. al., "Massage Therapy is Associated with Enhancement of the Immune System's Cytotoxic Capacity." *Intern. J. Neuroscience,* 1995.

[10] Rosa, L, et al, "A close look at therapeutic touch," *Journal of the American Medical Association,* 1998, p. 279.

[11] Krieger, Dolores, "Therapeutic Touch: The Imprimatur of Nursing," *American Journal of Nursing,* 75 (1975), 784-87.

Chapter Six

[1] Hafiz [in Ladinsky, Daniel]. *The Subject Tonight is Love.* Myrtle Beach, NC: Pumpkin House Press, 1996, p.9. Used with permission.

[2] Main, M., "Parental aversion to infant-initiated contact is correlated with the parents own rejection during childhood," Barnard, K.E., and T.E. Brazelton (Eds.), *Touch: The Foundation of Experience,* Madison, CN: International Universities Press, 1990, p. 495.

[3] Hafiz [translated by Daniel Ladinsky], *The Gift.* New York: Penguin/Arkana, 1999, p.160.

[4] Whereas sexual experience is an important and invaluable *aspect* of tantric practice, it is important to understand that the all-too-frequent association in the West of tantra with a series of sexual techniques designed to produce experiences of bliss and ecstasy, represents a diminishment of one of the least understood and most encompassing avenues of spiritual transformation.

Chapter Seven

[1] Cummings, E.E., "somewhere I have never travelled, gladly beyond," (poem copyright 1931); from: *E.E. Cummings Complete Poems 1904-1962* (New York: Liveright, 1973) p. 367.

[2] Pearce, Joseph Chilton, (Interview), *Mothering*, Spring 1985.

[3] It is for this reason that scientific discoveries are often made simultaneously in different parts of the world—the objective knowledge in the universe suddenly coming into a configuration that is accessible to the open receptacle of the scientific mind. By the time our mind is consciously aware of a piece of information, that information has already been "alive" for eons.

[4] Dossey, Larry, *Prayer is Good Medicine* (CA: HarperSan Francisco), pp. 3-4

[5] Byrd, Randolph C., "Positive Therapeutic Effects of Intecessory Prayer in a Coronary Care Unity Population," *Southern Medical Journal* 81, no. 7 (July, 1988): 826-29.

[6] Jigme Rinpoche, Public Talk, December 1995, Adelaide, Australia.

[7] Tweedie, Irina, *Chasm of Fire* (Wiltshire, England: Element Books, 1979), p. 202.

[8] For an excellent book on meditation see: Rick Lewis, *You Have the Right to Remain Silent*. Prescott, AZ: Hohm Press, 2002.

[9] Stevens, John, *The Essence of Aikido: Spiritual Teach-ings of Morihei Ueshiba* (New York: Kodansh America Inc., 1993), p. 13.

[10] Gold, E.J., *The Joy of Sacrifice* (Prescott, AZ: IDHHB Inc. and Hohm Press, 1978), p. 106.

[11] Nouwen, Henri, *The Wounded Healer* (New York: Doubleday, 1972), p. 91.

[12] Mother Teresa of Calcutta, *Life in the Spirit* (San Francisco, CA: Harper and Row, 1983), p. 93.

[13] Conway, Timothy, *Women of Power and Grace* (Santa Barbara, CA: The Wake Up Press, 1984), p. 264.

[14] Ibid., p. 112.

[15] Sister Chan Khong, *Learning True Love* (Berkeley, CA: Parallax Press, 1993), p. 249.

[16] Conari Press (editors), *Random Acts of Kindness* (Berkeley, CA: Conari Press, 1993), p. 37.

[17] Conari Press (editors), *Kids' Random Acts of Kindness* (Berkeley, CA: Conari Press, 1994), p. 105-6.

[18] Wilber, Ken, *Grace and Grit* (Boston, MA: Shambhala Publications, 1991), p. 405.

[19] Miller, Ronald S., *As Above, So Below* (Los Angeles, CA: J.P. Tarcher, 1992), p. 283.

[20] Gold, E.J., p. 28.

[21] Mother Krishnabai, *Guru's Grace*. Kasaragod, India: Anandashram, 1964, 47-8.

[22] Lozowick, Lee, *Poems of a Broken Heart* (Madras, India: Sister Nivedita Academy, 1993), p. 23

Books

Ainsworth, Mary. *Patterns of Attachment*. Hillsdale, NJ:
Lawrence Erlbaum Associates, 1978.

Anderson, Sherry Ruth and Patricia Hopkins. *The Feminine Face
of God*. New York: Bantam, 1992.

Attwood, Charles. *Dr. Attwood's Low-Fat Prescription for Kids*.
New York: Viking, 1995.

Barker, Sarah. *The Alexander Technique*. New York: Bantam
Books, 1991.

Barnard, Kathryn E. and T. Berry Brazelton. *Touch: The
Foundation of Experience*. Madison, CT: International
Universities Press, 1990.

Berends, Polly Berrien, *Whole Child/Whole Parent*, New York:
Harper Collins, 4th Edition, 1997.

Bowlby, John. *A Secure Base*. New York: Basic Books, 1988.

Bradshaw, John. *Family Secrets*. New York: Bantam, 1995.

Burmeister, Alice, et al, *Touch of Healing*, New York: Bantam Books, 1997.

Caplan, Mariana. *When Holidays are Hell...! A Guide to Surviving Family Gatherings.* Prescott, AZ: Hohm Press, 1997.

———. *When Sons and Daughters Choose Alternative Lifestyles.* Prescott, AZ: Hohm Press, 1996.

Chamberlain, David. *Babies Remember Birth.* New York: Ballantine Books, 1988.

Chan Khong, (Sister). *Learning True Love,* Berkeley, CA: Parallax Press, 1993.

Chesto, Kathleen, *Raising Kids Who Care About Themselves, About Their World, About Each Other*, Franklin, WI: Sheed and Ward, 1997.

Colton, Helen. *The Gift of Touch: How Physical Contact Improves Communication, Pleasure, and Health.* New York: Seaview and Putnam, 1983.

Conari Press (editors). *Random Acts of Kindness.* Berkeley, CA: Conari Press, 1993.

———. *Kids' Random Acts of Kindness.* Berkeley, CA: Conari Press, 1994.

Conway, Timothy. *Women of Power and Grace.* Santa Barbara, CA: The Wake Up Press, 1994.

Crenshaw, Theresa L. *The Alchemy of Love and Lust.* New York: Pocket Books (Simon & Schuster), 1996.

Davis, Phyllis K., *The Power of Touch*, Carlsbad, CA: Hay House, 1999.

Dossey, Larry. *Prayer is Good Medicine.* CA: HarperSan Francisco, 1996.

Dougans, Inge, and Suzanne Ellis. *The Art of Reflexology.* Rockport, MA: Element Books, 1992.

Dunham, Carroll, et. Al. *Mamatoto.* New York: Penguin Books, 1991.

Editorial board. *Massage: Total Relaxation.* Alexandria, Virginia: Time-Life Books, 1987.

Editorial staff. *Hohm Sahaj Mandir Study Manual (Volumes I and II).* Prescott, AZ: Hohm Press, 1996.

Feurstein, Georg, and Stephan Bodian. *Living Yoga.* New York: Jeremy P. Tarcher, 1993.

Field, Reshad. *Here to Heal.* Longmead, Shaftesbury, Dorset: Elemental Books, 1985.

Field, Tiffany M., *Touch in Early Development*, Mahwah, NJ: Lawrence Erlbaum Assoc., 1995.

———, ed., *Touch*, Cambridge, MA: MIT Press, 2001.

Fields, Rick. *Chop Wood, Carry Water.* Los Angeles: J.P. Tarcher, distributed by Houghton Mifflin, 1984.

Fifer, Steve, and Sharon Sloan Fiffer. *50 Ways to Help Your Community.* New York: Doubleday, 1994.

Ford, Clyde W. *Compassionate Touch.* New York: Simon and Schuster, 1993.

Gaskin, Ina May, *Spiritual Midwifery*, 4th Edition, Summertown, TN: The Book Publishing Company, 2002.

Gawain, Shakti. *Path of Transformation: How Healing Ourselves Can Change the World.* Mill Valley, CA: Nataraj, 1993.

Gold, E.J. *The Joy of Sacrifice.* Prescott, Arizona: IDHHB Inc. and Hohm Press, 1978.

Goldhagen, Daniel Jonah. *Hitler's Willing Executioners.* New York: Alfred A. Knopf, 1996.

Grigg, Ray. *The Tao of Relationships.* New York: Bantam, 1988.

Heller, Morton, A., *The Psychology of Touch*, Hillsdale, NJ: Lawrence Erlbaum Assoc., 1991.

Hover-Kramer, Dorothea, *Healing Touch: A Guidebook for Practitioners*, Australia: Delmar Thomson Learning, 2002.

Johnson, Anne and Vic Goodman, *The Essence of Parenting: Becoming the Parent You Want to Be*, New York: Crossroad, 1995.

Josipovici, Gabriel, *Touch*, New Haven, CT: Yale University Press, 1996.

Kitzinger, Sheila. *Homebirth: The Essential Guide to Giving Birth Outside the Hospital.* New York: Dorling Kindersley, 1991.

———. *The Complete Book of Pregnancy and Childbirth.* New York: Alfred A. Knopf, 1985.

222

Kozol, Jonathan. *Amazing Grace.* New York: Crown Publishers Inc., 1995.

Krieger, Dolores, *The Therapeutic Touch: How to Use Your Hands to Help or to Heal,* NY: Simon & Schuster, 1992.

————. *Accepting Your Power to Heal: The Personal Practice of Therapeutic Touch.* Santa Fe, NM: Bear&Co., 1993.

————. *Therapeutic Touch Inner Workbook,* Santa Fe, NM: Bear and Co., 1997.

Leboyer, Frederick. *Birth Without Violence.* New York: Alfred A. Knopf, 1984.

————. *Inner Beauty, Inner Light.* New York: Alfred A. Knopf, 1978.

————. *Loving Hands.* New York: Alfred A. Knopf, 1976.

————. *The Art of Breathing.* Paris, France: Editions de Seuil, 1985.

Levine, Stephen. *Who Dies?* Garden City, New York: Anchor Press-Doubleday, 1982.

————. *A Year to Live: How to Live This Year as if It Were Your Last.* New York: Bell Tower, 1997.

Liedloff, Jean. *The Continuum Concept.* Reading, MA: Addison-Wesley Publishing Co., 1977.

Lozowick, Lee. *Conscious Parenting.* Prescott, AZ: Hohm Press, 1997.

———. *Living God Blues.* Prescott, AZ: Hohm Press, 1984.

———. *The Alchemy of Love and Sex.* Prescott, AZ: Hohm Press, 1996.

———. *The Alchemy of Transformation.* Prescott, AZ: Hohm Press, 1996.

———. *Poems of a Broken Heart.* Madras, India: Sister Nivedita Academy, 1993.

Macy, Joanna. *Despair and Personal Power in the Nuclear Age.* Philadelphia, PA: New Society Publishers, 1983.

Mander, Jerry, *Four Arguments for the Elimination of Television,* New York: William Morrow and Co., 1978.

Mansfield, Lynda Gianforte and Christopher H. Waldmann. *Don't Touch My Heart.* Colorado Springs, CO: Piñon Press, 1994.

Martin, Chia. *The Art of Touch: A Massage Manual for Young People.* Prescott, AZ: Hohm Press, 1996.

Miller, Alice. *Banished Knowledge: Facing Childhood Injuries.* New York: Doubleday, 1990.

———. *For Your Own Good: Hidden Cruelty in Child-Rearing and the Roots of Violence.* New York: Farrar, Straus, Giroux, 1984.

———. *Thou Shalt Not Be Aware: Society's Betrayal of the Child.* New York: Meridian Books (Penguin), 1990.

Miller, Ronald S. *As Above, So Below.* Los Angeles, CA: J.P. Tarcher, 1992.

Montagu, Ashley. *Touching: The Human Significance of the Skin,* (Second Edition). New York: Harper and Row, 1978.

———. *Growing Young,* (Second Edition). Granby, MA: Bergen & Garvey. 1989.

———. *On Being Human,* (Second Edition). New York: Hawthorn Books, 1967.

———. *The Nature of Human Aggression.* New York: Oxford University Press, 1976.

———. *Touching: The Human Significance of the Skin,* (Second Edition). New York: Harper and Row, 1978.

———. *The Dehumanization of Man.* New York: McGraw-Hill, 1983.

Mother Teresa of Calcutta. *Life in the Spirit.* San Francisco, CA: Harper and Row, 1983.

———. *The Love of Christ: Spiritual Counsels.* San Francisco, CA: Harper and Row, 1982.

Nelson, Dawn, *From the Heart Through the Hands: The Power of Touch in Caregiving,* Forres, Scotland: Findhorn Press, 2001.

Northrup, Christiane, M.D. *Women's Bodies, Women's Wisdom: Creating Physical and Emotional Health and Healing.* New York: Bantam Books, 1994.

Ouspensky, P.D. *In Search of the Miraculous.* New York: Harcourt Brace Jovanovich Inc., 1949.

Pearce, Joseph Chilton. *Evolution's End.* San Francisco, CA: HarperSanFrancisco, 1992.

————. *Magical Child.* New York: Bantam, 1977.

————. *Magical Child Matures.* New York: E.P. Dutton, 1985.

Peck, M. Scott. *People of the Lie.* New York: Simon and Schuster, 1983.

Piercy, Marge. *The Moon is Always Female.* New York: Alfred A. Knopf, 1988.

Prescott, James. From: *Violent Behavior: Assessment and Intervention.* Great Neck, New York: PMA Publishing Corp., 1990.

Rahula, Walpola. *What the Buddha Taught.* New York: Grove Press Inc., 1959.

Reich, Willhelm. *The Function of the Orgasm.* New York: Farrar Straus and Giroux, 1973.

Rilke, Rainer Maria. *Selected Poems of Rainer Maria Rilke.* New York: Harper and Row, 1981.

————. *The Selected Poetry of Rainer Maria Rilke.* Edited by Stephen Mitchell. New York: Vintage International, 1980.

Sayre-Adams, Jean, et al, *The Theory and Practice of Therapeutic Touch*, New York: Churchill Livingstone, 2001.

Schaef, Anne Wilson. *When Society Becomes an Addict.* San Francisco, CA: Harper and Row, 1987.

Sears, William, M.D. and Martha Sears. *The Baby Book: Everything You Need to Know About Your Baby—From Birth to Age Two.* New York: Little, Brown and Company, 1993.

Sears, William, M.D. *Keys to Becoming a Father.* New York: Barrons, 1991.

———. *SIDS: A Parent's Guide to Understanding and Preventing Sudden Infant Death Syndrome.* New York: Little, Brown and Company, 1995.

———. *The Fussy Baby.* Franklin Park, IL: La Leche League International, 1985.

Sellner, Edward C. *Wisdom of the Celtic Saints.* Notre Dame, Indiana: Ave Maria Press, 1993.

Sen, Soshitsu. *Tea Life, Tea Mind.* New York: Weatherhill, 1979.

Sheldrake, Rupert. *The Presence of the Past.* New York: Random House, 1988.

Siegel, Bernie, M.D. *Love, Medicine and Miracles.* New York: Harper and Row, 1986.

Simon, Sidney B. *Caring, Feeling, Touching.* Niles, IL: Argues Communications, 1976.

Shiva, Shahram T. *Rending the Veil: Literal and Poetic Translations of Rumi.* Prescott, AZ: Hohm Press, 1995.

Somé, Malidoma. *Of Water and the Spirit: Ritual, Magic, and Initiation in the Life of an African Shaman.* New York: Putnam, 1994.

Sorell, W. *Story of the Human Hand*. London: Weidenfeld & Nicholson, 1968.

Spink, Kathryn. *Gandhi*. London, England: Hamish Hamilton Children's Books, 1984.

Staerker, Paul, *Tender Touch: Massage Your Baby to Health and Happiness*, Singapore: Twickenham Media Masters, 1999.

Stettbacher, J. Konrad. *Making Sense of Suffering*. New York: Dutton, 1991.

Stevens, John. *The Essence of Aikido: Spiritual Teachings of Morihei Ueshiba*. New York: Kodansh America Inc., 1993.

Stransky, Judith and Robert B. Stone. *The Alexander Technique*. New York: Beaufort Books, 1981.

Sullivan, Karin Horgan, *The Healing Power of Touch: The Many Ways Physical Contact Can Cure*. Lincolnwood, Ill: Publications International, Ltd., 1998.

Thie, John F. and Mary Marks. *Touch for Health*. Pasadena, CA: Touch for Health Foundation, 1998.

The Troops for Truddi Chase. *When Rabbit Howls*. New York: E.P. Dutton, 1987.

Thevenin, Tine. *The Family Bed*. Wayne, New Jersey: Avery Publishing Group, 1987.

————. *Mothering and Fathering: The Gender Differences in Child Raising*. Wayne, NJ: Avery Publishing Group, 1993.

Tweedie, Irina. *The Chasm of Fire.* Wiltshire, England: Element Books, 1979.

Verny, Thomas, M.D. and John Kelly. *The Secret Life of the Unborn Child.* New York: Dell, 1981.

————. *Nurturing the Unborn Child.* New York: Dell, 1992.

Wagner, Susan. *A Doctor's Guide to Therapeutic Touch.* New York: Perigee, 1996.

Wilbur, Ken. *Grace and Grit: The Spirituality and Healing in the Life and Death of Treya Killam Wilbur.* Boston: Shambhala Publications, 1991.

————. *The Spectrum of Consciousness,* Boston: Shambhala Publications, 1999.

————. *The Marriage of Sense and Soul: Integrating Science and Religion,* Boston: Shambhala Publications,1999.

————. and Tony Schwartz, *A Brief History of Everything,* Boston: Shambhala Publications,1996.

Zilbergeld, Bernie. *The New Male Sexuality.* New York: Bantam Books, 1992.

Articles

Ashford, Janet Issacs. "The History of Midwifery in the United States." *Mothering,* Winter, 1990.

Associated Press. "An Electrifying New Hazard." *U.S. News & World Report,* March 30, 1987.

Associated Press. "Report linking electric fields, cancer delayed by White House." *Arizona Republic,* December 14, 1990.

Baker, Beth. "The Changing Face of Social Work." *Common Boundary,* January/February, 1994.

Bar-Yam, Naomi. "The Nestle Boycott." *Mothering,* Winter, 1995.

Biemiller, Lawrence. "Lessons From a Sobering Age: 'Touch People. Hug Them When You Need To.'" *The Chronicle of Higher Education,* October, 1994.

Blackman, Nancy B. "Pleasure and Touching: Their Significance in the Development of the Preschool Child." Paper presented at the International Symposium on Childhood and Sexuality, Montreal, Sept. 1979.

Bassoff, Evelyn Silten. "Healing Love." *Mothering,* Spring, 1991.

Brandeis-McGunigle, Gayle. "Childhood and Ritual in Bali." *Mothering,* Fall, 1991.

Burton, Arthur and Louis G. Heller. "The Touching of the Body." *Psychoanalytic Review,* Vol. 51, no. 1, Spring, 1964.

Byrd, Randolph C., "Positive Therapeutic Effects of Intercessory Prayer in a Coronary Care Unity Population." *Southern Medical Journal,* 81, no. 7, July, 1988.

Davis-Floyd. "Hospital Birth As a Technocratic Rite of Passage." *Mothering,* Summer, 1993.

Edelman, Vladimir. "Touch Goes High-Tech: Dispatch from Virtual Reality." *Psychology Today,* January/February, 1996.

Editor. "Debate: Should You Ever Touch A Student," *NEA Today,* February, 1994.

Emma, Ushanda io. "Life With The Pygmies." *Mothering,* Summer, 1988.

Falbel, Aaron. "The Computer as a Convivial Tool." *Mothering,* Fall, 1990.

Fathman, Robert E. "Child Abuse." *Mothering,* Winter, 1991.

Ferguson, Eugene S. "How Engineers Lose Touch." *American Heritage of Invention & Technology,* Winter, 1993.

Field, T., Hernandez-Reif, M., et al, "Elder retired volunteers benefit from giving massage therapy to infants," *Journal of Applied Gerontology,* 1998, 17: 229-239.

Field, Tiffany. "Massage Therapy for Infants and Children." *Developmental and Behavioral Pediatrics,* Vol. 16, No. 2., April, 1995.

Field, T., Delamanter, A.M. et al. "Diabetic children's adherence and glucose levels improve after touch therapy," *Diabetes Spectrum,* 1997.

Field T., Seligman, S. et al. "Alleviating post-traumatic stress in children following Hurricane Andrew," *Journal of Applied Developmental Psychology,* 17, 1996, pp.37-50.

Field, T., Lasko, D., et al, "Autistic children's attentiveness and responsibility improve after touch therapy," *Journal of Autism and Developmental Disorders,* 1997, pp. 333-338.

Frankel, Max. "Do Computers Eat Our Paychecks?" *New York Times Magazine,* March, 1996.

Freedman, David H. "Playing God: The Making of Artificial Life." *Discover,* August, 1992.

Gagne, Deborah and Toye, Richard, C., "Effects of therapeutic touch and relaxation therapy in reducing anxiety," *Research in Nursing and Health,* 1994, pp. 184-9.

Giasson M. Bouchard, L. "Effect of therapeutic touch on the well-being of persons with terminal cancer," *Journal of Holistic Nursing,* 1998, 16(3): 383-98.

Goldman, Caren. "Prisons can be more than holding tanks. They can be sacred spaces where troubled souls are guided to mature manhood." *Common Boundary,* January/February, 1993.

Gorney, Roderic, "Hope for Humankind," *The Humanist,* January/February, 1996.

Haeuser, Adrienne Ahlgren. "Swedish Parents Don't Spank." *Mothering,* Spring, 1992.

Hovey, Pauline O. "The Quality of Mercy." *Common Boundary,* March/April, 1993.

Ironson, Gail and Tiffany Field et. al. "Massage Therapy is Associated with Enhancement of the Immune System's Cytotoxic Capacity." *Intern. J. Neuroscience,* 1995.

Jeffers, Frank E. "Love and the Relatedness of Things." *The Humanist,* January/February, 1996.

232

Klein, Paul. "The Needs of Children." *Mothering,* Spring, 1995.

LaCerva, Victor. "Dearest Papa." *Mothering,* Fall, 1984.

Lattin, Don. "The Problems and the Potential of 'Reaching Out.'" *Common Boundary,* September/October, 1991.

Liedloff, Jean. "Normal Neurotics Like Us." *Mothering,* Fall, 1991.

Levy, Steven. "No Place for Kids? A Parents' Guide to Sex on the Net." *Newsweek,* July 3, 1995.

Mathison, Linda. "Birth Memories: Does Your Child Remember?" *Mothering,* Fall, 1981.

McCarthy, Anna. "Reach Out and Touch Someone: Technology and Sexuality in Broadcast Ads for Phone Sex." *The Velvet Light Trap,* No. 32, Fall, 1993.

Palmer, Gabrielle. "The Politics of Infant Feeding." *Mothering,* Summer, 1991.

Pearce, Joseph Chilton. (Interview). *Mothering,* Spring, 1985.

Plaut, Michael S. and Heidi B. Ginter. "Sexual Boundaries Between Health Professionals and Clients: A Blueprint for Education." SIECUS Report, June/July, 1995.

Prescott, James. "Alienation of Affection," *Psychology Today,* December, 1979.

————. "Failure of Pleasure as a Cause of Drug/Alcohol Abuse and Addictions." *The Truth Seeker,* September/October, 1989.

————. "Hollywood Violence...First Do No Harm," *Imagine a World of Wanted Children,* August, 1995.

————. "NIH Violence Research Initiatives: Is Past Prologue?" Panel on NIH Research on Anti-social, Aggressive and Violence-related Behaviors and Their Consequences, September, 1993.

————. "Somatosensory Affectional Deprivation (SAD) Theory of drug and alcohol use," in *Theories On Drug Abuse: Selected Contemporary Perspectives,* 1980. Dan J. Lettieri, Mollie Sayers and Helen Wallenstien Pearson, Eds. NIDA Research Monograph, March 30, 1980. National Institute on Drug Abuse, Department of Health and Human Services. Rockville, MD.

————. "The Origins of Human Love and Violence." *Pre-and Peri-natal Psychology Journal,* 10 (3), Spring, 1996.

————. Time Life Documentary "Rock a Bye Baby," premiered at the 1970 White House Conference On Children.

Putnam, Robert. "Bowling Alone: America's Declining Social Capital." *Current,* June, 1995.

Remland, Martin S., et. al. "Interpersonal Distance, Body Orientation, and Touch: Effects of Culture, Gender and Age." *The Journal of Social Psychology,* 1995.

Rynearson, Robert R. "Touching People." *Journal of Clinical Psychiatry,* Vol. 39, no. 6, June, 1978.

Schwade, Steve, and Linda Rao. "Hospitals with the Human Touch." *Prevention Magazine,* Vol. 46, Issue 12, December, 1994.

Seligman, Katherine. "Sex Laws For Schools." *San Francisco Examiner,* May 30, 1993.

Snyder, Trish. "Touch." *Chateliane,* July, 1996.
Solter, Aletha. "Television and Children." *Mothering,* Fall, 1986.

Staff. "Mothering Interviews Joseph Chilton Pearce." *Mothering,* Spring, 1985.

Stetzel, John. "Teaching Good Touch." *Joperd,* August, 1994.

Turner, J.G., Clark, A.J., et al, "The effect of therapeutic touch on pain and anxiety in burn patients," *Journal of Advanced Nursing,* 1998, 28(1): 10-20.

Wellness Associates Journal. Issue 36, Spring, 1996.

INDEX

A

abuse, 75–80. *See also* sexual abuse
  causes, 93
    chemical component, 96–97
    passed down from generation to generation, 94–95
    complicity and being a passive witness to, 84–85, 117–18
    coping with, 102–8
    culture of, 111–23
    cycles of, 94–95, 116
    defined, 80
    ending it in ourselves, 126–27
    nature of, 80–81
    physical, 82–83, 114
    subtle forms of, 82, 84–85
    verbal/emotional, 83–85
abusive contact *vs.* no contact, 97–99
abusive tendencies within each of us, 101–2, 126
affection
  on demand, 67–68
  excessive and unwanted, 67–68. *See also* abuse
  people who have had an abundance of, xxiii, 97
  withholding, 65–66
aging, 156
ahimsa (non-violence), 196
AIDS, 15

B

AIDS patients, massage for, 136–37
Ammachi (Mata Amritanandamayi), 164, 194
appearance, emphasis on, 7
Aria, Barbara, 54–55
artists, 118
Ashford, Janet Isaacs, 47
attachment. *See* bonding
attention, need for, 99

bedtime, 55–57
Bhagavati, Ma Jaya, 15
birth, 104
  and early intimacy, 26, 38
  hospital birth *vs.* homebirth, 43, 45–49
  natural *vs.* with drugs, 43
birth chamber, 41–45
birthing procedures, 30–31
blame, xviii–xix, xxii
body, 141. *See also* women's bodies
  as dirty and unsanitary, 11–12, 147. *See also* sexuality, as dirty
  "getting in" the, 129–30
  gratitude for the, 155–58
  "selling" it cheaply, 150
  shame and the, 146–50, 154
  wisdom of, 151–54. *See also* women's bodies, knowledge in

237

COPYRIGHT PERMISSIONS

Every effort has been made to trace copyright holders of the material in this book. The editor apologizes if any work has been used without permission and would be glad to be told of anyone who has not been consulted.

OTHER BOOKS BY MARIANA CAPLAN

HALFWAY UP THE MOUNTAIN
The Error of Premature Claims to Enlightenment
by Mariana Caplan   Foreword by Fleet Maull
Dozens of first-hand interviews with students, respected spiritual teachers and masters,
together with broad research are synthesized here to assist readers in avoiding the pit-
falls of the spiritual path. Topics include: mistaking mystical experience for enlightenment; ego inflation, power and corruption among spiritual leaders; the question of the
need for a teacher; disillusionment on the path . . . and much more.
    "Caplan's illuminating book . . . urges seekers to pay the price of traveling the hard
road to true enlightenment." —*Publisher's Weekly*
Paper, 600 pages, $21.95   ISBN: 0-934252-91-2

WHEN SONS AND DAUGHTERS CHOOSE ALTERNATIVE LIFESTYLES
by Mariana Caplan
A guidebook for families in building workable relationships based on trust and mutual
respect, despite the fears and concerns brought on by differences in lifestyle. Practical
advice on what to do when sons and daughters (brothers, sisters, grandchildren...) join
communes, go to gurus, follow rock bands around the country, marry outside their race
or within their own gender, or embrace a religious belief that is alien to yours.
    "Recommended for all public libraries."—*Library Journal.*
Paper, 264 pages, $14.95   ISBN: 0-934252-69-6

THE WAY OF FAILURE: *Winning Through Losing*
by Mariana Caplan
This straight-talking and strongly inspirational book looks failure directly in the face,
unmasking it for what it really is. Mariana Caplan tells us to how to meet failure on its
own field, how to learn its twists and turns, its illusions and its realities. Only then, she
advises, is one equipped to engage failure as a means of ultimate "winning," and in a
way that far exceeds our culturally defined visions of success.
Paper, 144 pages, $14.95   ISBN: 1-890772-10-6

TO ORDER: 800-381-2700, or visit our website: www.hohmpress.com

CONTACT INFORMATION

By request, Mariana Caplan leads seminars in North America and Europe based upon her various books. She also works as a private counselor and as a consultant to aspiring writers. Further information can be found at: www.realspirituality.com, or by writing to her c/o: Hohm Press, Box 2501, Prescott, AZ, 86302.